QUEEN OF CLUBS

SIMON GLYNDWR JOHN

QUEEN OF CLUBS

A NOVEL BY
SIMON GLYNDWR JOHN

Copyright © 2010 by Simon Glyndwr John
All rights reserved.

The characters and events in this book are fictitious.
Any similarity to real persons, living or dead, is
purely coincidental and not intended by the author.

COVER ILLUSTRATION
Lynn Blake-John

BOOK AND COVER DESIGN
Andrea Blake/tomboywebdesign.com

ISBN 978-0-9566391-0-3

Printed and bound in Great Britain by
CPI Antony Rowe, Chippenham and Eastbourne

Published by Squiggles Press

www.simongjohn.com

For Lynn Blake-John

CHAPTER 1

Dai Williams stopped walking as soon as he saw the Glanddu village rugby clubhouse. He and his wife, Marilyn, had just been watching a TV series called, 'The ugliest buildings in Britain.' The eyesores displayed each week had fascinated them for the last six Wednesdays, and they were saddened that tonight's episode was the last. What puzzled Dai was why the clubhouse before him had not been included in the TV series.

Built on the cheap in the early 1960's, the building had been designed by an architect who had fled Hungary in 1956 following that country's abortive anti-Russian uprising. The clubhouse clearly reflected his training in the Stalinist school of the all-concrete, bombproof, anti-tank, blockhouse design.

At the time they commissioned him the architect told the Glanddu Rugby Club's Committee that concrete did not weather well in rain. Then he asked, 'Does Carmarthenshire get much precipitation?' Dai looked at the squat blob with its multitudinous, variously-sized, coloured stained patches and started to laugh.

He said loudly as he continued on his path, 'Does it rain much in Carmarthenshire? We have hard and soft rain, heavy and light rain, continuous and intermittent rain, solid and fine rain, blustery and driving rain; it drizzles, it pours, it rains cats and dogs, it rains stair rods, it buckets down; we get cloud bursts, we get thunder storms, we get deluges, we get downpours, we get squalls.'

He stopped and thought for a moment. Perhaps squalls only occurred at sea. 'Can't use that, then,' he muttered and decided to avoid any of the coarser expressions for rain just as a wasp flew at him at ankle height.

Dai aimed a kick at the wasp that the latter easily sidestepped. He stood poised, ready to battle the insect if it counterattacked. The wasp hung mid-air, thinking. The local season for wasps to annoy and sting humans was not due to open until September first - several weeks hence. The wasp knew that if he broke the start date rule, a hideous punishment would ensue. The rumour in the nest was that errant wasps would be forced to attend all Glanddu Rugby Club's home games.

As a knowledgeable wasp explained, 'Only queens survive the arrival of frost. Frosts might not occur here 'til November. If one of us worker wasps is punished, that means seeing as many as six of Glanddu's games. What right-minded wasp wants that to happen in the twilight of his life?'

'Can't they be stung into action?'

'No, not the team,' replied the knowledgeable wasp, 'but get in amongst the game's spectators and who knows?'

The wasp had watched the team's pre-season training as it foraged for food. Those few minutes had been enough to establish there was no way it wanted to see the team actually play. Keeping its sting firmly sheathed, the wasp abruptly flew off in search of early blackberries. Dai watched the wasp disappear and as he recommenced his walk, he broke into song: 'When August showers, they come to Wales, they bring the rain clouds that pour for hours.'

'Very musical, Dai, but the words could do with some work, a lot of work.'

A voice sounded through the open window of the shed that stood at the end of the rugby pitch.

'There's something else. Stay there,' commanded the voice.

Dai stopped and waited for the voice's owner, Tom Moses, to appear around the side of the shed, holding his dentures. When Tom emerged Dai was pleased that the man did not wipe his dentures on the oily rag he was carrying in his left hand.

Tom just popped them in with his right before he sidled up to Dai and whispered, 'I was watching on the driveway before you started singing.' He raised his eyebrows. 'You were talking to yourself nineteen to the dozen. You know what they say. . .' He tapped his temple with an index finger that left a black mark.

Dai shrugged. 'When people who lived in Glanddu worked at its coalmine, I saw my customers regularly. Nowadays everyone who has a job commutes to Cardiff, Swansea or Llanelli, so they all leave at the crack of dawn. Now if I want a chat I've got to provide both sides of the conversation.' He sighed. 'Commuting every day all the way to Cardiff — can you imagine doing that in your day, Tom?'

'No. In the old days, to go to Cardiff took over two hours by bus and train.'

Tom paused to spit, a habit from his days as a collier. That done, he remembered, 'It was a big occasion to go there so we took sandwiches. Egg was always my favourite with great dollops of Welsh butter, none of this bloody margarine rubbish the wife tries to get me to eat. I tell her the dust will get me long before the cholesterol does.' He spat again then grinned, 'I'd usually eaten the lot before the train had left Swansea Station.' He laughed, bringing on another coughing fit and a mouth wipe with the rag.

Dai had no desire to go down memory lane any further. He started backing away but Tom grasped his arm and said eagerly, 'Before you go, what do you think of the ground?'

Dai stood and looked at the rugby pitch. The last time he had paid any attention to the field's appearance was during the club's final match of the season in April. At that time of the year, after eight months of non-stop rugby matches, the pitch reminded Dai of Swansea Bay after the tide went out. The difference was that where the rugby pitch had the odd tuft of grass, Swansea Bay had shoes, dead dogs and the occasional supermarket trolley scattered around its expanse.

'It looks immaculate, Tom. The best I have ever seen it.' He nodded his head pitch at the green sward before him. 'It is a real credit to you and the boys of the Ground Committee.'

For a few seconds there was silence as the two men stared at the pitch. Dai then added, 'No doubt though, Tom, once the team has played a few games on it and we get our usual autumn rain, it will be the customary Flanders' Fields boggy brown morass.'

'Maybe not,' said Tom with a shake of his head. 'Yesterday the wireless said that because of this global warming we're predicted to have an exceptionally dry winter. These meteorologists reckon that Wales may soon be a desert just like the Sahara.'

'Really,' Dai replied, trying not to smile.

'Yes. When that happens, we'll definitely need to have a sprinkler system to get the grass to grow.'

Dai put his arm round the old man. 'If this place ends up like the Sahara it will be long after you and I have gone. Let us leave it to our grandchildren to decide on the sprinklers. In the meantime I take my hat off to you gardeners because you certainly know how to get the best looking rugby pitch in Wales.'

Tom looked at Dai quizzically. 'Well, the club owns the pitch so we have a duty to look after it.'

He frowned then after a moment shook his head, 'Dai, this is not gardening. Gardening is when the wife says, "I want a new border, or I want to move this plant or that plant." Then gardening is non-stop digging. Then, there are the visits to these mega-sized Gardening Centres that sell never-ending new and costly varieties of plants that the missus wants. Down here,' his arm swept across the pitch, 'we don't have to worry whether this colour flower goes with that colour flower, or this flower contrasts too strongly with the colour on the clubhouse windows.'

He spat again, 'Admittedly some weeds like plantains grow on the ground. But, unlike at home, we don't need to bother about them.'

Suddenly, Tom's voice took on a preacher's timbre. 'Being here on the pitch is all about peace, tranquillity and getting away from the wife. Our only problems are to decide whose turn is it to sit on the tractor or whose turn it is to bring the milk for the tea.' Tom winked, 'Because I'm the chairman I get to drive the tractor more than most.'

'What about them?' Dai thrust a thumb at the pitch. 'The Ground Sub-committee Chairman's job is to remove them. Or do you assign one of your minions to do it?'

Without a word, Tom's face changed to thunder. He placed his hands firmly on his hips, breathed out audibly, spat viciously and without a word to Dai, he strode out onto the pitch and began to clap his hands loudly. The pigeon flock slowly roused itself before it flew off towards the far end of the ground. Then it circled back and deposited its members a few feet from where they had just been grazing. Dai watched Tom walk further onto the pitch and clap his hands for a second time with exactly the same response as before. Tom turned and looked at Dai in exasperation, shaking his fist before beginning a determined march towards the birds, clapping and swearing.

Tom' dentures were not the best so as Dai continued his walk towards the clubhouse, he was unsure — as were the pigeons, no doubt — whether Tom's expletives were in English or Welsh or both.

As Dai neared the clubhouse, he heard a car approaching from behind and without looking he waved, knowing it would be someone he knew. The car sounded its horn in acknowledgement, as it overtook him and parked. The driver got out and then retrieved a briefcase from the backseat. Ramrod straight as always, the driver marched towards the clubhouse entrance where Dai stood waiting, holding the door open.

'Thank you and good evening, David,' said the driver, who was the only person, other than his wife when she was angry, who ever used his full name.

'Glad I've caught you. Toby is coming down this weekend with his girlfriend, so may I have an extra two pints on Friday and two on Saturday, please.'

Over thirty years in the milk delivery business had honed Dai's mental filing system and already he had opened his mental order book: G Bowen Thomas, Hillcrest.

'The usual - skimmed for her and full fat for him?'

'Yes, thanks. A supermarket wouldn't remember my requirements, would they, David?'

'No, they certainly would not,' barked Dai as he followed Mrs Gloria Bowen Thomas, chairwoman of Glanddu Rugby Club, into the clubhouse.

♣ 5 ♣

Chapter 2

Gloria Bowen Thomas paced up and down her living room, stopping from time to time to peer out of the window and then to glare at the clock. If one arranged a business meeting for two in the afternoon, then two o'clock was when the meeting should start, not two-fifteen. It was imperative that this meeting start on time because the man now overdue must not meet the gentleman due to arrive here at four o'clock.

It was seven years since she and Duncan had bought this house as a holiday home. Duncan, born and raised in a two-bedroom terraced cottage in the village, had always coveted this house, once owned by the local mine owner. Duncan always claimed he bought it for its views across the valley. Gloria saw the house as a demonstration of how successful in business they had both been.

Within two years of buying the house Duncan and Gloria had discovered what an absolute swine Angus McLeod was, their so-called friend and financial advisor. That pig had defrauded them and all his other clients of their savings. McLeod had possessed two Porsches; by the way, why would a single man need two Porsches? Still, at least the poor excuse for a man had the decency to blow his brains out.

As if the loss of their savings was not bad enough, property prices then collapsed, quickly followed by both her and Duncan losing their jobs. Both lost senior positions when companies undertook what they called "the re-organisation of their management structure." Everyone in business knew that firing older managers looked good on the balance sheet because it gave immediate savings - and a pay rise for the company directors.

To be mortgage-free Gloria and Duncan sold their London house and moved their home (temporarily, they hoped) to Glanddu, and there awaited an upturn in the job market.

Duncan's health began to deteriorate almost as soon as they moved from London and he never worked again, partly because of the illness and partly because his management skills were superfluous to modern requirements. During the first two years of Duncan's illness Gloria worked as a short-term contractor; for someone in their late forties it was the only type of work available. In the last year of Duncan's illness Gloria refused any work at all in order to nurse and comfort her lifelong friend and lover. It had taken Gloria two years to come to terms with Duncan's death but now she wanted a change and even more she wanted to be earning a living.

Gloria's dream was to move back to London from this provincial Welsh valley village, but with London's ludicrously high house prices and Duncan's tiny pension as her sole source of income, a relocation was impossible. Gloria thought that if she got a well-paid contract then a move to Cardiff was possible, but the cheaper and more likely alternative was Swansea.

Finding work was the problem. The problem was not just her age in an ageist market, but there was so much competition from an ever-increasing pool of out-of-work, capable people. Not having worked for three years was a nail in her coffin but she remained hopeful that a job might appear from Aladdin's lamp provided, of course, the lamp was rubbed.

Currently, Gloria had just one thing that she was pleased with in her life: being the chair of Glanddu Rugby Football Club. She was proud to be the first chairwoman in the Glanddu Rugby Football Club's hundred and ten-year history. Duncan had been Gloria's immediate predecessor in the chairman's role, though in the last year of his life she had done the job for him. Gloria knew that the club's committee had realised during that year how good at the job she was. She knew that they needed someone like her who, with her business knowledge and her competence, no local male could match.

She smiled with pleasure as she remembered the late Alwyn Prosser, shortly after Duncan's death, coming to see her.

'Gloria, sorry to bother you at this sad time but the club's committee members have unanimously deputized me to ask you one thing.'

'Oh, you will want all the papers relating to the club that we have here. I have them all ready if would you like to take them?' She indicated a cardboard box.

'Actually, Gloria,' Alwyn had smiled, 'I have come to ask you whether you would consider becoming chairman, sorry chairwoman, of Glanddu Rugby Club.'

Gloria was shocked. She thought back to her late teens when she had first developed an interest in rugby. She liked watching rugby games, not for the sporting prowess but because the players wore shorts that showed off both limbs and bums; she adored hairy legs. Duncan had had a nice bum (although his legs were smooth and hairless). Tears came to her eyes as she remembered how cancer had shrunk Duncan down to his playing weight and then reduced him to skin and bone.

She focussed back on Alwyn's suggestion. A woman to become the chair of one of the last bastions of the male preserve — the rugby club — was intriguing and gratifying.

'We on the committee all know that you did much of Duncan's work over the last couple of years. Ordinary club members recognised that as well, which is why they elected you to the club committee in your own right last year. You have the business and management background we think the club needs. And, there is one other thing.'

'I thought offering me the chairmanship was the one thing.' Gloria replied, knowing already what her answer would be.

'True, but we think having a woman as the chair shows how progressive the Glanddu Rugby Football Club is.'

'Nice to hear it,' Gloria responded with a smile. She was thrilled to be asked and said, 'Yes, I would love to be proposed as the chair.'

The rugby playing season lasted from August to May. There were committee meetings each month in the season; the chair was almost a full-time job. She sometimes regretted accepting the role because the volume of work restricted her freedom to visit her children in London. Still, it kept her brain active and gave her something she had always enjoyed: bossing men around.

Where and how she wondered, as she looked impatiently out of the window again, was she ever going to get employment? Gloria had worked as everything from programmer to project manager in the thirty years since she had left university. She possessed enormous IT and business skills. But in the year that she nursed Duncan full-time, the computer industry underwent one of its sea changes and her skills were no longer in vogue. In reality, people still working in IT told her that everything was the same; only the buzzwords changed. The real issue was that cheapness seemed to be the sole criterion for employing people, and the young held that card.

For Gloria, even more galling had been her last two job interviews back in the spring. People young enough to be her children carried out those interviews. Every interviewer, ironically all of them women, was a hardnosed, unsmiling, unfriendly clotheshorse who gave the impression that their generation had discovered everything about work in general and IT, in particular. At each meeting Gloria felt that the interviewers looked at her as though she should be using a Zimmer Frame or be on duty outside a school with a lollipop sign, ready to escort infants across a road.

'How do you keep abreast of developments in IT?' the interviewers had asked.

'I read the trade papers,' particularly if I cannot get to sleep, she thought, but did not care to mention.

'Any other ways you can keep in touch?'

'I have been both actual and acting chairwoman of my local rugby club for three years. This exposes me to the full range of processes for managing a business. This includes staff management, strategic planning and financial management. I can assure you that managing the Glanddu Rugby Committee, which,' she added the next bit hoping for a smile, 'consists mainly of men, is as difficult as anything I faced when managing a multi-million pound IT project.'

No smile was evoked by that response; instead Gloria got the following question at each interview: 'The majority of our staff are young, vibrant, go ahead and always enjoy each other's company outside work. We encourage socializing because it builds up team spirit. So how do you get on with young people, Mrs Bowen Thomas? What about your young players?'

'Well, they don't often ask me out for a drink,' was what she said at the first interview. That interviewer scowled and wrote something down on her pad of paper. If things had not been at rock bottom at that moment, they certainly went downhill after that.

When Gloria was asked the same question at the next interview, she replied, 'We get along very well. I always have a drink with them after the game.' She now went into po-faced lying. 'I always discuss their performance and how they can look to improve it both as individuals and, more importantly, as team members. I think the players respect that I know so much about the game.'

In truth, after each rugby game Gloria would have a drink in the club bar room entertaining the visiting committee if Glanddu had played at home or, if Glanddu's match was away, she was entertained in that club's committee room. After their post-match shower and meal the players would appear in the room, and she would speak to those who happened to pass by. Depending on whether the team had won or (more usually) lost, she would say, 'Well played, bad luck,' and add the name of the player she addressed.

The conversation only varied if the player was injured during the game, and then it would be, 'How is the knee/the elbow/ the ankle? How many stitches did you have?' Then to round off those remarks she always added, 'I hope you'll be fit to play next week; we cannot do without you.'

She never heard if she got either job. IT job agencies, it seemed, only informed people when they got the job; everyone else who had been interviewed for the post was ignored. Gloria could never understand why it was so difficult to make a brief telephone call or email, but calls take time, and time is money.

All of Gloria's friends working in IT and in the same age bracket were having exactly the same depressing experience in finding work.

It was Gloria's knowledge about the club's rocky financial situation that had led her to set up today's meetings; she hoped these meetings would change her life, particularly if her career was at an end. She looked at the clock. How could he be twenty minutes — she looked at the clock again — no, twenty-two minutes late? The man she was expecting had spent his whole life working at the local electricity board before he retired, and Gloria knew from long experience how people from service industries were oblivious to time.

Gloria clumped into her hall. 'Where the hell are you?' she snarled at the mirror hanging above a telephone. 'You live in Brynddu, the next village, precisely two miles up the road and a five-minute drive away.' Gloria began deep breathing in order to keep her anger in check; she could not afford to alienate this man.

Gloria stomped back into the sitting room, picked up the novel she was reading and sank into her chair, determined not to look at the clock again for at least fifteen minutes.

CHAPTER 3

'Money makes the world go round,' sang John Jones grimly to himself as he sat back in his chair and pondered the figures displayed on his computer screen. The name that one of his friends had given him years before was "Le chef de books," though his official title was Honorary Treasurer of Glanddu Rugby Football Club. The name, "Chef," was bestowed because of his skill in running two sets of accounts and his apparent ability to do anything by fair means or foul that financially benefited his beloved rugby club.

Money in the village of Glanddu and the whole area had always been tight, but since the mine had closed and local factories had started leaving Wales for the rich, low-wage pastures of Eastern Europe, money was becoming as scarce as rain in the Sahara. No matter, people expected him to continue to work miracles with what he had on the screen in front of him. The screen was displaying the "true" accounts on which he drew up his financial plan for the new season. He had another set of accounts — the fictitious "official" accounts - that did not show all the money that flowed through the club. These accounts were the ones submitted to the club's auditors. All the "official" accounts needed were to be plausible enough to pull the wool over the club's auditors' eyes. The rugby club's committee over the years had fully supported their treasurer's machinations because without such culinary manipulation, how could a small rugby club survive?

The positive side to keeping two sets of accounts was that less money ended up in Whitehall's coffers. Everyone in the village's general attitude was that "if our club accounts were accurate, the amount of extra taxes they would generate would only get wasted by the Government."

Jones speculated down which drains the government could empty the rugby club taxes. Tax money to pay either for some government minister's wife to work for a couple weeks (just before Christmas) in the Houses of Parliament doing what that all-encompassing money pit referred to as "research" or, for a castle in a Member of Parliament's duck pond. Hopefully, that sort of abuse was stopping but since most MPs were lawyers they'd find some other way of exploiting the system, and it wouldn't take them long.

As he stared gloomily again at the screen, Jones thought that it was all very well having the motto "What is ours, we keep," but what the club needed was some fiscal geophysicist to find a new well or lode that somehow had remained hidden.

As winning the National Lottery was more likely than finding such a well, Jones felt the club would be better off with the lottery. However, placing a bet was impossible because many older club members had been brainwashed in their youth by "fire and brimstone" Baptist ministers who were opposed to gambling.

Jones knew that the club's biggest monetary problem was its biggest expenditure: paying the players. There had been a tradition that players expected a few quid in their "boot" to cover any wages lost by working only half a Saturday shift down the pit. Now players expected payment as a matter of course. If a club did not pay its players, they just went looking for teams that did.

The sponsorship money raised from local, barely solvent businesses had made the difference in recent years to the club's ability to pay and keep its players. Tonight, Jones was meeting some of those club sponsors and he was expecting them to bring further doom and gloom thanks to the local economic situation. Tonight's meeting was 'hush, hush' but no doubt, as usual, everyone in Glanddu would know what was discussed in less than forty-eight hours and everyone who had attended the meeting would deny it was they who spilled the beans.

Happy that he had everything ready for the meeting, Jones removed a disk from the laptop before he switched the machine off. He took the disk into the garage where he stored it in the bottom drawer of a toolbox rarely opened. His garage was also the place where he stored any incriminating paperwork prior to shredding it (unless mice got to it first.) He kept the true accounts on a removable disk rather than on the laptop's hard drive for three reasons. First, he had to keep the true and the official accounts in separate places to prevent getting mixed up. Second, if some nosy government official were ever to come and investigate the club accounts, they would be shown the "official" ones stored on the hard drive. Third, if the true accounts on the hard drive were later deleted, they could be retrieved by Government officials (John knew this because he was an avid viewer of FBI and other American cop shows which always had techies who could recover the files).

If the Revenue performed an investigation, their search for evidence would include not just the clubhouse but surely his own home, as well. However, if any investigator looked inside Jones' garage and saw the unbelievable jumble that included everything from his grandfather's First World War army entrenching tool to an old television intended for the dump twenty years ago, he would baulk at the task. Jones himself could never find anything in the garage, so how could anyone else?

Anyway, Jones believed that any government official worth his salt must know that most sports clubs falsified their accounts.

As he re-entered the house Jones wondered how long he could continue in his post, which got more and more difficult each year. He'd like to stay because although his post was honorary, it did have its financial benefits — untaxed, of course. For example, a few years ago the club had paid for redecorating his house using the simple expedient of the decorator's invoice stating that the work was carried out in the clubhouse.

And now that he was retired from working in the Local Council's Accounts Department, what could he do with his life apart from the treasurership? Watch daytime TV? He shuddered at the thought.

There was, of course, golf. The thought of spending four hours on a golf course and then another four listening to people talk about their shots — only the good ones, naturally — filled him with dread. His stock answer to the inevitable question people asked when they found out he was retired was, 'Play golf? - no. May I point out that golf is not compulsory when one retires, is it? Being the club treasurer keeps my brain active which I think is rather more important than trying to catch pneumonia on some God-forsaken, windswept, bleak moorland, don't you?'

Jones usually worked in the clubhouse when on club business, not at home. The reason he always gave was that he needed to work where the paperwork was stored. In reality Gwladys, his wife, didn't want him around the house. If John was working on club business, Gwladys wanted the club to pay for any heating or lighting he required. In addition, since she cleaned the house thoroughly every day, she didn't want her husband under foot.

Because tonight's sponsors meeting was 'hush, hush' Gwladys allowed it to be held in her home (despite the mess the visitors would create). Jones was just in process of sliding the laptop under the bed in the spare room when he heard his wife open the front door.

Jones galloped down the stairs and gave his wife a peck on the cheek and she responded with an airy kiss that whistled past his ear.

'Guess who I saw in his car turning down the street where your Fuhrer lives?'

John made several guesses but he wasn't even close. When she told him who, John wondered why that gentleman would be going to see Gloria. Would it be club business or a social call? Hanky panky? He shook his head and stood pondering until Gwladys snapped her fingers. John helped Gwladys take off her coat and after he hung it on the coat stand, he followed his wife back into the living room where she squinted along the dining table. She exhaled loudly and pointed at a smudge on the otherwise gleaming piece of furniture, 'You've got finger marks on my table. I just polished it this morning! I did remind you to put a mat on it. I should have known better and done it myself before leaving.'

'I did,' replied Jones. Indeed, he had, but only belatedly after he began work and put a sweaty palm on the table whose imprint he had failed to remove with one of Gwladys' dusters.

Gwladys shook her head then patted him on the shoulder as one might a faithful old dog that retrieved yesterday's newspaper for its owner, who was already reading today's edition.

'I know you try, John.' Her voice changed tone. 'Cup of tea?'

'Oh, yes, please. I am absolutely parched.'

Gwladys stopped at the door and looked at him. 'John, if I had come in half an hour later would you have been dead from thirst?' John might be called "Le chef de books" down the club but his real culinary skills were non-existent unless one included opening beer or wine bottles and tearing the wrappers off chocolate bars or biscuits.

'Probably. Shall I put the kettle on?' John offered.

'No, I want it done properly.' Gwladys pointed at a pile of papers lying on a placemat on the table. 'Remove those so that I can dust properly.'

CHAPTER 4

Gloria walked to the telephone and, trying to calm down, picked up the instrument. Twenty-five minutes late was inexcusable; why couldn't he phone? Surely, even he had a mobile telephone. Just as she punched the last number of his home phone she heard a car slowing to a halt on the gravel outside. In front of the hall mirror she fluffed her hair, pasted on her most engaging smile and then marched to the front door.

Watcyn Watkins was a man who always wore, even when driving, one of those green felt hats with a feather in its hat-band, forever associated with the Austrian Tyrol. Whether Watcyn had ever been to Austria, Gloria doubted. His car, though old, was in pristine condition and shone as only a car can when its owner is in love with it. Watcyn eased himself out of the car with all the arthritic speed that an ex-rugby player who was closer to seventy than sixty years of age could muster. When he saw Gloria, he smiled apologetically.

'Mrs Bowen Thomas, I do apologise for being late. There was an accident on the main road where a bus had knocked down a cyclist. I left my mobile telephone at home so I couldn't contact you,' Watcyn said as he creaked up the steps. He doffed his hat before he gently shaking Gloria's proffered hand.

'Are you late?' She looked at her watch but could barely see its face because she was not wearing her glasses. 'So you are. I hadn't noticed.' She shrugged. 'It is so unimportant. Come on in. Was the cyclist badly hurt?'

'More grazes than anything else, luckily for him, Mrs Bowen Thomas.'

Gloria ushered Watcyn into the house and after placing his hat on the hall table, she led the way into the sitting room. 'I know we're on Rugby Club business but let us have no formality.'

Watcyn laughed. 'Quite right, Gloria. Call me, "Watcyn." Of course, a name like mine where the Christian and surname only differ by an "s" makes people unsure if they are using my first or second name when they chat to me. Of course, when I spell both names it becomes clear unless I'm speaking to a call-centre based on the Indian sub-continent.'

Gloria, fearing that last statement would be followed by a tedious dissertation on the Anglicanization of Welsh names, forestalled Watcyn by saying quickly, 'Absolutely fascinating, Watcyn, though to be politically correct should it not be Christian name, but given name? Would not your fellow Socialist members on the Borough Council Committee reprimand you for using that term?' Gloria grinned as she steered Watcyn to the sofa opposite her comfortable armchair.

'I certainly practise PC when I chair the Council's Planning Committee. I am sure that none of our minorities are tarnished at my meetings.' Watcyn grunted as he pulled up the legs of his grey flannel trousers before he sat down (as his wife had instructed because they were his best pair). 'If I call you chairman rather than chairwomen, please forgive me. It will be an accident, not an attempt to upset you because your club and mine are deadly rivals.'

'I will not be offended. I didn't realise you have minorities on your Council Committee, Watcyn.'

'Well, only one - Jessie Houghton, who is English.' He snuggled down into the settee. 'Though fair play, Jessie overcame that disability by learning Welsh.'

'Thank God for that,' Gloria laughed. 'How is Mrs Watkins?'

'Elizabeth still wants to retire to Spain because she suffers from the cold so badly and, in particular, the damp we have here. Unfortunately, like so many on a pension, we have a money problem and our only hope of salvation is to win the lottery. You know the odds of doing that.'

'Yes, but you never know what opportunities may come your way as a councillor.' Gloria looked for Watcyn's reaction to her implication that he might benefit from his position.

'A chance of someone wanting to do something in this valley and offering me money to achieve it is remote. Not that I would take it, of course.' He was old enough and wise enough to take gifts instead of money and he wasn't too greedy. Builders for whom he had done favours had, for example, fitted his house with a new toilet and replaced two rotten windows, whilst his large garden shed had a mains gas stove, electricity and running water - all as a thank you for his planning support.

'Perish the thought, Watcyn, that you, an old socialist, could be bribed. Now would you like tea, coffee, beer?'

Watcyn decided against a drink because his waterworks were not what they were, and he was sure he would embarrass himself if he had to use her toilet. Elizabeth Watkins had given him strict instructions on what to do if he had to use Gloria's facilities. He must not leave the seat up; he must check to see whether he had sprayed or dripped; and he must put the towel back exactly as he had found it. Remembering all his wife's instructions would, he knew, be impossible.

'No, I have just had lunch so I am comfortable, thank you,' Watcyn responded, just as he realised that he had forgotten to bring notepaper with him. Elizabeth normally reminded him what he needed for all his meetings; he hoped that she was not developing Alzheimer's.

Gloria nodded then announced, 'We need to talk about the condition of our rugby clubs here in the Ddu valley.'

Watcyn clasped his hands in front of him and his face took on a serious and a sad countenance. He shook his head and pursed his lips as he stentoriously announced in a voice reminiscent of the Baptist preachers of his youth: 'Rugby football in this valley is in a parlous state.'

Gloria chose her words carefully. 'That is precisely the reason why I invited you today. As I said on the telephone, this is an unofficial meeting between the chairman of Brynddu and the chairwoman of Glanddu rugby clubs. I felt that, as the leaders of our two clubs, we must demonstrate our leadership qualities to both our committees — committees who may not want to make the tough decisions that you and I know have to be taken.'

Gloria leaned forward and picked up her notepad. Watcyn, feeling himself redden as he pointed at Gloria's notepad, 'I left mine on our hall table.'

Without a word, Gloria got up and went to her desk. She placed a notebook marked 'Travelodge' in Watcyn's outstretched hand. 'Watcyn,' she said, 'I have given a lot of thought to what we should do in this difficult climate. I wrote down two things which I thought were relevant to the pair of us and that we must discuss.'

Gloria looked at her notepad. 'One is money or, as I suspect in both our cases, the lack of it. The other thing is players and the lack of them. Both our villages now have fewer young people than ever before.'

'And they want to do other things on a Saturday than we did when we were young.'

'So true, and compounded by the fact that people are commuting up to sixty miles to work. That eats up their spare time and leaves less time for rugby training in the evenings.'

'Which also means they are not as fit as we used to be, or as fit as they should be.' Watcyn sighed then continued, 'It was not that long ago when both our clubs easily ran two teams on each and every Saturday; now, we really struggle to get a full second team.'

Watcyn thought back to the previous season when Brynddu had a succession of injuries to key first team players and although the club had players to replace them, they were not the required standard.

It was so different, Watcyn remembered, from when he played in the 1950's and 1960's when Brynddu had players who fought to gain a regular place in the second team, yet who could perform adequately, if required in an emergency, in the first team. The lack of reserves at the required standard caused Brynddu to lose so many matches that at the end of last season they were relegated from the fourth to the fifth division Wales West.

Playing in the very bottom of the Welsh League was something Brynddu had never done before and meant that for the first time in years, Brynddu and Glanddu were in the same division. In days of yore whenever the clubs were in the same division, "Derby" games between them were inevitably a bloodbath. Watcyn had played in many a "Derby" and, indeed, his nose's odd shape resulted from one of those games.

Watcyn knew Gloria was a clever woman and so he would have to be wary and not allow himself to be out-manoeuvred. He shifted in his seat and studied the carpet as he heard Gloria's grandfather clock in the hall chime three o'clock; he thought very carefully. Watcyn's first language was Welsh so he chose his English words cautiously.

'I believe that an amalgamation between our clubs is a possible solution to this lack of players,' Watcyn hesitated, 'indeed, the only solution.' Then, as he imagined how people at the club would bellow if they learnt of his heresy he continued, 'Though probably not right away.'

Gloria smiled inwardly. If she ever needed to sell the idea that Glanddu should amalgamate with its bitter rival, she could say in all honesty, 'Watcyn Watkins, the chairman of Brynddu, was the one who suggested it to me.'

'I am not sure I would ever agree to that,' was her bogus protestation, 'nor would my committee. You cannot throw away over a hundred years of history for both clubs just like that, Watcyn,' said Gloria, snapping her fingers and shaking her head, hoping that she was not overdoing her objection to his statement.

'I'm not saying that my committee would welcome it either, far from it. Brynddu has always been a bigger and more important village and, indeed, rugby club than Glanddu. We have played as high as the second division in the national league, something Glanddu has never achieved.' Watcyn saw Gloria frown and before she could speak and no doubt argue with him on that last point he added, 'But as I said, if the last resort is amalgamation, then I'm sure you and I can pull it off. And what you said about maintaining community spirit between the two villages would be a key selling point.' He sank back into the settee looking at Gloria to gauge her reaction.

Time not to protest too much, Gloria thought.

'Despite both our reservations, Watcyn, let's brainstorm on how we would amalgamate if we had to.'

Watcyn leapt at the opportunity she had given him. He argued the merits of the two clubhouses, the standard of the playing pitches, the size and capacity of the stands. In every comparison, Brynddu was vastly superior. Even the colour of Glanddu's rugby shirts, shorts and socks, Watcyn eulogized, were inferior.

'You will be telling me next that the teacups used in your clubhouse are a better quality and cleaner than ours.'

'Undoubtedly,' replied Watcyn before he realised that Gloria was being facetious. 'No, of course they are not. On the key fundamentals like the quality of the pitch and the stand then Brynddu is undoubtedly better. Even many Glanddu people agree.'

Gloria knew that his last remark was true but she was not going to admit that yet. 'What about the weather, Watcyn? Brynddu is further up the mountain and its climate is definitely more extreme than down here.' As Watcyn opened his mouth, Gloria held her hand out to stop him. 'I can remember being here just after Duncan and I were married. It was raining in Glanddu but when we got to Brynddu, it was snowing.'

'The difference is only about sixty feet, Gloria, which isn't much,' Watcyn replied. Only a woman would say something so stupid, he thought.

'The difference is actually nearer to a hundred and thirty feet, Watcyn. When we have a windy day, you have a gale. And speaking of grounds, may I remind you that we own ours whilst you rent yours from the local council.'

Watcyn knew that Glanddu's ownership of its ground was probably the most important factor in deciding which ground the combined team would play on. He hesitated before he spoke.

'Of course, the Glanddu ground could be sold and the money raised could be used to develop rugby, not just for boys but for girls.' Watcyn had no time for female rugby, but times change. 'We could have a senior female rugby team in the valley but, of course, that would certainly require money.'

'Who would buy Glanddu's ground?'

Watcyn shrugged his shoulders, 'The local council might buy it for a school playing field or convert it into a park.' A thought struck him. 'Or, heaven forbid, it could be sold for houses. Think what that would do, Gloria.'

'More people, more players,' Gloria mused.

Watcyn, changing tactics completely, said, 'I hope you realise that after the game and a few drinks in the Brynddu clubhouse, anyone from Glanddu can walk home downhill - very important for our aging population. After a game and a few beers you don't want to struggle uphill.'

Gloria laughed and replied, 'Watcyn, I can just see myself presenting that point to my committee.'

'Yes, me too,' he paused. 'Got any thoughts, though, on the new season?' Without waiting for her response, Watcyn began to boast about the Brynddu team.

Gloria began to blank out but when he said that Brynddu was a certainty to win the league and gain promotion, Gloria just stopped herself from saying that she hoped so, too. Instead, out of loyalty to her club she retorted, 'I bet you ten pounds that Glanddu will win the league.'

Watcyn snorted at Gloria's statement but hesitated to take on the bet. He remembered Gwilym Henshaw, the Baptist Minister of his youth, decrying drinking, sex and gambling on those long ago Sundays. In the intervening years Watcyn had done a fair bit of drinking, had even had some luck with the fairer sex, but he was always afraid of gaming.

'No thank you, Gloria. I never gamble. Now, when I first played for Brynddu in 1956…'

Watcyn sounded like he could go on for several days and it was getting uncomfortably close to four o'clock.

Gloria interrupted, 'Watcyn, I have some club business to attend to. Time is marching on so we shall have we leave gamblers to another time.'

Watcyn was just about to reminisce about his favourite teams of the late 1950's. He was cruelly disappointed that Gloria had not the time to hear of his exploits.

'Of course,' he looked at his watch and rubbed his stomach, 'Elizabeth is making Welsh Cakes this afternoon.' He stood, 'She still uses butter, not margarine.'

For a moment Watcyn wondered if he should give Gloria a peck on the cheek but this was business, after all. He flexed his knee and hobbled into the hall.

'Next time we meet you must tell me all about those wonderful teams you played in,' Gloria lied as she escorted Watcyn to the door. 'Don't say anything to anyone about our meeting.' Watcyn nodded his agreement and doffed his hat at her before creaking into his car. Gloria watched him drive away before she raced to the telephone on the hall table.

'Toby Bowen Thomas, please. His mother. No, not bloody again.' Gloria moved the telephone away from her ear as Vivaldi's 'Four Seasons' reverberated loudly down the line. If Vivaldi were alive he would be worth a fortune from the amount of airplay he got.

Hearing a voice, she moved the phone back to her ear. 'Toby, darling, how are you? Guess what?' Then before her son could answer she said excitedly, 'He...yes, he...did it, I know it's stupid but I feel happier that he put forward amalgamation. It gives me a clear conscience. Of course, Watkins, as you would expect, wanted Brynddu to get everything. The significant point, however, is that the first phase of my plan is underway. So, as they say at Cape Canaveral, ten seconds to launch and counting. Oh, I expect him anytime now...'

Chapter 5

Gloria heard the car enter the drive dead on time. She sneaked a look from behind her curtains as the gleaming Mercedes glided to a halt. Gloria shrank back further from the window as the man swung out of the car and put on his expensive-looking suit jacket. He stooped to look in the car's wing mirror and spent several moments arranging his hair. Satisfied at last with his coiffure he walked to the boot and emerged with a laptop computer. Slamming the boot shut, he locked the car with a flick of the wrist and strode towards Gloria's front door.

'Mr Ball, I presume?' Gloria said with her most gracious smile as she opened the door.

'Mrs Bowen Thomas, very nice to meet you.' He took Gloria's hand and gently shook it. As an afterthought he gave her a perfunctory smile.

Gloria remembered her son Toby's description of John Ball. 'He has an abrupt manner with everyone and does not suffer fools gladly, so be careful how you approach him. His sense of humour was mislaid at birth. However, Mum, if he thinks there is money in your proposal he will move hell and high water to get his hands on it.'

Gloria led him into the sitting room. Ball requested a table for his laptop and a chair at the correct height for his bad back. A quick glance at the furniture left Ball shaking his head. Gloria then suggested the kitchen.

'Yes, Mrs Bowen Thomas, this will do,' said Ball in a supercilious tone.

(Gloria then expected him to run his finger along the furniture to check for dust.)

Ball took his laptop and the power cable out of the bag. 'I don't like to use the machine's battery when there is a power source available.'

Be nice of you to ask first, thought Gloria, before she offered Ball a cup of coffee.

'Black, no sugar. I'd prefer decaffeinated.'

As Gloria brewed the coffee, she made polite conversation to Ball's monosyllabic replies. As Gloria was asking a question, Ball's mobile telephone went off. Ball halted her mid-flow whilst he answered. Gloria didn't bother to finish her question.

'Time and tide wait for no man, particularly directors of large companies. So then, Mrs Bowen Thomas, why don't you talk about the status of the rugby ground and everything else that appears to be relevant whilst I make notes. Toby has told me something about the situation but you clearly have the deeper knowledge. Your position as chair of the club gives us an unprecedented insight into the club's intentions. Nothing compares to insider knowledge; it gives me a huge advantage over any other interested parties. It's also a big help because you can anticipate the reactions of the other locals.'

Gloria tried to think of whom Ball was referring. Rather like the law in Henry VIII's time stating that after church everyone must practise archery, Gloria thought there was a law in Wales stating that everyone who lived in a village with a rugby team must support it.

'My husband was born here but I was not.'

Ball waved his hand dismissively. 'Your status as chairwoman is the key. So tell me about Glandoo Rugby Club,' he smiled with all the warmth of the wind blowing across the tundra.

"Glan thee" is the correct pronunciation,' she corrected. Ball remained impassive so she continued, 'We can survive this year financially but I have found out that the local factory owned by Ffonelinc is closing down and moving to Estonia because of lower wages. So this is the last year that Ffonelinc will sponsor the Club.'

Ball exclaimed, 'These factory workers expect ridiculously high wages. The unions encourage the stupid oafs to price themselves out of the market. It's hardly surprising that the owners want to move to where production is cheaper. It's called globalisation.'

'Well, the global market is leading to other factory closures in this area which means that it will be impossible to find a replacement for Ffonelinc and its sponsorship money. In the Welsh League sponsors obviously concentrate their attention and their money on the higher divisions of the League, not where we languish.'

'Company money is too precious to waste on poor quality products.' Ball's eyes flicked up at her from his computer screen and raised his eyebrows for her to go on.

'I believe that there is little hope of promotion this season so we won't get the extra money that a team promoted to the fourth division receives. Then we have the problem with the number of players needed to ensure a club is viable. Two teams are the absolute minimum for a club like Glanddu. The role of the second team is to cover any injuries suffered by first team players. Glanddu is struggling to run two senior teams because of the shortage of youngsters wishing to play the game, and because there are a surfeit of rugby clubs in this area.'

'How many clubs are there?' Ball stared at her expectantly.

'Well, there are Brynddu, Pontarddu. . .'

'I just need a number.'

'Six clubs,' she exhaled loudly, 'within a ten mile radius.'

'What sort of state are they in? The same as yours?'

Gloria had prepared for this question. 'Well, everyone is struggling for players. But because their villages are larger than ours, they get a bigger crowd. If they play in a higher division, as a couple do, then they get more sponsorship money from the League. Most of a club's money comes from the bar. Several clubs have bars that open more frequently than ours which, when you see our building, you'll understand why.'

'That was very interesting, but my question is, "Are they in the same state as Glanddu?"'

Gloria flushed before she replied. 'So you did. I'm not sure, because at least two clubs exist in a state of grace.'

Ball blinked. 'State of grace is some sort of religious concept? I don't understand.'

'Just a little joke, that's all. I was referring to wealthy English immigrants who come and see what a marvellous place Carmarthenshire is. They retire here and invest in the focal points of their respective villages. In England, it might be the cricket club or the local soccer club. Here in Wales, it's the rugby club. My "state of grace" refers to the luck those Welsh clubs have in finding such benefactors.'

She ploughed on. 'Llangoed have an English benefactor who is putting in enough money (so I am told) to attract former players from much higher divisions. Llangoed are in the same division as we are so with all that new talent, promotion seems probable; if money can buy talent, they will succeed. Our near neighbours, Brynddu, who were demoted last season to join us, are the other candidate to gain promotion,' she said. 'Or so their chairman thinks.'

'What about a name? Do you know the name of the man sponsoring,' Ball scanned his computer, 'Llangoed?'

'I cannot think of his name,' Gloria replied after a long pause. She did know the benefactor, but she also knew not to give away everything at the first meeting. 'It will come to me, I am sure.'

Ball rested his chin on his hands for a moment. 'It would be useful to know who he is and his background. And financial support for you comes from. . .?'

'We have small local businesses, which mainly sponsor rugby balls and playing kit.' She added, 'We don't use a new ball for every match – they're too expensive.' In her mind's eye, she recalled the club's accounts. 'Last year the club only bought four balls. Our sponsors paid for the rest.'

Gloria watched Ball key furiously into his computer. 'What will happen or, dare I say, what would you like to happen if your rugby club were to go bankrupt? I assume the club will disappear.'

'No, not necessarily. I see us merging with one of the other local clubs. My favourite is the club situated at the top of the

QUEEN OF CLUBS

valley, Brynddu. It is a bigger village and, logically,' she saw Ball smile, 'the small should be amalgamated into the large.'

'That used to be the case in business but I can tell you that today, thankfully, anyone can take over anyone and these takeovers make fortunes for our banking friends.'

'Yes, I am aware of that, Mr Ball, having worked in the City of London for many years. I know well that whatever generates the most money for the banks will get preference.' Ball looked up from his computer and tilted his head in agreement.

Ball sat back, drummed his fingers on the table and thought for a moment. 'There is one important fact that you haven't mentioned, Mrs Bowen Thomas. Who, precisely, owns the Glanddu ground?'

Always save the best to last, her father had told her. 'The Glanddu ground is actually owned by the club. A local farmer donated the ground in memory of his one of his sons killed in the Boer War. When the ground was actually donated in 1903, the trust stipulated that it remains as a playing field for one hundred years.'

'Any other local clubs own their ground?'

'No.'

'Obviously I realise, Mrs Bowen Thomas, that you'd like to see the ground redeveloped either domestically or industrially; otherwise, I wouldn't be here. But what happens to the ground may fire fierce local opposition — developments always do.'

Gloria did not like the sound of the words "industrial development." Why would anyone want to put a new factory here when other local existing factories were closing down? Of course, industrial development would, without doubt, generate a grant from the local council to the developer. Gloria was sure, though, that new houses would generate a larger profit for the developer and for her own pocket. Did it really matter to her? No. She didn't care how the ground was developed; she just wanted her cut - a cut which she hoped would send her off to pastures new with all the speed of a startled rabbit.

'Developments still go ahead quite often, despite local opposition.'

Ball nodded. Then he keyed his initial thoughts. That done, he snapped shut the computer's lid. Buttoning his coat he ordered, 'I'll see the ground now.'

The big Mercedes might provoke questions if it was spotted in the ground, so they parked beside the mixture of concrete slabs, barbed wire and bricks that ringed the perimeter of what had once been Grindley's Garage. All that remained of the once busy filling station and workshop were the concrete footings of its demolished buildings. The rest of the site was a battleground between blackberries, dandelions and nettles. The former garage guarded the western side and the Baptist chapel guarded the eastern side of the narrow entrance to the rugby ground.

Ball looked at the entrance and commented, 'Whatever the type of development, this entrance needs to be wider. The chapel still looks in use, so I assume that the derelict plot is what one needs to acquire. Do you know who owns it?'

'Yes, of course I do. The chap who ran the garage still owns it. I'm talking to him about acquiring it for the club,' Gloria lied.

'Really? Pity. Just hold back if you can. Don't commit to anything without talking to me. Clear?' Without waiting for a reply Ball started walking into the ground. Gloria followed, feeling her temperature rising.

Inside the ground Gloria was relieved to see no parked cars or any of the ground committee working on the pitch. Gloria let him inspect the site on his own but watched Ball intently as he paced the whole area, studied the stand and the clubhouse, taking photographs with a camera no bigger than a wallet. When Ball wasn't taking photographs he spoke into a miniature-recording device. Finally Ball walked back to join her. In silence they returned to the car and drove to Gloria's house where Ball switched off the car engine but made no move to get out of the car.

'So, Mrs Bowen Thomas, if the ground were to become available and I and my company were interested in developing it, what would you want for the help I am sure someone in your position could provide?'

Gloria suggested a figure to which Ball replied, 'Seems reasonable.' He leaned across her and opened the car door, thanking her for her time and her hospitality. As Gloria eased herself out of the car as elegantly as possible, Ball said he would telephone her in the next few days and discuss his studied thoughts about developing the ground. Gloria hovered at the open car door. She volunteered to keep Ball abreast of any developments at the club, but Ball merely grunted and switched on his engine. As soon as Gloria shut the car door, Ball gunned the engine and shot off without a backward look.

CHAPTER 6

Gwladys Jones laid a white tablecloth on the dining table. In front of each chair she positioned a large place mat and then turned to her husband.

'John, you are under pain of death if you allow anybody at tonight's meeting to write notes anywhere other than on the mat.'

'Yes, dear,' Jones replied, straightening his back.

'Remember that if you allow people to smoke, it damages our paintwork and we'll have to get Colin Mabbutt in again to re-paint. You know how much he costs.'

'Yes, dear.'

'No smoking.'

'Yes, dear.'

The meeting was due to start at seven o'clock but by quarter past, only three of the five people expected had turned up.

'I think we better start, because the other two said they might not make it.'

'Any reason for skipping the meeting?' Marilyn asked.

Jones shook his head. 'Pressure of work, they said.'

'Why are you here, Marilyn?' Herbie Scurlock asked.

Marilyn fixed Herbie with a stare that made him shift in his seat.

'I am here, Herbie, because Dai's Uncle Ted Williams is expected to die at any moment. As his father's last remaining brother Dai felt that being at his hospital bedside was rather more important than attending a meeting about the amount of our hard earned money that is to be given to the Glanddu Rugby Club.

Furthermore, as you well know, Herbie Scurlock, Dai and I are not just married but we are a business partnership. Anything discussed here this evening I'll report to my husband. It will be a joint decision, as it always has been, as to what and how much Williams and Son Dairy Ltd. will support the rugby club in the coming year.'

'Sorry, Marilyn, my question didn't come out right. I just meant, where's Dai this evening?' responded Scurlock, his face a bright pink.

Herbert Scurlock was the Honorary Glanddu Rugby Football Club Bar Manager, a position that changed regularly every few years. The reason the role changed frequently was, of course, money. Running a cash concern like the bar was recognised by club members as an excellent chance to fiddle. The club tolerated some fiddling if the current bar manager was not too greedy and gave the club a reasonable return.

Bar managers changed every three or four years so that all members of the club had a chance of being elected to such a rewarding post at least once in their lifetime. There was also an assumption that because nearly every member of the rugby club drank alcohol since their early teens, they had an intrinsic knowledge of how to run a bar.

Herbie was in his third year as manager and the problem he faced in getting another year in the job was that bar takings had been going down each year since he took office. The continued poor performance of the rugby team and the death of old die-hard supporters meant a drop in match attendance; that, in turn, meant that fewer people followed the traditional rugby ritual of entering the club's bar immediately after the referee's whistle ended the game.

When he took on the job, Herbie had promised his wife that he would make enough money from the bar that by the end of his tenure he could afford to take her to Australia for a month-long winter holiday. The way things were going, however, he would be taking her for a cheap weekend in Blackpool.

'Tell Dai I am sorry about his Uncle Ted. Tell him. . .' Herbie's voice tailed off as he failed to find any appropriate words.

The others expressed their condolences in an equally inarticulate way.

'I accept your apology, Herbie, and thank you all for your sympathy about Ted.'

'Thank you, Marilyn,' Jones said. 'Now let's get down to business. Glanddu Rugby Union Football Club is in dire financial straits. It's a real possibility that we could go out of business next season.'

Everyone looked grim as Jones waved a sheet of paper.

'This is my financial plan for the club. All I've found, hardly surprising, is that expenditure will increase at a rate that exceeds any rise in income. Club revenue, as we know, has been declining steadily over the last three seasons. If the club collapses, the village's identity is also lost — forever.'

'It's the change in lifestyle,' said the glum voice of a depressed-looking Len "The Post" Penry, who owned the shop that was part grocery, newsagent and sub-post office.

Len's sub-post office was the last in existence amongst the villages in the valley. The supermarket closest to Glanddu was about to open its own post office and Len knew that his business was going to get tougher. 'People now do their shopping on the way home from work at the bloody supermarket. I just can't compete, not in range of stock and certainly not by price.' He looked at Marilyn.

'Same here. And not by quality. No one these days seems to realise that if they buy their milk for the entire week from the supermarket, the milk loses its freshness. Our milk is delivered straight from the cow each day.' Marilyn shook her head, 'I'm not sure how long we can or want to continue in business.'

'A pound to a penny supermarket prices will rise if all we local businesses disappear. And if Marilyn's and my shop go, then our support for the club disappears, too.'

One of the things that currently underpinned Len's shop was his business relationship with the rugby club. Either Len supplied the club with goods at prices that benefited both him and the club, or he supplied the club with goods that he charged for but never delivered. These "fictitious goods" were such items as bandages and first aid equipment that the players never needed. If they had actually used all the bandages that were ordered, the players would have looked like Egyptian Mummies as they ran out to play.

(There were a number of older supporters, often ex-players, who thought the current crop of players did play like Egyptian Mummies — just without the shrouds).

Len had no doubt that the demise of the club and its "business" with his shop would definitely force him to close. He still needed to work. But where? The supermarket? He shuddered at the thought of not being his own boss.

'The other problem we face is that people nowadays would rather watch rugby on TV than support their local team.'

'We all know that, John,' interrupted Herbie. 'But people might come back to watch Glanddu if they became a successful team.'

The top divisions of the Welsh Rugby Leagues were national whilst the lower were district-based. Glanddu were relegated to the bottom division ten years ago. In all the seasons since then they had never once looked like gaining promotion.

'Promotion for us is difficult for one good reason: the players. All the local village teams in our division are chasing a smaller and smaller pool of players because first of all, we have an aging population and second, youngsters want to do other things on Saturdays, like shopping'

'Even I can't get my head round that,' said Marilyn. 'Shopping in a mall rather than running round a field wearing a gum-shield, covered in mud, the wind coming straight from Siberia and the rain off the Atlantic? And the type of an opponent who, if he can get away with it, tries to re-arrange your teeth. Why would shopping appeal to our young people?'

'And if you're playing in Swansea at the end of the match you discover that your car isn't where you parked it. If you're lucky enough to get it back, the petrol tank is empty, the bonnet is dented and it smells of urine or worse: vomit. Otherwise, it's on its way somewhere for scrap.'

'God, what a load of miserable beggars you are. Can I get back to players? Each club has to pay larger and larger financial inducements to attract the players.'

Len interrupted, 'I heard via the grapevine that a couple of our competitor clubs like Brynddu have brought in new players from outside.'

'Or is it "bought," not brought?' Herbie Scurlock's interjection produced grunts of agreement.

Len continued, 'Yes, Herbie, "bought" is a more accurate word. Anyway, they have induced four players to join them who last season played for teams two or three divisions higher. The quality of these four players must make Brynddu one of the favourites for promotion.'

'We also must face that in our division, each of the five villages physically closest to us has a larger population than Glanddu. Larger population equals a larger supporter base which equals more income through match attendance and bar takings.'

He slumped back dispirited. 'How can we compete with them?'

'We must have faith, Len,' interjected Jones.

'I gave that up years ago, John, when I stopped going to chapel,' Len replied.

'Are we saying that there is no hope for the club? That we should give up and take down the rugby goalposts, level the clubhouse and give the ground back to Bob Rhys to run his sheep?' Herbie asked.

'I don't think Bob would want that,' replied Jones. 'He's in as dire a situation as the club for money and an extra piece of pasture is probably not what he wants.'

'Bloody supermarkets again,' snapped Len. 'The price they charge customers for lamb bears no relation to what they pay farmers for it.'

Marilyn chimed in, 'Oh, but Len, the supermarkets have to maximize profit for their stockholders; if they don't, some snotty-nosed kid in the City working for a Hedge Fund threatens them with a take-over by a shadowy outfit based in the Caymans. This kid has no idea how to produce or create or manage anything; it's only about the money (as he drives his Ferrari to spend a four-figure sum on a meal at a restaurant run by a TV celebrity chef).'

Jones wanted to get back to business before he lost control of the meeting. He did think that the new supermarket could become a sponsor, but if he said anything now about supermarket sponsorship there would be an almighty row.

Instead he said, 'Our only realistic hope of survival is to gain promotion. If we played in the higher division we would receive more money from the divisional sponsors. We would draw a bigger crowd and increase takings from the bar.'

'We have just been discussing how unlikely promotion would be. Even if we were promoted, would it be enough to ensure survival? To cap it all, I heard today that the Ffonelinc factory is closing.' He looked at Jones for confirmation.

Jones surveyed the room and said simply, 'True.'

'Golly,' said Herbie, glancing at Marilyn.

Marilyn laughed. 'The word that I was thinking, Herbie, was rather stronger than that.' She turned to Jones. 'So, found any replacement for Ffonelinc, John - perhaps a money tree between here and Llanelli?'

'Nothing. I have been discussing with our chairwoman what to do. We have come to the same conclusion: by fair means or foul, we must get promoted this year.'

Len snorted. 'Tell us, John, how it will happen. The players we have this season are the same ones who played last season, when they got to the dizzying height of sixth position in a ten team division.'

'Does anyone here, apart from me, think that our current team is overpaid?' Marilyn interrupted. She, along with many people in Wales, wondered why players in the lowest divisions of the league were paid at all. Everyone knew that paying players put an intolerable strain on the clubs.

'Yes, they are overpaid, Marilyn, but discussing their actual worth is counter-productive. We need to put fifteen players on the pitch and we have to pay them, like it or not.'

'What about your famous magic wand?' Herbie suggested.

Jones shook his head, 'I wish it were that simple. However, all is not quite doom and gloom, thanks to Tommy Harries.'

Tommy was the most famous player the village had ever produced and a local legend. Tommy had played for Wales in the 1950's. The lure of money and a good job saw him switch codes from rugby union to rugby league. First he moved to the North of

England then he transferred to an Australia rugby league club. At the end of his career Tommy stayed in Australia where he had recently died.

'In his will Tommy Harries left the club money for our players,' Jones announced and then grinned as he saw the shock on Marilyn's and Len's faces. 'Tommy bequeathed the sum of,' he cleared his throat, 'five hundred pounds, to be paid in bonuses. The club can devise the bonus scheme.'

Len exchanged looks with Marilyn. Both were thinking that one minute Jones was explaining how strapped for money the club was and now he seemed ecstatic about five hundred pounds. Five hundred pounds divided between the twenty plus players on the first team squad meant no more than twenty-five pounds to each player. Had Jones finally gone cuckoo?

'Twenty-five pounds is hardly enough to cover a player's night out with a girlfriend,' Len quipped. 'Nor is it likely to galvanise the team to win enough games to get promotion.'

Jones studied the table and saw something on the tablecloth. It was a piece of cotton. He put it in his pocket, thankful it was not something about which Gwladys could complain. He looked up to see the others staring at him, 'Gwladys likes a tidy ship. As for Tommy Harries' bequest well, yes, it's small but we must be thankful for small mercies. Herbie has a proposal about how we set up the bonus scheme. Over to Herbie.'

'What we propose is to pay a rolling bonus of two pounds for each win. For the first win the bonus is two pounds. If they win two games consecutively the bonus is four pounds per player, and so on. When the team loses, obviously, no bonus is paid. The first win after a loss in the preceding match the bonus starts again at two pounds.'

'Why would paying such a bonus to the players work now, when it has not worked when we tried it before?' Len remarked.

Herbie cleared his throat. 'Frankly, of course, we have no guarantee that it will get us promotion. We just have to do something with Tommy's money and a bonus scheme was what he stipulated.'

'I calculated what we would have paid out if we had this bonus scheme last year,' Jones interrupted, glancing at his spreadsheet.

'If both replacements got on the field each game and the team coach also got the bonus, then the total cost would have been three hundred and twenty four pounds for the season. If we have the same results this coming season, Tommy's bequest will cover total bonus expenditure.'

'But if we have the same results this coming season we will not win promotion and Tommy's money will achieve precisely nothing. Next May we'll be in the same division and one year closer to shutting down,' said Len.

'One can always hope.'

Marilyn sat and wondered at Herbie's statement. When it comes to sport, men live in cloud cuckoo land. She knew brainy men with degrees in philosophy, history, maths and physics. Yet when it came to sport even men with advanced degrees acted like the dullest man in the village; their logical faculties were replaced by pure emotion.

'You looked a bit sceptical when I mentioned hope, Marilyn.'

'Sceptical, Herbie Scurlock, not only is Marilyn sceptical but I am, as well – highly sceptical,' said Len.

'I bet you're both thinking that we are going to ask you for more money,' Jones said, 'But you're are right and wrong at the same time.' He stood, stretched his arms and flexed his aching back before sitting down again. 'What the club can't do is to be seen to pay the players bonus money.'

'Because we and the players would then have to pay tax,' interjected Herbie.

'No one wants to pay the government more than we have to. So will we pay under the counter?'

'Yes, exactly, Len,' responded Jones.

'Well,' Len looked down at his piece of paper, 'I've done some basic estimates. Over the last ten years sixteen wins have been the norm for a club gaining promotion from our division which, if we won that many, would cost us a minimum of fifteen hundred pounds in bonuses. Three clubs in the division won all eighteen games; if we won eighteen it would cost over three thousand pounds. Tommy's bequest is five hundred pounds. Where would the extra thousands come from?'

Jones knew Len's figures were accurate. 'It's possible that we may ask you both for more money when we've spent Tommy's bequest.'

'How much, precisely?' Marilyn snapped.

Jones looked at his paper. 'That obviously depends on our season. I've got a contingency fund of fifteen hundred pounds but we need some of that money for expenses other than the players.'

'So the club has enough to cover the bonus if we win sixteen games but if we are unbeaten, our small businesses would fund the rest,' Len said quietly.

'Correct,' Jones replied after a pause.

'Just under four hundred pounds per sponsor!'

'Yes, Marilyn.'

'I can't afford that amount.'

Len threw the pencil he was holding onto the table.

(Jones hoped he could wipe away the mark before Gwladys saw it).

'I'm not sure we could even find a couple of hundred extra, much less four hundred pounds,' Marilyn added with vehemence.

'What about the two sponsors not here tonight? Where do they stand?'

Jones replied, 'The four sponsors are meeting next week. At that meeting they can tell Arthur and Colin about our discussion this evening. Marilyn would have already put her husband, Dai, in the picture. Hopefully Arthur Davies, who has the biggest business of all the four sponsors would, if push comes to shove, come to the club's rescue.'

'What? If ever a man is all mouth and trousers, it's Arthur. We actually have a better chance of winning the league than getting more money out of him. Arthur hasn't bought my husband a drink in two years,' said Marilyn.

'Arthur bought him one that recently? – Dai's done better than me,' Len uttered.

'Marilyn, forget Arthur. How about this solution? If we do well and win lots of games in succession, say a dozen, we won't be able to pay the bonuses. If we can't pay the bonuses, the players will probably strike. Matches will be cancelled, the league will deduct points from us and hey, presto, we go bankrupt. So we'll have no problem with money.'

'Is that logic?' Marilyn said, genuinely perplexed.

Len quipped, 'Bertrand Russell or Aristotle might struggle. Are you on a new tablet, Herbie?'

Jones interrupted, 'Not a logic pill, that's for sure. We're all getting tired. Let's conclude the meeting.'

Chapter 7

Gloria was glad that the rugby club's bank was located in Swansea because it gave her a chance to spend time browsing the shops before she and John Jones met the new bank manager.

Gloria preferred to shop for clothes in the boutiques of Cardiff, Bristol or Bath but, sadly, the boutique fashions rarely fitted her anymore. Today was her a chance to visit the major retail chains in Swansea that could occasionally clothe her, something she disliked admitting. The stores were already gearing up for autumn and winter so she tried on the new fashions. As usual, nothing was quite her colour, nothing fitted right, and nothing flattered her figure.

Gloria was annoyed that she had allowed herself only an hour and a half to browse the shops, insufficient for thorough shopping. Free parking for two hours was available at the supermarket near the shopping mall. After her clothing expedition, Gloria returned to the car park just prior to expiration time, drove out, circled the block, and then returned to park in another bay. Then she bought her groceries.

When Gloria saw John Jones and his wife, Gwladys, standing outside the bank she stopped and looked at herself in a shop window; she looked fine though her hair might need a trim. She put a smile on her face and approached the Joneses. Gwladys was speaking to John in full flow and Gloria knew enough to stand silently until she finished.

'If your meeting ends within the hour,' said Gwladys, 'I most likely will still be in Berk and Hare in the High Street.' She turned to Gloria. 'Great name for a hairdresser. They were murderers, you know.'

'And grave robbers, too,' replied Gloria.

'My second cousin runs the place and she's been cutting my hair for years. I can recommend it if ever you're looking for a hairdresser in Swansea.'

Gwladys turned back to her husband. 'If I'm not there then I'll be in our usual café. Let's have a look at you.'

Jones straightened his back, a signal for his wife to lean forward and study him. She brushed something off his suit, and then nodded in satisfaction like the proud owner of a prize dog.

'You can't always see yourself as others do, eh, Mrs Bowen Thomas?'

Without waiting for a reply, she snapped, 'Good. I must be off.' Walking towards the hairdressers she said over her shoulder, 'And don't let those buggers bully you.'

John looked at Gloria and then raised his eyebrows. 'Maybe Gwladys should be attending the meeting. I'm sure she'd frighten them to death in there.'

Gloria thought Gwladys would merely put the bank manager's back up but she nodded and said, 'Are we waiting for our illustrious bar manager?'

'He's not coming.' Jones looked at Gloria and shrugged. 'He telephoned me and said had to go somewhere with the missus last minute.' He smiled. 'Probably got to buy a new towel or something. You know how she feels about rugby.' He muttered without thinking, 'Typical woman's attitude to the game.'

'Would you like to accompany this female club chair to our meeting?'

Jones smiled sheepishly. As they entered the bank, Gloria was surprised. 'What have they done in here?'

'The place was re-organised about a month ago to make it more customer-friendly. They want to bring the staff and customer closer together,' replied Jones, shrinking back as a scruffy individual smelling of urine and booze lurched past the pair.

Gloria wrinkled her nose.

'Poor old staff.'

The bank now had an open-plan design. A large round desk had the words "Customer Help Desk" engraved on a sign above it, but the long queue did not look like they were getting much of what was promised.

As Jones and Gloria walked past the line of customers she heard one man snap at the teller, 'All I need from you is to put my money in and take my money out of my account. If I want anything else from you, I'll just ask.' He stalked away muttering under his breath.

Gloria and John stood for a moment wondering whom to tell that they had arrived when the balding figure of David George, the bank manager, extended his hand to welcome them. George ushered Gloria and John into a bland room with a flat screen monitor and nondescript prints on the wall. The whole place presented an air of, 'Come in, get on with business and get out, ASAP.'

Gloria had drunk enough vending machine coffee in her working life to last her forever, but when George's PA offered tea and coffee she accepted a cup.

George reappeared a moment later and told them that the new manager would be with them shortly. Just as they were raising their cups a young man scorched into the room with a pile of papers. Jones and Gloria returned their cups to their saucers with alacrity and shook the newcomer's limp hand.

'Bryan Barker, George's replacement as manager for small businesses,' the man said and rocketed round to the other side of the desk and plonked a folder down on it. He then fell into the desk chair and immediately began pressing the computer keyboard before smiling at Gloria and John.

Gloria and Jones had to hold back giggles at Barker's entrance. Gloria had met a number of Toby's friends whose appearance was similar to Barker's: streaked hair upon which lashings of gel were used to make it stand up like railing spikes; a suit which was not what an older person expected to find bank staff wearing.

Gloria remembered the days when charcoal grey, black, or pinstripes was the norm, not the silver-grey, luminous cloth the new man was wearing. Gloria was glad the sun was not shining on the suit because otherwise it would surely dazzle her and Jones.

(She thought how much she would like to be a fly on the wall in the clubhouse bar on Saturday when Jones described Barker to his cronies.)

As Barker leaned forward and looked at the Glanddu pair, Gloria whiffed Armani Acqua Di Gio. Jones called it, "pong."

'I must confess to you I am not a rugby man myself; I much prefer amateur dramatics and that sort of thing, but I appreciate that in this part of the world rugby is important.'

Barker smiled before he added, 'Your rugby club, like all sports clubs, is a business and has to be run to my satisfaction, as the representative of the bank and its interests.'

'I've been looking at the figures of Glanddu's income and outgoings.' He looked down at the folder then up at the screen for a few moments. 'It seems to me that your income, particularly from the bar, is going down. Your outgoings, particularly player payments, are going up. You have some monetary reserves but you will have to repay the last loan we gave you within the next twelve months.'

He smiled at Gloria and John. 'I'm not quite sure how you are going to do that. Can you enlighten me?'

Jones looked at Gloria with a frown. 'Our bar takings have gone down over the last three years for no apparent reason. But,' looking first at David George and then at the expressionless face of Barker, 'apparently the local pub is closing down and we are thinking of opening the clubhouse on more evenings if it does so.'

'How often are you open now? How often will you intend to open the clubhouse if the pub closes? Am I right that you don't have a professional bar manager but rely totally on unpaid help?' Barker looked dismissively at Gloria and expectantly at Jones.

'In the rugby season we're open for much of the day on Saturdays and the two evenings in the week when the players attend for training. In the light of the pub's possible closure. . .'

Jones turned to Gloria.

'We are seriously thinking of hiring someone full-time. We'll open each evening except Sundays, when we'll have a carvery at lunchtime provided, of course, that we get permission from the local council.'

'What are your predicted takings?'

'We've never opened on a Friday,' Jones said, 'but traditionally Friday is a big night out. We hope to turn over one or two hundred pounds initially.' (Jones felt himself go red since he was sure they wouldn't even take £50.)

Barker frowned, 'It will hardly solve your financial problems.'

He looked down at his folder, flicked through a couple of pages and without looking up said, 'I understand that Brynddu, who are your closest competitor, keep their bar open each evening. Why will people come to your clubhouse, which I understand is a bit of an eyesore, when they can go there?'

Jones smiled broadly. 'Mr Barker, clearly, you have much to learn about valley life.'

Gloria continued, 'People from Glanddu will come to us simply because they live in our village. They want to help the club survive. It's called loyalty.'

Actually, it was tribalism, but perhaps that wasn't an appropriate term to use in a bank.

George interrupted, looking intently at Barker.

'Bryan, the villagers do not want to support their deadly rivals if they can avoid it. And another reason for using the Glanddu bar is that there are a couple of miles between the two clubs and nobody wants to drink and drive these days.'

George's voice died away; to Barker, he was yesterday's man.

Barker wrote something on his notepad, pausing now and again to read. The sound of the electric clock could be heard distinctly through the room. Gloria stared at Barker, a nasty piece of ambition. Eventually, after what seemed an age, Barker looked up.

'I would like you to let me know what you intend to do by next week.'

'All right, Mr Brewster,' said Gloria.

'It is Barker, Mrs Bowen Thomas, not Brewster.'

'Oh, I am so sorry. Anyway, Mr Barker,' Gloria drawled, 'we are a rugby club which is run by a committee and Mr Jones and I are members of that committee.'

She turned and looked at Jones.

'I think I can say important members, though?'

Jones nodded so she turned her gaze back to Barker.

'The news about the public house closure has occurred just since our last committee meeting and the next meeting is not until...'

Again, she looked at Jones, though she knew perfectly well when it was.

Jones' eyebrows furrowed as though he was having difficulty remembering. 'Three weeks yesterday, I think, Madam Chairwoman?'

Gloria imperiously rummaged slowly through her handbag before retrieving her diary. She opened it deliberately and slowly turned the pages.

'Quite right as usual, John, three weeks away.'

'Still, better to be safe than sorry,' Jones said, looking at Barker. 'I have already started looking at the various alternatives arising from the new situation. We obviously need to talk to our brewery representative, but we may not get hold of him before our next full club committee meeting.'

Barker looked away from the pair in front of him. He then stated that, despite the potential to earn a few more pounds, he wanted a revised plan to show how the outstanding bank loan would be paid on its due date. Then he shot out of the room to another meeting.

'New breed,' said George as he stood awkwardly waiting for Gloria and Jones to gather their things. 'All about money now and there is certainly not much local leeway in making decisions.'

'Mr George, you're a bit young to retire, aren't you?' Jones said, snapping his bag shut.

'Fifty-five is old these days in the bank. Re-organisations used to occur about every ten years, then about every five years and now, it's about every other week.'

'And a jolly good way of getting rid of people without actually paying any redundancy money,' Gloria spoke knowingly. 'It keeps the City of London happy, the share price high, and all the senior managers more than pleased with their share options.'

Once outside the bank Jones suggested a cup of coffee. Gloria agreed, though she felt a gin and tonic might be more appropriate.

'Mrs Bowen Thomas, do you think we will ever open the club bar more often than now? Our village hasn't got the money; one can't get blood out of a stone.'

'I agree. I'm sure the committee will not want to open the club bar more often since it won't generate any extra money. We've just tried to play a waiting game with Mr Barker. Can you, Mr. Chef de Books, once again consult your Mrs Beaton cookbook for guidance?'

'I think I've been through all the recipes; it looks like the end is nigh, particularly after meeting Mr Smelly in there.'

'This time you could be right, John.'

CHAPTER 8

Gloria heard the doorbell ring followed by the voice of her daughter, Evelyn, opening the door and greeting her brother, Toby. There were sounds of perfunctory kissing and the tread of two pairs of feet down the hall and into the sitting room. Toby pecked his mother on the cheek and accepted the offer of a drink before he dropped into a chair beside Gloria. Evelyn disappeared towards the kitchen.

'Am I still in the dog-house after cancelling the other weekend, Mother?'

'It is not the fact you cancelled but when you cancelled. I had enough milk in the refrigerator to last me a month. It was most inconsiderate of you,' Gloria snapped.

'You could have cancelled the milk, Mother,' said Evelyn, re-appearing with a glass of red wine for Toby before refilling her own and her mother's glass.

'Yes, I could have done, but David Williams would have already ordered it and I know what a struggle people like him have in today's world.'

'Do you want me to pay for it?' Toby thrust his hand into his back pocket and came up with a few copper coins.

'Typical,' said his sister to Gloria when she saw the coins.

'I don't need for you to pay me for any milk.'

'Fine. I love Australian Shiraz,' said Toby holding the glass up and staring at its contents.

'Yes, don't we all, Toby, even more than milk,' his mother exclaimed.

'Pax,' Evelyn interjected. 'You two can argue later. I've coursework to finish marking this evening.'

'And I've a meeting to go to in an hour,' Toby said, looking at his watch. 'So we'd better make this quick.'

'I come all the way from Wales to London and now one is going to disappear to her room and the other is going out. I do expect to see my children for more than a few minutes.'

'Mother, we both work. Anyway, you've been shopping successfully in the West End today so you can't say your trip is just to see us.'

'I never said it was, Evelyn,' her mother exclaimed. 'I came for several reasons, one of which is the Grindley's garage situation. I'd like to discuss Grindley's if you both can spare some of your precious time.'

'You came all the way up from Wales to discuss Grindley's garage? It's been closed for ages,' Evelyn said.

'Evelyn,' said Toby, pretending shock. 'Didn't you know Mother is going to retrain as a mechanic? Then she can re-open the garage, repair the rugby club tractor, and start earning a living again.'

'What is it with my children? It is no laughing matter, the pair of you,' Gloria said, as Toby and Evelyn giggled at the prospect of their mother wearing overalls and covered in grease.

'Toby could not resist winding you up, Mother,' Evelyn said, wiping her tears away.

'So what do we need to know so desperately about Grindley's Garage?' Toby asked.

When Gloria first spoke to Toby and Evelyn after Ball's visit, they spoke primarily about Ball's vanity and rudeness. Gloria now needed to explain to them in detail what Ball said when he telephoned after looking over the rugby ground. Gloria wanted to discuss her plans with her children when they were together in the same room.

'Ball thinks that the rugby ground has clear potential as a development site for houses.'

'You told us that after his visit,' said Toby.

'Yes, if you could find that fact hidden amongst his copious failings, according to Mother.'

'Thank you, children. Now, pay attention. Mr Ball said that the current single track entrance to the rugby ground is a major problem. The entrance would have to be widened to accommodate a two-lane access road onto the site. Only then would the council give any planning approval for houses on the rugby ground. There is no way that the Baptist chapel is going to sell or give up any of its land. Grindley's Garage on the other side of the entrance is, therefore, the key to whether the rugby ground could ever become a housing development site.'

Gloria took a deep breath and looked at her children who were now all ears. 'So what I have been thinking is that perhaps as a family we should try and buy the Grindley site as an investment.'

'I thought you have no money.'

'I do have some, Evelyn, but certainly not enough to buy the site on my own. If you listened, I said "we as a family" — not myself, alone.'

'You haven't told us what the site's value is, Mother.'

'That I don't yet know, Toby. Before I develop any plans I need to know whether you both would be interested in investing money in my proposal.'

Gloria looked expectantly at Toby who sat back frowning. Then she switched her attention to Evelyn.

'Obviously, you need to talk to Ron. Where is he this week?'

Evelyn had to stop and think before replying. Her husband was a whiz kid in telecommunications and was invariably away.

'India this week, Germany next week, and Canada in a fortnight. Then,' she said, 'he's here with me – hurrah!'

'Lucky man,' said Toby sarcastically.

Then, after he had caught the cushion his sister threw at him, he turned to his mother.

'Isn't this a bit premature? First, because we don't have a valuation of Grindley's. Second, because you don't know if the club will make it through this season. And third, it could be years before it folds. You don't actually know when the ground will become available for a housing development. Isn't it all too risky?'

'Yes, but if we wait until the club folds by then other people might see the ground's potential and realise that Grindley's holds its access key. Anyway, yesterday I talked to the council planning department about possible developments.'

'Wait a moment,' said Toby. 'You went into the Planning Office to ask about the club ground and Grindley's? You know that will spark talk and other people might start sniffing around and interfere with your plans.'

Gloria smiled benignly and halted his diatribe. 'Toby, there are no flies on your mother. I went into the Planning Department yesterday to discuss whether or not I could put a new house in my garden.'

'God, you surely aren't going to do that?'

Gloria smiled broadly. Her daughter might be academically clever but her knowledge of the way her mother's mind worked was clearly limited.

She then recounted the conversation. The planner could not say whether she would get permission to put a house in her garden until she actually submitted a planning application for what she wanted to do.

'In my discussion with the planner he said that any housing development within the boundaries of villages — what they call "infilling" — is more likely to be granted today than it would have been five years ago. What is not acceptable is development on green field sites. Then I asked the planner, purely out of curiosity, could any development of Glanddu's rugby ground ever take place? He said, "Yes, in the unlikely event that it no longer remained a rugby pitch." I, of course, said nothing at that statement.'

Gloria rummaged in her bag and produced a diary-sized book with the title, "Glanddu Rugby Club Membership Book."

'You two are already club members and I have now paid for Ron to become a member.'

She handed the book to her daughter.

'He doesn't like rugby and loathes coming down to Wales, so why bother?' Evelyn said, taking the book and idly flicking through it.

'This membership might earn him a few quid if the club folds,' said Gloria.

'What on earth do you mean, Mother?' said Evelyn.

'Club members would be deemed the site owners so they would get the money that a sale would raise, after all debts are cleared.'

'Ron will like that.'

'I bet he'll like Wales and Glanddu a whole lot more if he makes a pile of money out of being a club member,' interjected Toby.

Gloria had pointed out to the planner that, as chairwoman of the Glanddu rugby club, she was interested in whether the Grindley's Garage site could ever get approval to be used as an overflow car park for the rugby ground. The planner said there would be no obvious reason for the Planning Department to object.

Gloria then asked the planner, 'What about the application for housing on Grindley's that failed a few years ago? Would an application now be more favourably received?'

Because the planner looked at Gloria suspiciously, she clarified that if approval to allow housing on the site was granted, the club would want to move quickly to avoid any greedy developer getting his grasping mitts on it. When the planner continued to look doubtful, Gloria emphasized that the price of the site would be beyond the capability of the rugby club if in competition with a developer.

'Wouldn't want that to happen,' said the planner. 'I know people need houses, but Wales needs good rugby players and they need to be able to park their cars. Looking at the site today, however, the council would probably be more favourable to a housing application than it was last time.'

'Basically,' Gloria added, 'the chap then gave me a look that said, "Get your arse into gear."'

'You're asking us to gamble based on this look?'

'Yes, Toby, I am.'

Toby and Evelyn sat silent for several moments mulling things over.

Then Evelyn said, 'Mother, whilst I am impressed by this plan, are you being fair? Aren't you, as chairwoman of the rugby club, being devious and, dare I say, unethical by investigating the possibility of developing the ground?'

'It depends what you mean. If the club folds, there's no reason not to make some money. And if it doesn't fold, we're left with the White Elephant of Grindley's Garage. It's our loss or our little earner, but we're not asking anyone else to take a risk.'

'Have you been able to speak confidentially to anyone about your plans?' Evelyn asked.

'Just with your Uncle Tim and Auntie Jean. When they came down for a visit back in May I asked them, just out of curiosity, to see if I could build another property in the garden of my house, like they did. They thought it would be feasible to build a four-bedroom house using a self-build kit called, "Scandiahus." After I met Ball, I spoke to Tim on the telephone about the Grindley's site. Your Uncle has often wondered why it has been derelict for so long and he thought we could build at least four houses on that plot. Since none of us are builders we could use Scandiahus to provide the prefabricated building materials and also to manage the whole job.'

Toby, who had been doing some rough calculations on an envelope, pointed out, 'Building four houses could cost from two to four hundred thousand pounds depending on the house size. Do any of us have that kind of money? I don't.'

Gloria replied,' I do know how expensive it is to build houses. One alternative is to work with a local developer as a partner in the scheme, but it's far too early to investigate who that might be. Ball said that he is only interested in developing Grindley's site for housing if he also develops the rugby ground.'

'Back to the crucial question, Mother. How likely is it that the club will actually fold? John Jones has been crying wolf for years, yet the club still exists.'

'Well, Evelyn, we have met the new bank manager and he is clearly not a rugby fan. He wants us to repay our loan when it is due at the end of the season. At the moment it seems that without a miracle, the club won't make it.'

'Any chance of a miracle occurring?'

'Well, promotion to the fourth division would be a miracle.'

'So, basically, no chance.'

'No, Toby.'

'So what we need to do now is find out what amount money Mr Grindley wants for the site?'

'Yes, Evelyn. He's going on holiday this week but I have arranged to see him in Swansea when he returns at the end of September.'

Toby leaned forward and glanced at his sister before he said, 'I'm interested, provided I have the money to meet his price.'

'I'll talk to Ron and, like Toby, it's a question of how much money is required. In principle, I think we're in.'

'I thought you were questioning mother's principles about this earlier. Money talks, eh?'

'We would be doing this to help Mother,' Evelyn replied tartly.

Toby laughed at the reply and then asked, 'How are you going to approach Grindley without raising his suspicions as to why we're buying it?'

Gloria tapped her nose with a forefinger. 'I have it all worked out. You two have other things to do. Just trust me.'

'So we are all hoping that Glanddu Rugby Club goes bankrupt. Daddy would be so upset at the club's disappearance.'

'If Glanddu does go bankrupt it probably would amalgamate with Brynddu.'

'Shit,' said Toby, 'Daddy would turn over in his grave if he heard that.'

Chapter 9

Marsha Bolotnikov watched her husband's car draw up outside the house. His chauffer, Yuri, got out and, after a glance both ways, opened the car's back door. Boris Bolotnikov leapt out of the car and sprinted to the front door, just as Marsha swung it open. Marsha received a perfunctory kiss on the cheek as Boris ducked inside. Whilst Boris divested himself of his suit jacket, Marsha moved into the sitting room and made him a drink.

Boris appeared a moment later and took the drink before he flopped down heavily into an armchair. His wife perched on the chair opposite and watched him swig his drink and munch nuts from the large bowl she had placed on the coffee table. The sound of a key in the front door presaged the arrival of the chauffer who stuck his head in the door.

'Eight o'clock in the New Indus Curry House in Whitfield Street.'

'Right, boss.' Yuri withdrew and headed out through the kitchen into the tiny garden that housed a shed just big enough for his bed, a chair and a TV.

'God, I hate this house. It is so small for London,' Marsha said, with the good grace to wait until the chauffeur had disappeared.

'Marsha, compared with how we both grew up in Moscow, this is a veritable palace. Also, this company house is only temporary.'

'You have been saying that for two years.'

'Well, we will be here only until. . .'

Marsha's face, wreathed in a beaming smile and, unable to contain her excitement, blurted out, 'I have found the perfect house in the posh area called St John's Wood. It is not huge, just six bedrooms, four baths and a flat over the garage for you know who.' She flicked her head towards the garden.

'I am not worried about Yuri.'

'I know that, silly.'

'Now, how is the security?'

'A high fence, electronic gates, CCTV everywhere with a control room in the cellar. There are houses opposite, but no high ground to overlook the place, so it seems ideal. I spoke to your secretary and she suggested tomorrow at one o'clock? OK, by you?'

Boris stood and went into the hall before reappearing with his laptop. 'Yes, she has put it in my schedule. One hour, only.' He looked at his wife. 'And that includes travel there and back.'

He stopped speaking and glanced at the security monitor as he heard the sound of a key unlocking the front door. A moment later, the door crashed shut with such violence that the whole house shook. A red-haired teenager with a large training bag appeared, wearing a pained look on his face.

'I may have tweaked a hamstring so I quit training and arranged to go to that sports physiotherapist over in Goodge Street. Is that OK?' Without waiting for an answer the boy disappeared in the direction of the kitchen where he removed a meat pie from the refrigerator and walked back to join his parents. He began to demolish the pie with huge bites and dribbled pastry crumbs down onto the floor.

'Is a hamstring important?' Marsha asked. When her husband and son had stopped laughing, she remarked, 'Silly me.'

'Yes, particularly if, as Mr Parry my school coach believes, I have a chance to play for the Welsh schoolboys this year.'

'Sergei, you are Russian. How can you play rugby for Wales?' Marsha asked, and saw her son and husband exchange exasperated looks.

'Mother, I have been boarding at a Welsh public school since you sent me to Britain five years ago. I'm perfectly eligible for the

Welsh team. If I went to school in England, I might play for the English team.'

Marsha got up and turned to her husband. 'I am going to get changed after I have telephoned Larry Lord to confirm tomorrow's visit. I do not want anyone else getting a look in.'

She switched her gaze to her son. 'Do you want to come to the restaurant with us or was that pie enough?'

'Mother, that was a snack. Of course, I am coming. I'll be starving in an hour.'

'Put something decent on.'

Marsha picked up some pastry crumbs from her son's trousers and gave him a playful cuff round the ear.

Boris leaned forward and waited till Marsha had left the room before he spoke.

'Would you like to transfer to an English school? You know I can arrange that.'

The boy shook his head. 'No, I like my school.'

Sergei paused, and after clearing his throat he said, 'One of my schoolmates asked me today if I could get a DVD of "The Billings Range War" and a copy of "The Attack of the Venus Flytrap." He is a good friend. I said it might be possible.'

'Neither of those films is yet available on DVD in this country and will not be for three or four months,' Boris said, looking stern.

But when he saw his son's pleading look Boris added, 'OK, I will get you copies but you must say that a friend got them from a market in India or Hong Kong.' Boris made a note on a piece of paper and stuffed it in his wallet. 'I'll make sure to get them before you return to school. Any particular reason for those two films?'

'Rhiannon Griffiths.' The boy winked at his father, who nodded sagely.

Charleston as always was sweltering in August. The star of the "The Billings Range War" and "The Attack of the Venus Flytrap" was shooting some location scenes for her latest film, the American Civil War epic, "Attack on Fort Sumter."

The humidity of the late American summer was exacerbated by the heavy, ornate costume that Rhiannon Griffiths' character, a wealthy plantation owner's daughter, was wearing (or rather, it was wearing her). Her air-conditioned trailer was her oasis and when the weather became unbearable, Rhiannon was not above throwing a tantrum and storming off the film set just to get to her trailer and cool bliss.

Henderson Glitter's excessively violent grip on her arm was the alleged cause of today's tantrum. The scene called for Henderson, her co-star, to grasp Rhiannon's arm, wrestle with her, whirl her round before throwing her onto the floor. After eight attempts to get the scene right, a heavily perspiring Rhiannon noticed not only that her co-star but that she, herself, was beginning to pong. As soon as she entered her trailer, Rhiannon shooed out her assistant before washing under her armpits and spraying with deodorant. That done, she picked up the telephone and immediately began talking nineteen to the dozen.

'Hello, Mam, just having a break. God, it's hot here. What's it like in London? Sounds wonderful. How's everybody there? Good. Well, we finish here, thank God, at the end of the week then back to Hollywood for some interiors. It looks like I won't be back home for a few weeks because I've been signed to do a murder film. I'll be playing a cop. Amber Golightly was going to do it but she's pregnant... I assume her husband's the father, but you never know with her. . . The producers wanted me because both of my last films have done so well at the box-office. I'm now on the A list of stars, not before time... The working title of the cop film is, "Mindless Murder in Milwaukee." They're definitely going to do another Venus Fly Trap film. A draft script is ready but nobody is sure if it's a sequel or a prequel. Well, I know it's not highbrow stuff but the money will be fantastic. I'll be able to buy Wales. No, I know that's not a good investment. No, Mam, I'm not interested in the Costa del Sol... the Mafia owns it already.'

'Hey, I'm doing some advertisements for a new perfume in a couple of weeks. They're paying me loads of money. The perfume is going to be marketed in the UK next year. Maybe I'll make some UK-based adverts for them. Of course, I'll get some samples but believe me it is crap. . . but the money is so good. I've got to make hay whilst the sun shines.'

'Have you been down to Glanddu to see my uncle? How is he? Oh. Yes, I know I haven't been for years. When I come back I'll go down to visit him. Anyway, I'm sufficiently cool now so I'd better get back outside and finish the scene before someone thinks of suing me. Before I go, tell my brother to make sure that he videos all the autumn rugby games that Wales are playing, and if he can get the commentary in Welsh, so much the better... Mam, I know, November, but he forgot to video one game last year that Wales won and I missed it. Just remind him to do it on pain of death!'

There was a knock on her trailer door, Rhiannon covered the telephone mouthpiece and bellowed, 'Come.'

A head tentatively materialized and a voice whispered, 'Ms Griffiths, are you ready for the scene?'

'Yes,' replied Rhiannon, who looked in the mirror and snapped, 'I'll need the hairdresser.' The head disappeared and Rhiannon resumed her conversation, 'Well, I best go, Mam. I gather Milwaukee can be a bit chilly but I can't wait to get there. Give you a call tomorrow, love to you all, bye.' Rhiannon put the telephone down and walked to the door. 'Shit.' Picking up her voluminous dress in one hand, she began fanning herself with the other as she glided onto the film set.

Boris and his brother, Ivan, sat at the tiny bar in the entrance of the Indian restaurant.

'You are eating with us?'

Ivan shook his head. 'No, I have a business dinner over in Kensington,' he looked at his watch, 'in about eight minutes so I have to be quick. I had a late call at the bank from our paper merchant friend. You know, whose wife was a ballet dancer with the Kirov.'

Boris nodded, 'And?'

'He needs to move a few hundred thousand pounds out of a company account and put it into a personal account. I thought we could run the usual bogus market survey. We'll "charge" £300,000 for the survey and take our twenty percent commission; everybody will be happy. As always, all you have to do is make some cosmetic changes to the documentation.'

'I'll need a couple of days to research the subject to make sure the survey looks real. I think we'll survey the EU countries that existed before the EU expansion.'

Ivan grunted, 'Any reason for that restriction?'

'Well, since our client is a Russian company, they may have already done a market survey of the countries in the Soviet bloc.'

At that statement, both men started to laugh uproariously.

'I will have to tell the wife that one, she will laugh her socks off,' Ivan dabbed his eyes. 'A Russian company doing a market survey of the East European countries within the old Iron Curtain!'

'Actually, we may be over-using this market survey scam. We are going to have to come up with something new eventually. But for now, do you recall that survey we did for a wood merchant based in Murmansk? Since the pulp and paper businesses have many similarities, it should not take long to refine the survey. Will Friday morning do?'

'Yes. When you provide the survey, give me six copies. Backdate the invoice thirty days so he can transfer the funds to us on Friday.'

The two men shook hands. Boris watched his brother leave the restaurant before he joined his wife and son who were studying the menus. As Boris sat down, he kept an eye on the restaurant door. Yuri entered and walked to a table between the Bolotnikovs and the door and waved away the half-hearted attempts by the waiter to seat him elsewhere.

'Successful?'

'Yes. I can see us living in St John's Wood already.'

CHAPTER 10

The four club sponsors were jammed into the clubhouse's smallest room. The room usually was a jumble of old rugby balls, discarded playing kit and broken chairs but someone, no doubt on orders from Mrs Bowen Thomas, had cleared the place during the summer so there was enough space for a table and four chairs. Len Penry explained to Colin Mabbutt and Arthur Davies what had transpired at the meeting in Jones' house earlier in the month.

'Two pounds? Two measly quid? Are they all mad, Len?' said Arthur Davies. 'What the hell can you buy with two pounds? A couple of pints of milk from Dai, a few stamps from Len, and that is it! The players will laugh at us, bloody laugh. I think this is Tommy Harries' revenge because of how we treated him; I bet he is laughing in his grave.' Arthur sighed. 'It ought to be more if we want to see the club move up; otherwise, we shouldn't make fools of ourselves. It is ridiculous to offer two quid.'

'We haven't all got bank accounts in the Cayman Islands, or in Switzerland,' growled Dai Williams.

Dai had often wondered why a successful businessman like Arthur Davies still wanted to be involved with his hometown club. Arthur had lived for years in Swansea where he owned thriving businesses. Dai imagined that people of Arthur's status would prefer the glamour of one of the four Welsh rugby clubs that played in the multi-national Celtic League, where they were immune from the vagaries of promotion and relegation that clubs like Glanddu faced.

Dai figured that because Arthur's businesses were mostly cash-in-hand — a second-hand car showroom, a scrap-yard and a number of houses that he rented out to students at Swansea University — the last thing Arthur wanted was publicity. If Arthur sponsored a big club, his businesses would get a higher public profile. The higher profile might then interest the Inland Revenue, particularly its VAT division. But Marilyn said that even worse than the Inland Revenue would be increased attention from Arthur's three ex-wives. Arthur was currently on his fourth wife and as he had recently been spotted coming out of a divorcee's house at seven thirty one morning, he could be moving on to his fifth.

'How could I have accounts in the Cayman Islands when I couldn't even find them on a map?' Arthur said with mock innocence.

'You don't have to know where they are. You just need to send your money there by computer,' interjected Len Penry.

'How would a shopkeeper cum postmaster know anything like that?' Mabbutt asked with interest. As the local jobbing builder, he was interested in any good place to hide money far from the prying eyes of Her Majesty's Government.

Penry replied, 'Because, Colin, we need to know about money laundering in the Post Office. Now, let's just get on without further argument. The point is that none of us has much money to spare.'

'All I was saying is that a win bonus of two pounds is derisory,' said Arthur, before taking a swig of his beer.

'Bloody pipes in the bar need cleaning as usual,' he grunted before slamming the glass back on the table.

'Christ, Arthur, the bar is run by volunteers. It's not a pub where they clean the beer pipes as a matter of course,' Dai said wearily.

Len interrupted, 'Come on boys, enough. What the club is proposing is that the win bonus be an accumulator. If the team wins four games in a row, they get eight pounds. We know it is not a princely sum, but we do play in the bottom division.'

'When did we last win four games in a row?' Mabbutt asked.

'Not so long ago - March 2000, actually,' replied Len, then added, 'Remember, eight pounds untaxed is worth about nine pounds, depending on your tax rate.'

'Len, since when do most of our players pay tax? Many of them are on the dole and working for him,' Dai said, pointing at Mabbutt.

'Which, I might add, keeps them playing for the club. You don't employ players anymore, Dai,' Arthur snapped.

'Oh, yes, and how am I meant to do that? May I remind you I am competing with a supermarket. I can't even buy my milk wholesale for what the supermarkets charge retail.'

Dai looked round the table.

'My father employed four milkmen on deliveries when we were all growing up. When Eurof Cooper retires next week, I won't replace him. It'll just be me as the sole milkman delivering in this area.'

He banged his fingers hard on the table.

'I cannot afford any more money for the club.'

'Whoa, Dai,' said Mabbutt. 'The club is going to pay the players the bonus with boot money. None of us has to find this money.' He looked at Len, 'Do we?'

'Maybe. If the team wins more than a certain number of games, the club definitely won't be able to pay the bonus. If that happens the club wants us to step in and take over the payments. John estimates that if we won all our games the bonus payments to the players would cost us each an extra four to five hundred pounds over and above sponsoring rugby balls, meals and whatever.'

'That's a lot of money for us small businesses," said Mabbutt. Like Dai, I'm not sure I could find any extra money.'

'Me, too,' chimed in Arthur, receiving catcalls from the other three. 'You try running four wives and girlfriends and see how much money you end up with.'

'I am struggling,' said Len Penry who, since his wife died, had increasingly focussed on the rugby club. He was a member of six of the club's committees and never missed a meeting. His business was no more viable than Dai and Marilyn Williams' dairy but with his daughters married over in England, he wanted to support the club to the best of his ability.

Len cleared his throat and said deliberately, 'I've changed my mind. I will find the money by hook or by crook. The thing that strikes me, boys, is that if somehow the team plays well, would we want to scupper our chances by not paying the players this bonus? The maximum total sum is thirty-six pounds, thirty-two if the replacements don't get on the pitch. That boys, divided by the four, equals eight or nine pounds.'

Dai laughed sarcastically. 'Nine pounds, Len, is roughly the profit I make on about ninety pints of milk. But there is one glaring error. We would only have to put our hands in our pockets if they win twelve games. If the games are won in succession, the players will be on £24 each. Fifteen players and the coach brings the sum to £384 but even more must be paid when replacements get on the field. Eighty to a hundred pounds for each of us, not bloody nine, Len Penry, you prize idiot. That is nearly a week's profit.'

Len started to stammer. 'I don't care. I'll find the money somehow.'

'Hearing Len's unselfishness, I've also changed my mind; I'll front up the money,' Arthur said.

'Me, too,' Mabbutt said, hoping nobody would hear him.

Dai's face began to turn red. 'Our lads are playing for a fifth Division Club, not a first or a Celtic League club. They cannot expect more than what the club already pays them. If they were better players then they would not be playing here. This whole thing is an absolute nonsense.'

'The greatest player ever to come out of our village triggered this bonus scheme concept,' Len said, looking into Dai's eyes. 'We must ensure that if his bequest is exhausted, we must continue the bonuses, come what may.'

'You know what I think: the players will love the concept of an under-the-counter payment, no matter how small.'

'Typical of you to say that Arthur,' replied Dai.

'Oh, yes, and are you a chapel man?' responded Arthur. 'Come off the holier than thou pedestal. You can't tell me that you're not above doctoring the books.'

'Oh, yes, he can,' Len chimed in, 'because Marilyn does the books.'

Even Dai forced a smile.

'OK,' Dai said, grudgingly. 'We can put up some money on one condition.'

'That we drink more milk?'

'No, Arthur. If we have to start paying the bonus say, after win fourteen, then we will be liable for four hundred and fifty pounds. That means a hundred and twelve pounds fifty pence for each of us. I can go this high, but if we win the following week I won't pay a single penny more.'

'Christ, would it be that much, Dai?' asked Mabbutt.

'Yes, I propose we agree not to pay any more money than that amount.'

'Let's vote on Dai's proposal. All those in favour? Right, carried three to one because I oppose' said Len. 'But now it's time for the full committee meeting.'

CHAPTER 11

Before Gloria became the club chair committee meetings rarely started on time, but woe betide any latecomers now. Len and Dai surveyed the bar and saw at its far end Declan O'Grady and Granville Beck, the captain and the club coach, respectively. Len and Dai looked at the clock.

'We have ten minutes to talk to them, Len, before it starts,' said Dai and led the way through the throng of committee people who were fortifying themselves with alcohol.

'Right,' said Len, as he ushered captain and coach to an empty corner. Len told Dai that he would do the talking but nervousness got the better of him and Dai addressed Declan and Granville.

'Four of us have just had a meeting about how we can encourage the team to win promotion and we have come up with,' he lowered his voice, 'an under-the-counter win bonus for each player.'

'How much?' Declan's eyes narrowed as he looked at the sponsors because he had already heard about the bonuses via the grapevine.

'Two pounds,' Dai announced.

'It's not a lot, Dai.'

Granville chimed in, 'Derisory, really.'

'Dai forgot to mention that it's a rolling bonus based on the games you win consecutively,' Len stuttered.

'I know the structure,' said Granville, 'If the team wins two games in a row the players get four pounds, three in a row they get six and so on. Is there an upper limit, by any chance, like,' he forced a laugh, 'eight pounds?'

'No, but if you lose a game then the next game you win the bonus reverts to two pounds.'

'However, if you win every bloody match we would struggle to pay you.'

'You don't expect us to win the league?' Declan tried to look shocked.

'Of course, we do.'

'We will get promotion,' Granville spoke from the heart, despite disagreement from his brain. 'You said, Dai, that you might not be able to pay the players if we won a lot of games. Think again. You will just have to find the money.'

Dai was in a corner. 'If we get into that position, we'll try to find the money by hook or crook.'

'Good,' Granville looked satisfied.

Declan was not so sanguine. 'Try? I've got family commitments and, as professionals, the team expects agreement to be honoured because. . .'

Declan's voice tailed off as he saw the look on Dai's face.

'Declan, the club plays in the fifth Division. I am afraid you are not a professional. You are, like every other player in our team, a part-timer. We aren't a big professional club whose players have more money than sense. We four sponsors are local businessmen struggling to keep our heads above water. We are going to pay you what we can afford, and possibly more than you are worth.'

Dai saw Len stiffen and look anxiously at the two younger men.

Declan had not batted an eyelid at Dai's announcement. Instead he blurted out, 'What about the tax? How does this affect our regular wages from the club?'

'Declan, your regular wages stay just the same. There's is no tax on the bonus; it's what we used to call "boot money." Nobody knows we're paying you this bonus except one or two people on the committee and we'd like to keep it that way,' Len said, knowing that if anyone on the committee didn't know already about this bonus, the secret would be out by the end of this evening.

'If you could increase it a bit, say to three pounds, I'm sure the players would respond more positively,' said Granville.

'No, not possible,' said Dai.

'The meeting is about to start so we had better get up there, before Madam Fuhrer loses her cool,' Len said.

Declan piped up, 'Is the bonus scheme for League and knock out Cup Games?'

'Gentlemen,' said Len, grasping Dai's arm and pulling him towards the stairs. 'The bonus applies to the League only. We must get to the meeting.'

'Like a beer, Len?'

'Yes,' Len replied before heading out of the room with Declan and Granville.

Dai went to the bar and bought two pints. To avoid spilling any he took a mouthful from each glass and set off to the meeting.

CHAPTER 12

The committee meeting was held in what was, on Saturdays, the players' dining room. Tonight the white plastic dining tables were in a rectangle. Gloria arrived at seven o'clock for the meeting and found John Jones already working on his laptop. Jones did not hear her enter so Gloria reflected for a moment on what Duncan had told her about him.

'John Jones sacrificed his whole working career for Glanddu Rugby Football Club. At eighteen, he got a job as an accounts clerk in the local Council and stayed in the same job for forty years. He could have qualified as an accountant but he didn't bother because it would have interfered with his work for the club. They reckon' — Duncan had never said who they were — 'that John completed his daily tasks at the council in about four hours. After his official work was done, John spent the rest of his day on Glanddu Rugby Club accounts.'

Duncan also told her, 'John, as well club accountant, has at different times run the ground staff, been team manager, team selector, catering manager and just about everything else except team coach and bar manager. He told Gwladys before they were married that though he loved her, she had to share him with the club. I don't think Gwladys quite believed him,' Duncan paused, with a twinkle in his eye. 'She does now. John is a walking encyclopaedia of the club, all its functions, all its players, all its supporters, all their children, and all their dogs. I am not sure about cats, though.'

'How sad,' Gloria said when Duncan had finished, 'that anyone would devote himself so slavishly to the club and sacrifice a career that, no doubt, would have benefited him and his family. He could have earned far more money if he been a qualified accountant.'

Duncan shrugged, 'Well, every rugby club and, I suspect, cricket and soccer club has a John Jones. People like him ensure that a club can survive because in reality they are the full-time staff that every sports club needs but cannot afford to pay.'

'Found any problems with the software, John?' Gloria asked, as she came back to the present and began to manoeuvre herself to her position at the centre of the top table.

'No. As always, absolutely spot on with your repair or, should I say, enhancement?'

'Well, I have worked in IT for a long time. Rather longer than I care to remember.'

'Any jobs on the horizon?'

As she unloaded her briefcase Gloria snorted, 'Absolutely nothing.'

As Gloria settled herself down Jones reached into the pile in front of him and handed her a CD.

'Whilst I remember,' said John.

'Right, and I'd better give you one in return.'

Both CDs were then carefully stowed in their recipients' briefcases. The CDs contained back-up copies of the latest company official accounts.

The club had a more sophisticated computer system than one might expect in a rugby club the size of Glanddu. When Toby's company in London replaced its perfectly good PCs with the latest equipment, Toby bought, virtually for nothing, a PC from his company and presented it to the club. Gloria and Duncan, anxious to maintain their computing skills, developed a computer system for the club. The system handled the accounts, bar management, membership, players' weights and even match statistics.

'Anything I should know about?' she asked, putting on her spectacles before flicking through her papers to ensure everything was in order.

John pressed the save button on the laptop. 'Two pieces of information since I last spoke to you.'

John telephoned Gloria on average three times a week in the playing season and once or twice at other times.

'I'll give you the bad news first. Ffonelinc has now officially announced a date for closing down. They are dismantling the plant and moving every piece, lock stock and barrel, to Estonia.'

'Another victory for the so-called global economy, I suppose.'

'Undoubtedly, Mrs Bowen Thomas.'

'Estonia, eh, where the company will pay abysmal wages and where people will work in atrocious conditions with few benefits. But by moving manufacturing to a low wage economy, the managing director of Ffonelinc will see the company stock price rise. And just before some catastrophe occurs he'll sell his shares at an enormous profit. Then he'll go somewhere else, do exactly the same thing and ruin more people's lives.'

'I think you're right on all counts there. We'll have you voting Labour yet, Mrs Bowen Thomas,' Jones said laughing.

'We've got a Labour government now and they do nothing about any of this; they're too dominated by Wall Street. I'd rather vote Welsh Nationalist than for the present incumbent of Number 10. Any chance of getting any money from Ffonelinc before they disappear?'

'Yes. Denis Hopper, their Marketing manager, sent us the cheque for this season two weeks ago.' Jones pushed his glasses down his nose as he beamed at her. 'Denis must have known that this move was on the cards because he sent us the cheque before the season starts; this is the first time we ever had any money from them before September first. I bet when that bloody managing director finds out what Denis did, he will be beside himself with anger. Not that Denis cares because he has taken early retirement and is returning to live in Manchester. His move back to the North of England is a shame because his experience would be useful to us. We could think about co-opting him onto the committee until he moves.'

'I'll keep him in mind.'

'I wasn't implying that his background is as comprehensive or as varied as yours. I thought that, being retired, he would have time to do things for the club. Anyway, we can still consider him since he won't be able to sell his house in this market.'

Marilyn nodded, 'Nobody local could afford it now. But, as always, there are Cardiff people looking for a country home.'

The pair sat in silence for a while before Jones spoke again.

'Did you know that "The Fox" closing date is now set for the first of November?'

'What about the publican?'

'Don Bennett. He's still trying to get permission to convert it into dwellings. He'll continue to live on site but I think the shutters will go up on the windows. It'll look awful.'

'I hate seeing derelict buildings; they make the village look run-down.'

'So, on the agenda tonight is whether the club wants to open the club bar more often to serve customers from "The Fox" who no longer have a place to drink. You did a straw poll?'

'I did. Nobody wants it.'

'Good. So at least we can look our Bank Manager, Brewster, in the eye and we can tell him we tried (holding our noses as we do so).'

'Mr Barker is his name, as you well know, and once smelt, never forgotten.'

'I had to wash my sweater after we met him to get rid of the pong.'

Gloria drummed the table.

'We need to set up a meeting with our lovely Abertawe Ales salesman, Iory Isaacs.'

'Do we really need to have a meeting with him?'

'Yes, we do. Tell Iory that with the Fox closing, the club bar will stay open longer; he won't know that we've already rejected that possibility. We need to discuss whether Abertawe Ales is going to give us the new cash registers it is installing in some of its pubs. Also, will he have any new deals for us?'

'Such as what, apart from the cash registers?'

'Who knows? That's why we need to meet him. We haven't seen him for ages.' She looked at her diary. 'I'm free a week on Tuesday, so why not arrange it for twelve thirty? Iory can give us a working lunch in that nice pub on the marina. Anyway, John, it is about time he took us out again.'

'It is time to meet him again, Madam Chairwoman, but new cash registers — is that wise? New tills leave less scope for fiddling our bar accounts.'

'Oh, John, we'll just talk about it. We're never going to install new tills, for exactly the reason you've just said.'

'Oh, of course, the penny's dropped. This meeting is just an excuse to get us a free lunch; I must be having a senior moment.'

Suddenly the door burst open and a tidal wave of committee members, drinks in hand, flooded the room.

CHAPTER 13

Dai told Marilyn that the committee meeting could have ended a half-hour earlier but for the garrulousness of certain individuals. Marilyn knew how long winded rugby club committee meetings could be; she was originally from Bryntowy, eight miles away, on whose rugby team committee her father served after he retired from playing. Many times he came home complaining of the loquaciousness of committee members after meetings and threatened to give it up and sit in front of the TV. Marilyn had once asked him "Dad, why are rugby club committee meetings so longwinded?"

'Good God, what a question. What else is there to do in Bryntowy on a wet Wednesday night? Rugby club meetings give people a chance to express their passion about the game and its importance to the community. Rugby is an escape from being down the pit and gets the whole community together, particularly when you beat a neighbouring village like Glanddu. There is nothing finer than working with someone in the mine who lives in another village and whose team you have beaten the previous Saturday. Also, a rugby club committee meeting is a cheap night out because you can't drink when you are talking, yourself, and you can't drink when someone else is talking,' he laughed, 'because you are asleep.'

Her father did one committee job or another until coal dust ended his life.

It was hardly surprising that Marilyn met Dai at a Bryntowy rugby club dance, called a "hop" in those days. As usual, the hop ended in a fight between the Bryntowy players and their opponents from that afternoon's match, Glanddu. Dai and Marilyn's brother, Joe Powell, were participants in the fight where Dai got a black eye and Joe, a bloody nose.

That unlikely meeting led to courtship and marriage. Marilyn was glad that Dai was a milkman and not a collier. If he had been down the pit, then he might already be dead. Her father was Dai's age when the dust got him. After her marriage Marilyn learned how to run Dai's family's dairy business and learned to support the Glanddu rugby team - except when they played Bryntowy. Marilyn had never been passionate about the game although she enjoyed meeting friends and acquaintances in the club bar. Now, she only went to the game when Glanddu played Bryntowy.

Marilyn made Dai a hot drink and as she handed him the mug she asked, 'The bonus payment. What did everyone say?'

Dai sipped his drink and sighed, 'I did as you suggested and pretended that I wasn't happy about our paying the bonus if Tommy Harries' bequest money ran out. Len vowed he would pay it come what may. Of course, Arthur, after saying he wouldn't cough up, changed his mind. He then accused me of not having the best interests of the club at heart. It was only then that I grudgingly conceded that we would pay – but only to a maximum of a hundred pounds. That maximum was agreed three to one – Len opposed.'

'You told the players?'

Dai nodded.

Marilyn snorted, 'I bet they accepted, though?'

'They did.'

'Any thoughts on how we might afford to pay if the unthinkable happened?'

'We could increase the number of "full broken bottles" that the business suffers during milk deliveries.'

'I thought we were already at the limit.' Marilyn sounded doubtful.

'Well, I think we could increase it by one a day. Alternatively, we could increase the number of thefts from the van.'

'That would work unless we get some real thefts; then we'll have to involve the police.'

'As the village is currently morgue-like during the day, I expect any milk stealing to be purely imaginary except in our accounts.' Dai looked at his wife with raised eyebrows. 'Anything you can do to generate some money?'

'I can do some cash deals with our delivery-man and not show them on the books. Don't worry. We'll find a way if we have to. Now, bed,' she said, glancing at the clock. 'You'll only get five and a half hours. I'll be up in a minute.'

Dai stood, finished his drink, and put the mug in the dishwasher. Just as he was going through the door he stopped and turned to his wife. 'You remember the fire about three weeks ago at that nice pub on the Llandybie Road, the "Prince of Wales"?' Marilyn nodded. 'They had some slot machines which were not damaged and they disappeared somehow or other. Well, one was offered to Herbie Scurlock for a song. He fell on the offer like a vulture on a carcass'.

'Would I be correct in thinking this slot machine will not appear on the club books.'

'How did you guess that correctly?'

'Women's intuition. So we are getting people to gamble their hard-earned money on a slot machine to pay these worthless players their bonus. I wonder if our priorities are right.'

'What about the motion to open the club more frequently?'

'No decision until after a meeting with Abertawe Ales. Do you think we should start the broken and stolen bottle scams now to generate our sponsorship money?'

'No, we're not discussing that tonight. Bed,' she pointed and Dai disappeared through the door.

Chapter 14

Gloria parked in the supermarket's car park as always, and after she bought the requisite groceries to qualify for free parking, she crossed the main road and entered the Marina. She and Duncan in those early days of their relationship rarely visited Swansea. Duncan, like many from the Welsh speaking hinterland beyond the town, had an almost pathological aversion to all things Swansea.

The town's inhabitants were disparagingly referred to as either "Swansea Jacks" or simply, "Jacks." The term "Swansea Jack," Duncan told Gloria, had two possible origins. When English-speaking traders, particularly the scrap metal merchants from Swansea, travelled into the Welsh-speaking villages, they always tried to swindle the inhabitants. When Gloria asked why "Jack" and not "Swansea Smart Alecs," or "Swansea Wide Boys," Duncan said, "Nobody knows." He then told her that the alternative meaning was down to a dog named "Swansea Jack" that rescued several people from a sinking boat in Swansea Bay in the 1920's. The dog even had a plaque commemorating his achievement on the entrance wall outside the Swansea rugby ground. Duncan favoured the canine origin of the term because it insulted the Swansea inhabitants to an even greater degree.

As she walked past the port's Victorian and Edwardian buildings, she was impressed at how well they looked following their restoration and renovation. The buildings were no longer warehouses or shipping offices but shops, pubs, and museums. There were blocks of flats where once the gantries and cranes had stood like guardsmen round the docks.

When Duncan and Gloria had first talked about buying a holiday home in Wales, a Marina flat was one of their options. Gloria was particularly keen to buy a flat overlooking the sea rather than the yacht basin. Duncan, whose antipathy to Swansea had mellowed over the years, agreed to inspect a flat.

Three minutes inside the show flat was an eye-opener. It was so small that Gloria could hear her father say as he always did when he saw similarly-sized places, "You could sit on the toilet and cook your breakfast."

There was a flat available with a view of Swansea Bay but it also included a vista of the Port Talbot steelworks, with its never-ending smoke belching chimneys. Glanddu suddenly became attractive.

Gloria entered the packed pub. It took her a few moments before she spotted Iory Isaacs sitting at a table with John Jones and Herbie Scurlock. She set off through an obstacle course of tables and chairs jumbled together and picked her way to her companions.

'Christ, Iory, I know the pub has to make money but they could space the tables out a bit. I've got beer spilt on my trousers,' said Gloria grumpily.

'Hello, John and Herbie,' she added as an afterthought.

Iory shook her hand, grunted a welcome, and then made sure Gloria sat down before handing out menus. When everyone had decided what they wanted they all went in a group to the bar and ordered. Iory added a couple of bottles of wine. That done, the four navigated their way back to their table where Iory was the first to speak.

'You all know about "The Fox" closing and I can tell you that Abertawe Ales will not take it over. I understand that you think your club might try and act as "The Fox's" replacement. I'm all ears.'

Herbie cleared his throat and opened the discussion, 'Yes, we are thinking about opening more frequently. The first thing, though, is to find out if the council will grant us a licence to open for more hours since "The Fox's" has closed. Second. . .'

'Wait a minute before we go into all this,' Iory covered his mouth with his hand as he finished chewing. 'You want some money from us to help you? How much extra beer do you think you will sell in a week?'

'Twenty to thirty gallons.'

Iory dropped his fork with a clatter.

'I have pubs who sell that amount of beer in about ten minutes! You know what I could offer you on sales of that magnitude? A packet of cardboard beer mats with the words "Abertawe Ales" on them. Are you going to do food?'

'Maybe, if we can get a chef.'

'For a start, can your kitchen pass the Health and Safety Gestapo's EEC Directives?'

'The local Health and Safety chap is the second cousin of Len Penry's late wife. He always gives us a few days warning about when he's coming for a visit. We heed the warning and go into the clubhouse to hide all the mouse-traps. Then we put the dead mice out for the birds.'

'Who eats them?' asked Iory.

'Gulls, crows, possibly buzzards, or even red kites who've just started re-appearing over the rugby ground for the first time since...' Herbie looked at John Jones.

'1951. I remember seeing the kite flying over the stand at half-time. We were playing Bryntowy and we won 10-3.'

'Good,' replied Iory, 'I'm glad the kitchen is sorted out.'

He refilled his glass and looked at his companions.

'So, your estimated increase in beer sales is pretty paltry. Your clubhouse is not attractive enough for serving meals and you can't afford a chef to offer decent food. The place wants re-painting and I know the men's toilets need work and the women's, the same?' Gloria nodded vigorously. 'Then you have to think about heating and lighting. You also might like to know that I have met your bank manager recently who told me about your precarious financial position. In a word, lady and gentlemen, you have no money to do anything. Abertawe Ales won't be giving you any money because at the moment we only have cash to invest into expanding businesses. Yours isn't that. How's your food?'

'Fine,' was the reply in unison.

'You have got to try the chef's cheesecake, it's fantastic.'

Once outside the pub the three stood staring at the boats in the Marina.

Gloria spoke first, 'So we can confirm to the club committee that Abertawe Ales will give us nothing. So no need to waste any more time on this matter. Still, we had a nice free meal. My steak was really tender.'

'Yes, but you have an advantage over us two men,' said Jones, 'you have your own teeth.'

'Which is why I had the pork belly in gravy,' Herbie said, clicking his dentures.

Gloria looked at her watch.

'Right. I've got ten minutes parking left so I'm off to the car. I imagine on your drive back you'll spend the whole time discussing the all-time dream Welsh team.'

'Naturally.'

Chapter 15

Glanddu won their first two games of the season. The club's pundits expected the wins since the club's opponents were the two weakest teams in the Division. More difficult matches against better sides were scheduled to begin this coming Saturday; the pundits were not hopeful.

On Thursday as Dai was driving home after his deliveries, he saw a removal van outside Robin Roberts' house. Robin recently left Wales to travel to a university in America on a one-year sabbatical and, whilst there, was renting out his house. Dai dithered as to whether to call in; only when he was a hundred yards past Robin's house did he swing his van round and park. With his milk delivery book firmly in his hand he strode up to the house's front door. As he arrived at the door, two perspiring men appeared from inside the house and one of them took one look at Dai and emitted a shout over his shoulder, "Milkman."

A voice bellowed out, asking Dai to come into the living room. Dai switched on his famous smile — the one he used for enticing new customers. The voice's owner was unpacking in the corner of the room. He straightened up and turned to look at Dai. Dai heard his own jaw crack as it fell roughly level to his chest. The potential customer appeared not to notice Dai's gaping mouth as he extended his hand in Dai's direction.

'Bloody hell, you're Clive Wilson,' Dai spluttered as he shook the proffered hand. He had to crane his neck to look up at the six feet eight inch former England rugby player. Dai had only ever seen Wilson from a rugby stand or on TV. Wherever it was, Dai automatically hated the man because Wilson was a great player, a talisman for England and a perpetual thorn in the sides of Welsh teams for at least ten years before recently retiring from the game. Wilson's friendly smile and handshake were already changing Dai's view.

'I have been Clive Wilson since birth, maybe even before that, Mr—?' Wilson replied.

'Yes, of course,' Dai responded, feeling foolish and beginning to blush. 'I just did not expect to find the scourge of Wales living here. I'm Dai Williams, the local milkman, and I was wondering if you want milk delivered.'

'Yes, please,' said a female voice from the door. 'I'm Nora Wilson. Pleased to meet you, Mr Williams.'

Dai turned to see a pretty blonde woman holding a baby in her arms. Nora moved towards Dai, tucked the baby under her arm and offered him her right hand. Dai then tickled the baby under the chin and got a toothless grin in reply and from Nora, a joyful laugh.

'I deliver every day round here,' Dai said in his official voice and opened his book and wrote in the number of pints Nora wanted. When he finished writing he snapped shut the book and said, 'I must say it's a surprise to see such distinguished people coming to live in Glanddu.'

'I'm doing a course at Swansea University this academic year,' replied Clive, 'and as our new house in England won't be built until next year, we have rented this in the meantime.' He looked round the room. 'It will do us nicely.'

'We felt it would be quieter here than in the metropolis of Swansea.'

'That it will be for certain; you've very peaceful neighbours. I'll leave the milk by the front door. Friday is payday. If you want to leave the money, that's fine. I can also deliver eggs and butter. I usually deliver here between seven and five past.'

'You couldn't be more precise as to the time, could you, Mr Williams?' laughed Nora.

Dai smiled at the joke and then shifted from one foot to the other, knowing that he should go but he could not move — well, not till he had done his duty. Nervously swallowing, he looked up and asked, 'Clive, You wouldn't fancy coming out of retirement and playing for Glanddu, would you?'

The baby gurgled and the removal men's conversation on how they were going to manoeuvre something round the stairs all became audible. Wilson exchanged glances with his wife then started to laugh as Dai felt himself go beetroot red.

'You would not believe the amount of money I have been offered to play here, there and everywhere since I've given up English rugby. Mr Williams, Dai, I've retired and I've a post graduate course to which I must give my full attention.'

Nora then asked, 'How often do you train? What level does the club play in? And is that the rugby ground behind the derelict garage we saw on our way here?'

Hardly the questions Dai expected Clive's wife to be asking.

Dai answered Nora's questions then watched husband and wife exchange looks, clearly communicating something significant. Suddenly Dai began to get knots in his stomach.

'You always said that you would like to play in a junior team and put something back into the game,' said Nora, looking at her husband.

'Yes, but not in bloody Wales, though.'

'He's kidding, Mr Williams,' Nora explained, worried that her husband's humour might have fallen on stony ground. 'Ironically, he has always said he would love to play in a country where rugby is the national game.'

'That's all I need, for people to know my inner secrets,' said Wilson who then walked over to his wife. He put his arm round her and kissed the baby. 'You wouldn't mind my playing?'

Nora shook her head and turned to Dai. 'You don't play in Europe or Australia or South Africa, do you? I've had enough of this lunk playing all over the world.'

Dai did not know whether to have a heart attack or jump up and down. This could not be happening.

'We often play in Ireland and Scotland.' He saw Nora's look of shock so he added quickly, 'Just kidding. We mainly play locally, up to a thirty- or forty-mile radius. The only time we travel further is when we play in the Welsh cup and, sad to say, we haven't progressed beyond the first round since the early 1990's.'

'Good,' Nora smiled. 'For a moment, there I was thinking you might play in Perpignan or Toulouse.'

'I wish we did, Mrs Wilson, but I don't foresee it. Rest assured, every game Clive plays will be within an hour's drive. He'll be home by six on Saturdays.'

'Oh, you can keep him a bit longer than that.'

Nora saw her husband's happy face and looked at Dai.

'Just give him the details of when you train and try not to get him hurt.'

'Of course not, Mrs Wilson,' replied Dai expecting that if anyone was going to get hurt it would be the Glanddu's opponents.

'Nora, call me Nora.'

'I will, Nora.'

The two men talked for a few minutes with Dai increasingly believing that this was all a dream. Dai told Wilson about the match fee and the bonus but Wilson didn't want any payment; he was just glad to have a run around every Saturday.

Wilson then poured further fuel to Dai's flame when he said he would come and train that very evening although he didn't expect to play this Saturday.

Not expect to play? Dai almost burst out laughing but then remembered that the team was selected on Tuesdays and someone would have to volunteer to drop out for the Englishman to play.

'Clive, people do drop out with injuries on Thursday evening; it's very likely that we could get you on the team.' A thought struck him. 'We have to register you with the league; otherwise, if you play without being registered they deduct league points.' Leave registration to me. I have a form in the van.'

The form had been there for at least four years just in case something like today actually happened. It was Marilyn's idea — just wait until he told her about this!

He needed to get home; the excitement was stimulating his bladder and there were things to do quickly. 'I'll get that done this afternoon.'

Dai wanted to see everyone's face in the clubhouse that evening when he arrived with Wilson in tow. He even decided not to tell Marilyn immediately but leave it till tonight, though she knew him well enough to know that something was up.

A thought than struck Dai: how was it that nobody in this village knew that Wilson was renting a place here? 'Who was the estate agent who rented you the house?' Dai asked.

'William Isaacs of Pontnewydd showed me the house,' replied Nora, before pointing at her husband with her thumb. 'He was too busy to come down. Why?'

'No wonder that no one knew who had rented this place. Bill Isaacs is that rarity amongst Welshmen: he has no interest in rugby.'

'How awful,' laughed Nora.

Dai returned to his van where sat for several minutes until he felt calm enough to drive.

CHAPTER 16

'You're Clive Wilson,' said Gloria, astonished. Then she turned and glowered at Dai. The milkman had telephoned her earlier in the evening and suggested that if she came to the ground, she might get a nice surprise.

'Yes,' replied the giant. 'Mr Williams suggested that I might like to come and play for my new home club.' He smiled. 'I thought I would just meet everyone, have a run round the pitch. If your coach wants me to help tonight I'd be happy to do so. I'm available for selection, if and when you need me.'

Granville, standing with eyes agog whilst Wilson was introduced to the chairwoman, had nearly fallen over when he heard that Wilson was not only going to play for the team, but was offering to help with the team's coaching. Granville had been an assistant coach for five years with teams in higher divisions prior to coming to coach Glanddu. He had only taken the Glanddu coaching job because it gave him sole charge of a team for the first time. Granville could already hear himself saying in future years, 'My number two coach at Glanddu was Clive Wilson. Yes, that England player. It was Clive's first foray into coaching. He just needed a gentle hand from an experienced coach to guide him.'

Granville just wished he had his camera in the car. Perhaps he could ring Sharon, his wife, and get her to bring the digital one down. The sooner he had a photograph of him and Wilson together, the sooner he could get it put on the club website. If only he could get Wilson to impart the knowledge he had gained from playing all over the world; what would that be worth? Granville strode over to the knot of people surrounding the Englishman with a heart beating like a machine gun.

'I'm Granville Beck, the club's coach, Clive.' He almost called him "Mr Wilson" as the pair shook hands. 'I couldn't help overhearing your offers of coaching and playing.' He took a deep breath and said tentatively, 'You could start now, tonight, with the coaching. I'll have to talk to Declan, the club skipper. Maybe you could start as a replacement on Saturday.'

'Happy to do that, provided I don't stop anyone else from playing,' replied Wilson.

'No, we'll put you on the replacement bench and bring you on during the game.'

Granville turned to the players, who had congregated in the bar to stare.

'Right, boys, go and get changed.'

He whispered to Wilson, 'It will be an interesting session tonight, I should think. After they warm up, perhaps you'll give them a few training exercises?'

'Be delighted, but I need to get fit as well, remember.'

'Len and I sent three copies of his registration form by recorded mail, fax and email this afternoon,' said Dai.

Colin Mabbutt arrived in the room and stood behind Dai with his mouth open, staring at Wilson.

'Yes, it is Clive Wilson so you can stop trying to catch flies,' Granville said, smirking with delight. 'In case you are wondering, Colin, we are just going to have a look at Clive this evening and see if he is fit enough to come on as a replacement on Saturday. Never know what you find doing a milk round. Well done, Dai - just try to find us another couple of ex-internationals.'

Granville looked at the players and clapped his hands.

'Go on, lads, no more gawping, things to do for Saturday.'

Obediently the shell-shocked players began to leave and as they passed Wilson, they shook his hand or else, if they could reach it, they patted him on the shoulder. Declan was the last player to leave the room and as he introduced himself to the giant, Granville said in as loud a voice as possible, 'Switch on the training floodlights on your way downstairs, Declan. We don't want Clive falling over something and getting injured before he starts. The lads will show you the changing room, Clive. I'll be down in a moment.'

Colin watched Wilson till he had disappeared and then punched numbers into his mobile telephone so excitedly that he dropped it on the floor. Picking it up, he began talking breathlessly.

'Arthur, it's me, Colin, Colin Mabbutt. I know you are busy but I thought you might like to know that Clive Wilson just walked through the door and is going to play for the club.'

'And coach,' shouted Granville as he passed Colin on the way down to the changing rooms.

'Coach as well. Dai found him. He's living in the village. Len,' Colin handed over his mobile phone, 'Arthur would like a word with you.'

'Is Colin hallucinating about Clive Wilson?'

'He's right. Dai brought Wilson down tonight without telling a soul. Not sure he'll start the game on Saturday because the team's been picked already. He'll be on the replacements bench and will get onto the field, without doubt. Christ, he is a size when you see him in the flesh. He actually stooped to come through the door and had to turn sideways as well because his shoulders are so wide.'

Len had not actually seen Wilson come through the door into the clubhouse but he liked a bit of poetic licence. He handed the phone back to Colin who walked a few paces to recommence his conversation. Len swung round with a big smile and playfully shook Dai by the shoulders.

'How, when, why?'

Dai opened his mouth to explain when Mabbutt came up to the pair.

'Arthur will be down within half an hour,' Colin said, snapping his phone shut and thrusting it in his pocket.

'He's in Birmingham,' said Len.

'No, that's where he told his wife he was. He's in that widow's place again. I saw him getting out of his car with his flies undone.'

When he saw the look on the others' faces he added, 'I am speaking metaphorically.'

'You'd think at fifty-six he'd be cooling down,' Len said.

'Len, I thought you were in Tenby today. Why were you driving past the widow's place?'

'Tenby? No, I had a job in Swansea.'

Len looked at Dai. Reliability and honesty were characteristics not normally associated with builders and car-dealers; both Colin and Arthur were truly of that mould.

Arthur arrived half way through Dai's story and insisted that he start again at the beginning.

'What car does he drive?' Arthur said when Dai's story was complete. He wanted to meet the legend and was frightened that the Englishman might disappear without meeting him.

'I couldn't see any parked car that could remotely belong to a bloke of his stature.'

Gloria decided that it was time to leave since she didn't care what car Wilson drove. She thanked Dai for the nice surprise and told everyone that she would see them on Saturday. She glided out of the room, aware that everyone was glad to see her go so they could gossip about man things. If they only knew. . . She was worrying that all her plans could come to nothing if Wilson led the team to victory.

After he saw Gloria disappear Dai tried to remember what cars he saw outside Wilson's house earlier.

'They had a blue one and a Range Rover, I think. Wilson came down with me tonight, which is why you wouldn't have seen anything here. Why do you ask?'

'A blue one – how very helpful. Any particular blue, was it?' Arthur's asked sarcastically.

'Sky, azure or royal, I think,' Dai replied.

'Dai, those shades are completely different,' said Mabbutt, a self-confessed expert on colour (though some of his customers would beg to differ).

'I'll ask him after training. Tomorrow is collection day but for once I don't care if I get to bed late. I'm taking Wilson home.'

'Are you sure? I could take him,' said Arthur. Dai's face was all the reply Arthur needed, so he returned to his original subject.

'Any idea how old his car is?'

'Even though you are a car dealer, Arthur, your interest in his transport is a bit excessive, isn't it?'

'Business is business. I was thinking about getting him to drive one of my cars with my company's name plastered all over it. It is a longish drive from here to Swansea University and the car would be seen by loads of people.'

He then mused out loud, 'Arthur Davies Cars Ltd, sponsor of Colin Wilson, England, British Isles and Ireland Lions.'

'Don't forget Glanddu RFC. And what about that English club he played for?'

'No chance of an English club's name appearing on one of my cars.' He hesitated whilst he thought. 'I wonder if putting Glanddu on the car is a good idea?'

'Certainly. When people see that he's playing for Glanddu they'll come to our games in droves.'

'Yes, Dai,' grinned Len. 'It may bring in as many as thirty or forty extra spectators.'

'Sponsoring a car for Wilson is probably the best idea you've had since you took the decision to retire from playing in 1989,' Dai said, laughing.

Len and Mabbutt joined in but when the Mabbutt saw Arthur's face, he decided to change the subject.

'Mrs Bowen Thomas left quickly. She seemed not to be too happy. I can't imagine why.'

'Obvious,' said Arthur. 'Wilson didn't give her a second glance.'

'He's married and about twenty some years too young for her. That can't be the reason,' Len replied.

'Sex is my reason for everything,' said Arthur. 'I can't help my amazing virility; I was born with it.'

'Can we get back to rugby?' suggested Mabbutt as he turned towards the bar.

'Agreed,' replied the others in unison.

Normally when the players finished training, they drifted off to wives, girlfriends and, in one instance, a boyfriend. Not tonight. The players hung round the bar telling all and sundry about who had just joined the club. Mobile phone profits skyrocketed.

Granville hung limpet-like round Wilson, constantly asking technical coaching questions. Eventually Granville asked Wilson for forgiveness, claiming that his over-excitement in meeting Clive had got the better of him. Wilson, used to too much attention during his long playing career, gave the club coach a friendly squeeze on his arm. Then he finished his lime and lemonade and looked for somewhere to put the glass.

Before Granville could re-start his grilling, Wilson picked up his kitbag and headed for the door. He wished everyone, 'Good night,' and received a deafening response of, 'Good night, Clive' from the entire room.

Like a cat hunting a mouse, Arthur rushed after Wilson and caught him by the door. For the first time that evening Wilson seemed impatient as the car salesman explained his line of work. When Arthur stopped speaking he thrust a business card into one of Wilson's pockets, grasped his hand and then pumped it vigorously. After Wilson exited, Arthur sprinted back to join his companions with a smug smile.

'So I think Mr Wilson and I will be doing some business.'

'Right, then,' suggested Dai, 'how about buying us a drink.'

'No. Best be getting back to the little woman.'

His mobile phone rang.

'Hello, darling.' Arthur' face fell as he realised who it was. 'How did you know? I had to come back from Birmingham on urgent club business. The England player Colin Wilson, that's right, the one you like. Well, he may be driving one of my cars about the place. Well, he is joining Glanddu. Well, I played for Glanddu so the standard can't be that bad. No, he really is. No, I have not been drinking.'

He held the mobile out and the others shouted, 'No, he hasn't.'

'Yes, I'll be home shortly.'

He snapped the phone shut and announced, 'Shit, I've got to go home.'

Without a backward glance he set off out of the bar, his phone pressed to his ear. The Sponsors committee watched him go.

'That'll be the widow he's phoning,' said Mabbutt.

'You're probably right, Colin,' said Len. 'I wonder, lads, how long Wilson will sit on the replacement bench before Granville sends him on to the playing field on Saturday. Ten minutes?' Mabbutt pondered.

'However long it is, our opponents are in for a mighty shock.'

'Oh dear, what a shame,' mocked Dai.

'Let's go and talk to Declan and Granville and see what they have to say.'

CHAPTER 17

Gloria had finally managed to arrange a meeting with Grindley. It had taken six weeks because the man seemed to be permanently on holiday. The old mechanic lived in a large Victorian House, obviously converted into flats from the intercom and panel of buzzers outside the building's door. After speaking to Grindley's distorted voice over the intercom Gloria pushed the front door open. The smell of cat was almost strong enough to make her turn round and leave the building. As she began to climb the steep stairs, she held her nose with one hand until she reached the first floor where, after testing the air, she thankfully inhaled.

She could not help remembering her post-student days in London where everyone she knew lived either in a dingy, damp basement or high up in a garret. Why would an old man live all the way up in the gods? Was she going to be surprised by a gorgeous penthouse? A smell wafted round her. No, he lived high up to avoid the stench of cat and stale, boiled vegetables.

Finally, she got to the top and Grindley greeted her. The flat itself was barely large enough for one person and that, Gloria thought, implied dire financial straits. She smiled to herself and hoped her deduction was correct. The one redeeming feature of the place became apparent to Gloria when she sat in a chair and peered through the window: the tide was in and Swansea Bay looked beautiful.

When Gloria and Duncan bought their house in Glanddu five years ago, Grindley's Garage had just ceased trading. However, Gloria had known Grindley for thirty years, ever since her marriage to Duncan. Grindley's charges for working on a car were far lower than those in London. So, in the first ten years of their marriage when a car needed repair, Gloria and Duncan arranged to stay a weekend in Glanddu. On those weekends, a couple of nights were booked at the no-cost dinner, bed and breakfast establishment of Duncan's parents. After Duncan's parents died, visits to Glanddu were rare and, thanks to their improved finances, cars were repaired in London. Today was the first time Gloria was meeting Grindley in many years.

Gloria accepted Grindley's offer of a cup of tea. When her cup arrived, she was shaken by what she saw: for the first time in human memory, Grindley had clean fingernails. In the old days, Grindley spent fifteen minutes cleaning his nails every night (before his wife would allow any "hanky panky").

Grindley came originally from the East End of London where soccer was king and Rugby was the name of a town "Up North." Grindley moved to a flat close to the ground of the local soccer team, the Swansea City "Swans," so he could watch them regularly. Just his luck when the club moved to a new ground not in walking distance.

Grindley started to reminisce about Gloria's cars which he repaired from thirty years ago. He remembered the car colours, the car makes and even the particular repairs he had carried out. Gloria politely listened, bored out of her mind, but when Grindley finally paused to draw breath, she changed the subject.

'You know I am now the Glanddu Chairwoman?'

'Yes, Mrs Bowen Thomas, I've guessed that you've come, as the club's chairwoman, to see me about my garage. I remember all the damage rugby players did to my garage after drunken evenings in the clubhouse. They broke windows, stole anything and everything that wasn't nailed down. I was told that it wasn't Glanddu players; it was always their visitors. I have a long memory concerning your rugby club and its impact on my business.'

Gloria had rehearsed what she was about to say several times in front of her mirror.

'I wasn't chairwoman then but if I had been, I would have done something about it. Please let bygones be exactly that. I have come to talk about the present and the future. Mr Grindley, today more locals actually drive to the ground rather than walk like they used to, and every visitor drives him or herself.'

'Really?'

'Yes, so on Saturdays we have a parking problem; we're even parking in the chapel car-park.'

Gloria shook her head as though God might be appalled at such effrontery. 'After the match people are blocked in and that sometimes leads to fights.'

What Gloria had described was only partly true; fighting occurred just twice in the last five years. On those two occasions Glanddu played teams from higher divisions in the Welsh Cup competition. Both those teams brought a large group of supporters who had over-imbibed in the club's bar and referred to Glanddu's club as a bunch of "Welsh speaking bastards," a sure trigger for a punch-up.

'Too much drinking in the club bar - that's what leads to fights,' Grindley said.

'Yes, true, but the bar brings in much-needed cash. However, what we need is more parking spaces.'

'Ah! So you want to rent my old place.' He rubbed his hands when she nodded. 'Good, but some of the back is too rough. The old forecourt just needs some re-tarmacing and it will be fine. Don Ringer would do that work cheaply for you, and he's a good and reliable worker.'

'Don sadly developed Alzheimer's and moved to his daughter's in Bristol.'

'God, that only leaves that cowboy, Colin Mabbutt. Still, beggars can't be choosers, eh, Mrs Bowen Thomas?'

'He's not so bad.' Then she added after a pause, 'Well, not as bad as he used to be. He just needed experience.'

He smiled, 'I'll accept that. Now, about the site. I would expect the club to clear all the rubbish people have dumped there.'

'We can do that.'

'I assume you would want to use the place as soon as possible?'

'Yes.'

'I'll work out a fair rent and get back to you.'

'Actually, Mr Grindley, I was thinking about purchasing the place.'

Grindley thought about his time in the village. Despite the rugby players smashing up the garage, he'd been very happy there once his wife had gone off, some twenty-five years ago, with someone she met at Bingo in Llanelli. Grindley rarely saw his children because one lived in Ireland whilst the other lived in Newcastle upon Tyne. If he sold the site, he could visit them more often, particularly the one in Newcastle; he could even get a season ticket for Newcastle United's home games. Six hundred miles round trip by car to Newcastle was a long journey at his age, but if he sold the garage he could afford to fly up from Cardiff.

'Actually,' Grindley said, 'you have not been totally honest with me, Mrs Bowen Thomas.'

'What?' Gloria felt herself reddening.

Grindley picked up the local newspaper and opened it to the sports page and the article about Wilson's arrival.

'I'm sure this man will make a huge impact at the rugby club, particularly its finances. How much does he cost?'

'He plays now for enjoyment. He gets the same as anyone else and we had to persuade him to take that.'

'Blimey, that's fantastic.'

'He is a good man and he will, we hope, attract a few more people through our gates. But we need promotion to ease our financial worries.'

'According to this newspaper, he's only in Glanddu for the season?'

'Yes, sadly.'

'You won't be able to build on my site,' Grindley said. 'I tried a few years ago to get permission for houses, but no dice.'

'God forbid and perish that thought. All we want is a club car-park,' Gloria's face went red at her lie, so she fanned her hands in front of her face. 'Just having a hot flush.'

'Shall I open a window?'

Gloria shook her head so he continued, 'I reckon that bugger Watcyn Watkins was the one behind my refusal. He accused me once for over-charging on a car service.'

'Watcyn is a typical old socialist who never likes people to make money,' replied Gloria.

Grindley frowned, 'Talking of money, I heard that the club is having financial problems. So how can it afford to buy my place?'

'In memory of my husband, my children and I are thinking of buying the site, provided the price is reasonable. Perhaps the club will buy it off us when their finances improve.'

'That's very commendable,' muttered Grindley.

'Would you have a price in mind, Mr Grindley?'

Grindley shook his head. There was trouble on the site since he had retired to Swansea. Once, gypsies camped there for three weeks and he had the devil of a job to get rid of them.

After that, Grindley had the water supply cut off and the site fenced. The last time he had been back to the site the fence had been damaged but he had put off the repair work to save money. The fence repair would be unnecessary if the site became a car-park.

'Not sure I want to sell at the moment; I may prefer to rent the site to you, Mrs Bowen Thomas.'

'Fair enough, but what if we get two or three valuations of the site and see how you feel and whether my family could afford it? I could organize viewings by three local estate agents. Would that be an acceptable first step?'

Grindley blinked his approval so Gloria continued, 'Can I suggest that we not say anything to anybody from Glanddu, as my family and I want it to be a big surprise?'

'Glad you are doing this for Duncan's memorial,' said Grindley. Duncan worked at the garage during university vacations. Grindley had never once doubted Duncan's honesty in handling the cash, more than could be said of some others he had employed, like Arthur Davies. Grindley was impressed that someone had had the gumption to think about the use of his old site for car-parking. What had an old friend from Glanddu said recently when they met in Swansea: 'That Gloria Bowen Thomas is like a bloody dynamo around the rugby club. Always wanting to do something, paint this, and clean that, a typical woman who always wants us men to be seen to be busy. We come to the club to get away from that woman nonsense. God knows what she will be dreaming up next. But she does have good ideas, is more forward thinking than any bloke and generally is a first-rate chief executive.'

With that conversation in mind Grindley thought that if you can't trust someone you have known for thirty years and her husband and his family for longer, whom can you trust?

'As you say in rugby, let us run with the ball, Mrs Bowen Thomas.'

'Yes, and now I must go and do some shopping.'

Gloria stood and took a business card out of her handbag and gave it to Grindley who slipped it into his pocket. Just another four hundred and thirty-six cards left, Gloria thought, before I have to re-order.

Grindley escorted Gloria to the flat's door and shook hands with her. Shaking hands with a woman still felt odd to him as he had always either kissed them or smiled a greeting or farewell.

Once he closed his front door, in anticipation he began to sing the Newcastle anthem, "The Blaydon Races."

Returning to his living room he found the local paper and saw that Glanddu were playing at home whilst Swansea City were playing away. So this Saturday, for the first time ever, he was going to go up the valley to watch Glanddu play and see if Mrs Bowen Thomas was, after all, telling him the truth about the car parking.

Chapter 18

When Grindley appeared at Saturday's match, it shocked all the Glanddu locals. He didn't enjoy the rugby match but he did like the bonhomie in the club bar after the match. He enjoyed himself so much that he announced to all and sundry that he'd watch Glanddu play all its games, except when Swansea City was at home.

When Gloria heard the news that Grindley was going to start watching the club, she was worried. Nobody had said anything to her on Saturday about her plan for the purchase of the garage site so Grindley must not have told anybody — yet. It was only a matter of time before Grindley mentioned it and then everyone in Glanddu would know within the hour. Then people would start speculating why Gloria was actually acquiring the site. There was always the chance then that someone from the village who had a rich uncle would buy the site for their own nefarious purpose. Gloria was glad that she had arranged to see estate agents this coming week.

There were no estate agents in Glanddu but the nearby town, Pontnewydd, had several. William Isaacs and Sons was the only independent estate agent left in the town. It was where the locals went if they wanted a fair deal; Grindley would definitely expect one of the three valuations to be from him. The following Tuesday Gloria arrived at Isaacs' office. Gloria had met Isaacs when she and Duncan went backstage after several amateur dramatic productions in town. Bill Isaacs was not only in every play put on in the town by its four amateur companies, but because of his size, every drama group within an eighty-mile radius of Pontnewydd wanted him for the title role in the pantomime, "Humpty Dumpty."

As Gloria entered Isaacs tiny office she reckoned that the only way he could get to his chair behind the desk was by being winched into it.

After a gasping struggle to get to his feet, a feat that Gloria thought would induce a heart attack, Bill Isaacs extended his sweaty hand to Gloria who controlled herself enough not to wipe her hand on her coat. Gloria didn't fancy giving mouth to-mouth resuscitation, not just because of his fat florid face, but because she was almost overcome by the smell of his armpits as soon as she entered the room.

Isaacs began, 'I was driving past Grindley's sometime in the middle of August and saw you on the site with a very natty looking man.' Isaacs was actually dying to ask if he was her toy boy.

Because Isaacs knew Grindley, Gloria had to hide her devious intentions.

'Can you believe he wanted to pick blackberries for his wife? Some of the best and biggest in the village are at the back of what is left of the old workshop.'

Isaacs' mouth dropped open in surprise, so Gloria added, 'He's a friend of my son Toby and he's in the building trade, so I thought I'd kill two birds with one stone. I picked his brains about using the old garage as an overflow car park for the rugby club as our gate has increased recently.'

'I thought it a bit early for blackberries.'

'I think all the concrete traps the heat so the blackberries always arrive early there.' Gloria had often seen children picking on the site long before the ones near her property were ripe.

'Overflow car-park?' It had taken him a moment to realise that when Gloria mentioned "gate" she meant paying spectators to a game — not some physical barrier — hence, the car park idea.

He asked, 'You really need one?'

'Yes. People don't like walking anymore and many of them are getting older.'

She remembered something she had not mentioned before to Grindley but she'd tell Isaacs. 'And we've had trouble with people being given parking tickets by the police.'

The police did give one ticket when Cardiff thrashed Glanddu in a cup match a good twenty years earlier. The policeman involved assumed that a big, shiny BMW had to belong to a Cardiff supporter, but it was actually Duncan's car.

'I got done in Llanelli the other day,' Isaacs said, looking morose. 'It was absolutely pouring with rain. I was only gone five minutes to buy four 500-gram bars of chocolate that were on sale.' He shook his head. 'I came out to find a ticket on my windscreen and the traffic warden nowhere to be seen. They employ phantoms, Mrs Bowen Thomas. You never know where or when they will strike. I was so stressed I ate all four bars, then and there. I was going to have them for tea.'

Gloria tried to look sympathetic and made a clucking noise in her throat. She took out a handkerchief as if to blow her nose, but really to mask Isaacs' body odour. Meanwhile, Isaacs keyed into his computer and after surveying the screen told her that he would be able to visit the site this week. He keyed in her address and promised to send the evaluation post haste.

As Gloria stood up to leave he said, 'I seem to remember that old Grindley tried to get planning permission for houses and failed. I wouldn't mind betting he'd get a more favourable response now.'

Gloria felt her heart sink but she remained stony faced when she responded, 'Bill, a car park is what is needed on the site and Mr Grindley, as a loyal villager, agrees. Don't forget, it can be used every Sunday as an overflow park for the chapel.'

'They get a good turnout, do they?' Isaacs said in astonishment. 'Attendance at all the chapels round here has tumbled. My mother would be horrified, God rest her soul.'

'Well, whenever I've been there, the chapel definitely needed extra parking space,' said Gloria, who had attended the Baptist Chapel for three funerals in the past two years. The funerals had all been for former Glanddu rugby players, always a guarantee of a large congregation.

Before Isaacs could reply, his telephone rang. Quickly, Gloria shook his hand, shot out the door and took a deep breath.

Gloria then went to two other estate agencies where their staff showed about as much enthusiasm for valuing the Grindley site as they might for visiting a dentist for a root canal filling.

CHAPTER 19

'Your face tells me it's bad news, John' said Gloria. She handed the club accountant a cup of tea. Jones took a sip before placing the cup carefully on the place mat in a manner that Gwladys would have approved.

'Yes and no. I had a letter from Australia about Tommy Harries' bequest.' Jones stopped rocking and put his chin in cupped hands. 'Tommy didn't leave as much money as he anticipated, so there's no money for the bonuses.'

What wonderful news, thought Gloria as she got out of her chair and stared out over the garden hoping to hide her happiness. Her plan was coming together.

After she stood for several moments, she took a breath which she made as audible as possible, and without turning round uttered as sadly as she could manage, 'That is very bad news. This bonus scheme without the late, lamented Harries' bequest puts us in a very bad financial position earlier than expected.'

Gloria saw the reflection of Jones shrugging his shoulders in the window glass. Then she got angry. Her eye had alighted on a number of smears on the glass. What had her cleaning-lady been doing when Gloria was out of the house? She squinted at the adjoining windows and was equally displeased at what she saw. Gloria marched back to her chair, picked up a pad and wrote "windows" on it.

'You're right to get angry, Mrs Bowen Thomas. Seems he was more gaga than we thought. However, all is not lost.'

'Really? Why not? Where does this leave us, John?'

'We have been able to fund the bonus for our first five games more easily than expected.'

'How?'

'Nothing illegal,' replied Jones. 'The weather has been exceptionally good, the arrival of Wilson has stimulated interest, the unbeaten team is a big attraction so altogether we're getting more paying spectators than we've had in years. And that new slot machine Herbie acquired is an absolute gold mine.'

'Also, I've asked Wilson to sign autographs outside the changing rooms only after he has showered and had a bite to eat. People have nothing to do whilst they wait except play the slot machine and have a drink. This plan is working well.'

Jones' excitement grew. 'Then it gets even better. On training evenings, spectators as well as players are coming down to the ground to talk rugby to Clive, poor bugger. Fortunately, Clive doesn't seem to mind all the attention; he's a fantastic human being. As you know, you cannot talk rugby and not have a drink. Result? Bar takings are up. Bearing in mind our parlous position re the bank, I am building up funds and, if we go on as we are, we still may not be able to pay back our loan but we will be much closer to being solvent than I expected.'

'This includes paying the bonus?'

'Yes, but the club will struggle to pay the bonus once the team have won, maybe, eight or nine games.'

'Will we or won't we be able to pay them?'

'We won't.'

'The players won't like it if we can't pay them what we promised. There could be trouble,' said Gloria.

'Remember, our four local sponsors agreed to cough up some money even though I know all are struggling for cash. Hopefully, they'll provide enough for another four or five games after the club money runs out. It is winning all the games that will be the problem.'

Gloria did her arithmetic and worked out at which match the money would finish. 'So, unlucky thirteenth match for the players' bonus payments if we go on as we are.'

After Jones grunted an affirmative Gloria continued, 'I heard the long-range weather forecast this morning. We're in for a very wet November and December.'

Bad weather, it was said by all the game's pundits, was the great leveller in rugby.

'John, if that forecast is accurate, what are our chances of going on winning? Doesn't the wet punish the team with the higher skills because the ball becomes so slippery?'

'Yes, but it won't bother Clive. Nor will it bother the two other players who have just joined the club. Our team is not going to stop winning because of a bit of rain.'

Jones looked gleeful as he told Gloria that two men who had recently retired from playing in the League's first division had joined the club as players.

'Whilst they are not from Glanddu, we are glad to welcome them. Obviously, they have come here only to play with Clive. I don't blame them. I even thought about coming out of retirement myself but Gwladys would never allow it.'

All this good news about the team seriously worried Gloria. So much for her plan coming together. She went from happiness to despair in under five minutes.

John continued, 'It is impossible to say whether we can go on winning. I suspect it depends on whether we get a lot of injuries, rather than a lot of wet. Do you know what Clive told me?'

'No,' Gloria said, anticipating a new boost to her depression.

'That he was impervious to hurt. Anyway, we have been very lucky so far. We have had no broken legs, arms or pulled hamstrings. Maybe it's just our time to be lucky.'

God, I hope not, Gloria prayed as she saw Jones' smile turn into a beaming light and felt her heart sink into her shoes.

CHAPTER 20

Gloria was surprised that old Grindley kept quiet about her interest in acquiring his site, particularly since he now watched Glanddu play and had many opportunities to spill the beans. As she climbed the stairs to his garret, her heart beat faster as she wondered if her written offer for the site would be accepted. Of the three valuations, Isaacs' figure was the lowest but probably the most accurate, so that was the amount Gloria and the family had decided to offer Grindley.

'So what do you think of the three valuations and my offer?'

Grindley picked up his copies and scanned each of them in turn.

'Naturally, I was hoping for more. Unfortunately, I can't expect a huge amount since only a car park was proposed. I had a chat with Councillor Watkins in the Brynddu clubhouse about an hour after Glanddu had beaten them. He was very upset at losing to us,' Grindley laughed. 'It was not the best of times to ask him, as chairman of the local planning committee, but I thought I'd run this idea past him. I asked him whether we could build houses on the garage site and his reply was, "Not if he had anything to do with it." He thought it should be converted to a remembrance garden for all the miners killed in the old pit.'

When tears came to his eyes, Gloria felt guilty and selfish that she just wanted to make money for herself from the old garage site.

Grindley cleared his throat after a few moments and wiped his face with a sleeve. 'In one way it would be nice to have a memorial. But why is it down to me to provide it? I need the money to live now. When I suggested that the council buy it from me to develop a remembrance garden, Watcyn changed the subject (so typical of a politician). He said that on Saturdays he was chairman of the rugby club and couldn't talk council business. All he wanted was to discuss was that Glanddu were wrong to have such players as Wilson in their team. I told him he was a bad loser.'

'Perhaps not the best thing to have said,' Gloria commiserated.

'No,' Grindley slumped back into the settee.

Watcyn's reaction to his team's loss in Saturday's match was so typical of men who liked sport. Gloria could never quite understand why men got depressed as to who won or lost a game. Yes, she enjoyed watching a game of rugby but when it was over, why spend all evening discussing that if so-and-so were not such a greedy bastard and had passed the ball, we would have scored and won. As chairwoman of the Glanddu Rugby Club, Gloria had to put on an emotional display about a match result for a good half-hour after the game but then she dropped all pretence and went back to normal life.

'So where does that leave us then, Mr Grindley?'

'Hywel Thomas, a good friend of Watcyn, told me in the Brynddu bar last Saturday that Watcyn is definitely retiring at the end of his term of office next year He says we can expect a more flexible approach from the Council when he retires. Also, I telephoned Billy Isaacs on his view of the site. He thought that it would be worth applying again now for planning permission. Watcyn's negative attitude to new housing doesn't hold the sway it used to.'

Gloria was sure she heard her heart hit the floor.

'In the light of that news, what is your reaction to my offer?'

'Your offer is fair for the site if it were used solely for parking. But it wouldn't be high enough if we get planning permission.'

Gloria slumped back in her chair.

'So I take the answer as a "no" because you want to build houses there, if you can.'

'Yes and no. First, whilst Watcyn is still in post, my application might be rejected. Rejections are recorded in the Council's files and might influence a second application. So I'd rather wait a year and apply to the council after Watcyn retires. Second, how many and what kind of houses would we propose? I need an architect but I don't have the money to pay for one. Could we use your cousin?'

'You mean my cousin, Teddy? He hasn't been in Wales for...?'

Gloria only ever saw Teddy at weddings and funerals. Had he been to Duncan's funeral? No, he was out of the country. Was it ten years or more?

'I can't remember.'

'It must be thirty years since he came into my garage. He drove a red Triumph Spitfire, good car they were. He needed rear light bulbs.'

He paused, puzzled. 'Why did he think I would have stocked light bulbs for a sports car? That will annoy me until I remember why. I'll give you a call when I do.'

'No, Mr Grindley, please don't bother. The Triumph has been replaced by a Porsche.'

Grindley looked suitably impressed, so Gloria went on. 'Can we get back to my offer?'

'Certainly. The club is in a bad financial way despite its current good form. True?'

'Yes.'

'Is it possible that the club could go out of business? If so, what would happen to the ground? Could it be used to build houses?'

'God forbid that could happen,' uttered Gloria, appalled that she had misjudged the man in front of her. Her judgement was based on the perception that because his fingernails had always been filthy, he had no business sense. How could she have been so arrogant?

Grindley interrupted her thoughts. 'You and I both think ahead. I suggest that you and I go into unofficial partnership. I lease the site to you, not the club, for three years.'

'Why three years?'

'We wait a year for Watcyn to retire, then we submit planning permission, and then we wait several months for the Council's first reply. Undoubtedly, they'll want changes to the plan, which takes another six to twelve months. Final approval will take at least two years. Then it will take time to finalise the finances and find the right people to build the houses. So I think we're three years away from development.'

'That's a long time.'

'Yes. Over the next year you should investigate planning permission for housing and financing the development.'

Gloria chose her words carefully. 'Why would you want me to do that? You could do it yourself.'

'Simple. You are the one person in the village who has the brains for this job. You have the cousin who is an architect and I'm sure that he would do it cheaper for you.'

'Whilst it's nice to be flattered, what's in it for me?'

Grindley smiled, 'I've thought of that. I'll give you an option to buy a share of the site for which you won't pay me until we sell it to a developer – unless we develop it ourselves.'

'What are you thinking?'

'Ninety percent for me, ten for you?'

Silence descended before Gloria asked, 'Let me think for a moment about what you've just said. Let's go back and talk about how much money would you want in order to lease the site for parking.'

'Will you or the club charge for parking at matches?'

Gloria had not thought about that. 'I don't know yet.'

Grindley pondered then, 'Rent at, say, five, no, four hundred for the remainder of this season; then five hundred for a full season. A special price just because it's you and it'll help the club.'

'I just need to talk to the family but I am sure that they will willingly put money into renting the place on behalf of their father's memory.'

Gloria's voice was steady though she did wonder how the family would react.

'I came here thinking about a car park and now we're talking about my investigating planning permission. Meanwhile, remember, I'm still looking for work.'

'We'll cut your cousin in on the deal if the Council approves our plans. If you can't do the work, I'll try and get someone else,' he grinned. 'Councillor Watkins?'

'No, never. I'm happy to do what I can. I know my cousin is away in Poland on a housing development. Then he'll be at his Spanish villa; I'll contact him by email to see what he thinks.'

'No problem. I've said I'm in no rush. Think about it.'

'We'll need to involve lawyers.'

'I don't want the future spelled out on paper. I give you my word that if building permission is sought and given, I will honour our agreement.'

Although Grindley had sworn after his divorce that he would never trust another woman, at least this one in front of him was not a money grabber like his ex-wife.

Gloria smiled, extended her hand, and gripped his hand as hard as she could to emphasise that what she said next, she meant.

'Provided my family agree to the price for the parking lease we will act on that as soon as possible. As to the prospect of my acquiring a share in the site I have to think about your offer. My word will be not only my bond, but my family's, too.'

It was several days later that Grindley telephoned Gloria.

'Gloria, now that I'm a supporter of the club, I don't want to make money out of you. That said, in my experience people value something more if they have to pay for it. You give me. . .'

'Two hundred pounds for this and for next season is all I can afford,' Gloria said.

Grindley waited in silence for what seemed an eternity. 'On the proviso the club tidy up the site.'

'Meaning?'

'Clear the weeds and put a layer of tarmacadam down on the old forecourt and anywhere else you can. I saw a crew doing road repairs on the Pontardawe Road. It looks like this crew will be working there for another couple of weeks. I'm sure they'll have tarmacadam to spare; they always do. All you need is a couple of blokes doing two or three hours work laying it and you have a better looking site immediately. This work will cost a maximum of a couple of hundred pounds – less, if someone on your committee knows the road gang foreman. A much nicer looking car park will encourage people to pay for the privilege of parking there.'

'True. I'll pay for the lease and a lawyer friend of Toby's will carry out all the legal work.'

'No estate agents.'

'Of course not. My cousin says he can't do anything till the spring because of work pressure. Once he comes down and evaluates the place, we can start the ball rolling. So as for that other matter, I accept your offer.'

'Good. Suggest to John Jones that the club pays for the site clearance work since the club can pay the workers in cash. The workers, I am sure, will be willing to give the club a receipt for twice that amount using a fictitious company.'

CHAPTER 21

'Thank you for coming round on such short notice,' Gloria said, ushering Jones into her living room.

Then she blurted out, 'John, I've been keeping this under my hat but I want you to know that my family has acquired the Grindley site for use as a club car park for a couple of years, at least.'

'What?'

'I thought this would be a nice surprise, considering the amount of cars that have appeared following our success.'

She could see that nice or not, it was certainly a surprise to the club treasurer. She went on quickly. 'Though the deal has not yet been completed, Grindley said we could use the site immediately.'

Jones sat and digested the information. 'You're buying this for the club?'

'Actually, no.' Gloria could feel herself flushing. 'I should have said my family are renting the site for the club to use.'

'He tried to get housing on it a few years ago. I wonder why he hasn't tried again,' mused the club treasurer.

'He spoke to Councillor Watkins after our game; no chance of that.'

Jones threw back his head and laughed. 'Not the best time to ask Watkins about new housing when we've just beaten his team. Still, it won't cost the club, will it?

'No. Part of the deal is that the club tidies the place, including a layer of tarmac. I think we can get thirty cars in there.'

'That sounds a good idea and it'll make us a few quid. What is this about tarmac?'

'Grindley told me he wants tarmacadam put down. Sadly, the family cannot pay for that. Can the club?

'At a push.'

'Grindley also said you know one of the gangs doing road work round here on the Pontardawe Road, and they will do it for you.'

Jones' face lit up, 'Ah! I know who Grindley means. The foreman of that road gang, Jeff Huws, is from Porthcawl. Jeff played for Neath until his knee injury. Ironically, I drove up that way yesterday and when he saw me, he waved. I'll go and have a word with him, see if he can do the job and what he'll charge. We can get a receipt from him showing that we paid more than we actually did.' He paused as the thought struck him. 'We'll need the key for that padlock on Grindley's gate.'

'I could go into Swansea and pick it up,' suggested Gloria feeling buoyant.

'No, car parking comes under the aegis of the ground committee; tread on their toes and there will be hell to pay. The committee's chairman, Tom Moses, will go. We'll start him thinking about preparing the site immediately. It will give Tom and the others something different to do and get them away from the wives.'

'The weather is set fair for the next few days, so the sooner we start the better.'

'I nearly forgot. I have some good news.'

Gloria's exhilaration about the site evaporated when he told her.

'The money promised by Tommy Harries has arrived after all. Tommy Harries' sons had decided to honour their father's final wish out of their own pockets. The cheque had arrived this morning.'

Gloria was so upset by the arrival of the money from Australia that immediately after Jones left the house, she drove to Swansea. In fact, she was so upset that instead of parking for free she put the vehicle in a pay car park. But no dresses took her fancy. Indeed, some of the styles and all the prices made her feel even more depressed.

As she trudged back to her car she passed an office block and saw the dreaded name etched into a plate screwed to the wall: "Her Majesty's Inland Revenue and Customs."

Suddenly, out of the ether, a thought so dark emerged that she was amazed she could even think such a thing.

CHAPTER 22

Gloria's dark thought of several weeks earlier came back on the Saturday evening following Glanddu's eighth successive victory, keeping them top of the Fifth Division League Table. After the match even Gloria was excited over the team's winning performance and thoroughly enjoyed gently ribbing the losing chair about his team's defeat.

After any match, all anyone talked about was what had happened, what should have happened, how the climatic conditions impacted the game and which team was lucky or unlucky. The referee's performance usually merited a whole hour of discussion. When talk about the day's match ran out, a discussion about previous games between the two teams followed. When all else failed there was the fallback debate on who was going to play for Wales this year. The talk in the bar could go on to eleven o'clock depending on what explanation a man could give his wife for not coming home when he promised he would.

Gloria never stayed beyond six o'clock because by then she was exhausted by such talk and wanted to brain someone or simply scream.

When she got back to the house Gloria's earlier exhilaration left her. Yes, the house was big and it was decorated as she liked, but there was more to life than her house. Gloria was lonely and dreaded never working again. The people in the village were nice enough but none read her type of books. Few went to the theatre.

Then there was the fare on television. Every year there would be a new production of British classics like Dr Jekyll and Mr Hyde or The Pickwick Papers. Why keep making new versions of these productions? It was only five years since the last version, but this latest masterpiece was marketed as the best since the seminal 1955 version. Gloria said that she would burn her TV if she ever again saw mutton chops, Victorian bonnets or beautifully applied grime. Was she going to spend the rest of her life watching classical dramas?

Then there were the Hollywood films. Gloria was a firm believer that a story should have a beginning, middle and end. Now, it was common for a film to begin in the middle and arrive mysteriously at the end with no logical sequence of events. And in most films, the multi-million dollar stars play themselves and the minor characters, who make a story so interesting, are often absent. Gloria liked thrillers, but the body count in modern films inevitably ran into scores whilst the hero, if wounded, could operate on himself with a tin lid and a bit of fuzz from an old carpet. It had been years since Oscar winners were worth watching.

Was she just getting old?

Gloria poured herself a goblet of wine and picked up the Radio Times in the desperate hope that there would be something worthwhile to watch. She threw down the magazine then marched to her DVD storage cabinet and selected Gavin and Stacey. After one minute she stopped the DVD player and hurled the remote control onto the settee where it landed with such a crash that its batteries fell out.

Gloria sat with her heart beating so hard that she could feel it. She had to get work for sanity's sake. She had to get out of the house. After a moment's thought she leapt to her feet, grabbed the telephone and pressed her friend Jack Day's number.

'Jack, it's Gloria. Are you just on your way out for the evening?'

She replied in surprise at his response. 'You've got a job and you're working on a Saturday?'

'Gloria, I've just finished my shift at Housebase and I'm knackered. Marlene is due to finish her shift at Sainsco in a couple of hours. Before you ask, I've given up getting another IT job, as has Marlene. Her last interview for a proper job was a year ago and mine was over nine months ago. Mine took place in London at nine in the morning, so I had to travel during rush hour. Not one person on the train was under forty; I didn't see a single grey hair. I have a friend in his early forties, an ex-rugby player, who dyes his hair to look younger. But he can't go down to his old rugby club because his mates will laugh at him.'

There was silence for a moment before Jack's voice, laden with sadness, asked, 'You telephoned me to say you got a job?'

'Nothing like that. Just to bounce this idea off you. If I were to go to some of the offices in London where I have worked...?'

'Like?'

'The Shell building or that place in Covent Garden,' Gloria started to giggle at the ludicrousness at what she was about to say. 'Do you think that if I hung around outside them at lunchtime, someone I know might come out? That someone would be sympathetic and know of jobs going in their office?'

'Well, I've heard that employers are trying to get even more work out of their employees. Everyone is having food delivered to their desks, all toilet facilities are being converted to office space, and every employee will sit on a commode with their laptop plugged into the cistern.'

Jack then became serious.

'When you worked for Shell nearly all the staff was permanent, and they filled three large office buildings, north and south of the Thames. Now, nearly all the staff are on short-term contracts and they occupy just one building; the number of employees is horribly reduced. Of the other two buildings one, if not both, are converted into flats. Anyway, what makes you think anyone you knew when you worked there is still there?'

'I don't. I'm at my wits end and I'm willing to do anything to stop relying on those bloody contractor agencies to find me work. You should have heard the intellectual remedial who telephoned me this week.'

'Go on.'

'Well, he sounded about fifteen years old. He kept calling me Glo-rear-ha. He asked me why I didn't have the skill, "technical author," on my Curriculum Vitae. I replied that I did have "technical writer" on my CV. When I told him that author and writer were synonyms, he asked me, "What's a synonym?"

Despite my explanation, he insisted that I use the "correct" word. So I said, just change it. Do you know what his reply was?'

'No.'

'He was not allowed to change my CV and that he wanted me to email him an updated version immediately because this was a rush job. Then this idiot told me the job was in London - Putney - and that the interview was that evening, with work to start on the following day. When I said I lived west of Swansea, he asked if that was near London, to which I replied "yes," if you think two hundred miles can be classified as "near." What *do* these kids learn in school?'

'Keyboard skills and how to program DVD players; definitely not geography. Perhaps you should have gone to see what they were offering.'

'The only available interview slot was 6 p.m; the telephone call was at 3.30 p.m. When I said that I couldn't get there till at least 7.30 he replied, "No dice"; the agency couldn't take a chance and he had other clients closer to London.'

'That's agencies for you. Any bum on a seat will do because that's what makes them money.'

'Twenty minutes later this same agent rang back to offer me a 6.30 appointment. After counting to ten I said as nicely as I could that 6.30, too, was also impossible for me.'

Jack started to chuckle.

'This heinous child then had the effrontery to say that I didn't seem to be putting myself out to get work. Should he take it that I was no longer looking for work and did I wish to have my name removed from his agency's database?'

Gloria joined in Jack's laughter and for a few minutes they forgot about the world of agencies and unemployment. At the end of the conversation Gloria was cheered up as she put the phone down.

But after her second sip of wine, Gloria's mood changed. She started to think about her dispiriting conversation with the team coach, Granville Beck, earlier in the evening. She was just about to go home when Granville bounced up and backed her into a corner of the bar.

'It was a wonderful performance by the boys today, Mrs Bowen Thomas. All the boys are training so hard that we must be the fittest team in the league. The lads are unbelievably keen. Nobody can equal us.'

Granville then broke into a smile illuminating gaps caused by stray boots, fists and elbows during his playing career.

'Don't worry. I'm trying to dampen down the talk about getting through the season unbeaten. Let's face it, we've only won the first eight games. Clive and I don't want them to get overconfident.'

'Clive's learning from you?' Her voice dripped with sarcasm.

'He told you that? Fantastic.' Granville bounced delightedly. 'Clive did say to me that I seemed to have a knack of getting the best out of the players.'

At that moment they both saw Wilson about to leave the bar.

'It's been good talking to you, Mrs BT.' (Gloria hated being called that.) 'I must catch my number two before he goes home. Don't worry, Mrs BT,' patting Gloria's shoulder (Gloria also hated shoulder patting). 'I'll keep them focused on winning the League and going up to the fourth division next year.' With a wink (which she also hated), he trotted over to Clive Wilson.

Gloria observed Wilson listening to Granville's gems, nodding or pursing his lips from time to time. Finally, Wilson gave Granville a playful tap on the head and left the bar. Granville then thrust himself into a coterie of Glanddu committee members, clearly enjoying the claps on the back and the smiles they gave him.

Back home Gloria drank her wine and contemplated her options. Gloria had learnt about "boot money," or under-the-counter bonus payments to rugby players on her first visit to Glanddu as Duncan's girlfriend. The pair was in their final year of University and money, as always, was tight. During his vacations Duncan played for Glanddu if they needed him.

On this particular Easter Saturday Duncan was selected for the first team. Before the match he gave Gloria his wallet for safekeeping. Duncan showed her the contents of his wallet: two one-pound notes to cover their night out. After the match he took his wallet back from her and waved another pound note under her nose. With a grin he said that she could have steak for dinner accompanied, not by the house wine, but by a bottle with a real label. Payments to amateur players were really a no-no, so Duncan smiled and put his finger to his lips.

Gloria had never understood why the Inland Revenue didn't investigate rugby clubs. She was sure Inland Revenue and the clubs' auditors knew that sports clubs must fiddle their accounts simply to stay in existence. Perhaps the problem was that if the Revenue investigated the small clubs, someone would call "foul" and ask, "What about the big clubs — particularly the big soccer clubs?" Gloria was sure that if the Revenue investigated the big boys, questions would be asked in Parliament and protesting fans would riot in the streets in case overpaid soccer players left the UK for pastures new.

Gloria didn't wish any Glanddu player to suffer a serious injury but a few pulled hamstrings, she thought, would not go amiss. Perhaps there could be an outbreak of influenza, say, after the Christmas festivities. There must be some way to end the winning streak.

She refilled her glass and wondered if she had barked up the wrong tree in getting involved with the Grindley site. If Glanddu won promotion, surely the games would attract bigger crowds and more money would be spent in the bar. Instead of imminent bankruptcy the club would go into the black. Gloria could forget about a new housing development.

Nevertheless, the paperwork for leasing Grindley's Garage site was completed. Teddy, her architect cousin, had emailed his preliminary thoughts about the site. He thought six houses looked reasonable. The Council required that one of the houses, at least, would have to be affordable to the less well off. Alternatively, Teddy wondered if a small block of flats or a block of sheltered housing for retired people might be a good use of the site. And one more thing: there might be environmental issues with the old petrol storage tanks. He would come down in April or May and do a proper survey.

Teddy gave Gloria the "rule of thumb" formula that a site is worth a third of the final selling prices of all the houses on that site. Based on new builds in the area, Gloria estimated the houses might raise £500,000 - making the plot worth about £165,000. Her family couldn't afford to pay that much for the site.

Gloria negotiated an increased finder's fee of fifteen percent from Grindley when the time came for her to start preliminary work on their project. At fifteen percent, Gloria calculated that she might end up with only about twenty-five thousand pounds. She'd never afford to move to London with that, even after selling her own house. Nevertheless, she had to put her plan into action and stop waiting for her life to happen.

CHAPTER 23

Gloria parked, as usual, in the supermarket car park and then walked across to the Swansea shopping mall. The mall had the usual early Monday morning shopping crowd of about three people traipsing forlornly, ducking the rain. Gloria, too, moped around the mall for a while till finally, with her heart in her mouth and her hands shaking as if she was suffering from St. Vitus Dance, she found an increasing rarity: a public call box. She looked round nervously.

'This is the Swansea Office of the Inland Revenue and Customs. Please note that this call may be recorded for training purposes. Press one to speak to an operator in a normal voice. Press two to speak to an operator discretely.'

'Fraud Office?' Gloria said, speaking in a lower voice than usual, trying hard to imitate Marilyn William's accent. Nervously she gabbled, 'Glanddu Rugby Club is making under-the-counter payments to their players and these players are not paying tax.' Before the clerk could reply, Gloria replaced the receiver.

As she replaced the telephone, Gloria suddenly realised that in every detective story she had ever read the villain always makes a mistake. What was hers? She had disguised her voice, put on a scarf and wore gloves.

Cameras - there were cameras everywhere. All the Inland Revenue need do was looking through the surveillance tapes and tie them up to the time of the call. Should Toby have called for her? No, she had to do her own dirty work. Surely, as club chair she would be the last person to be suspected. Of course, the Revenue would not bother with the TV footage, would it?

Gloria suddenly felt disgusted with herself. Face down and a scarf covering her hair, she slunk back to the car park.

Gillian Gayle at the Inland Revenue took the call. She played the tape recording several times. She checked Glanddu on the map. Puzzled and clutching the tape, she wandered, via the coffee machine, over to her boss, John Evans. Evans was a rugby follower and listened attentively in shocked silence to the recording of Gloria's voice.

'Why would the woman telephone this office? Glanddu is in the Llanelli district.'

'It certainly is Gillian, well done.'

Evans was careful to pay Gillian a compliment because her boyfriend had broken off with her recently and she needed cheering up. Evans had even offered to audit her boyfriend's last tax return, but her ex wasn't stupid and he'd know who instigated it; he might even become violent. What about auditing him the following year? Evans made a note on the man's file, with the proviso to check first that the pair had not got back together again.

After playing the tape for the eighth time, Evans said authoritatively, 'This woman is from Bryntowy.'

When he saw Gillian's look of wonderment, he explained.

'Simple. There is no love lost between any of those villages in the back of beyond. Glanddu are currently first in their division and Bryntowy are second. If Welsh Rugby Union investigates the Glanddu club because of this call and they find fraudulent payments, then they would dock points from the club. They would probably remove enough points from Glanddu to reduce their chance of promotion to nil. Bryntowy have the most to gain from this telephone call. All but one of the clubs in that division of the Welsh League lie within the jurisdiction of the Llanelli Inland Revenue office. You may guess which one is the exception.'

'Bryntowy?'

'Exactly. It must be someone from Bryntowy who telephoned us, unaware that Glanddu is in the Llanelli area. Elementary is it not, my dear Watson?'

'You have to be on your toes in this job, Mr Evans,' replied Gillian, impressed by the power of her boss's deduction.

'No need to do anything. We'll let Llanelli deal with it.'

'There's the tape and tape log, though.'

'Yes,' Evans hesitated whilst he thought.

'Just log as, "tape copied," and leave the copy on my desk. I will forward it to Don Devereux over at the Llanelli office and then I'll discuss with him what to do about this obviously crank call.'

'Who is he?'

'The Llanelli office fraud man. Remember, "Mum's the Word."'

CHAPTER 24

Jane Devereux rang the doorbell but hearing no movement in the house, she walked round to the back and smiled at what she saw. Her father's elder brother, John Jones, was lolling back in a wooden garden seat, legs akimbo. John was tucked out of the wind with a newspaper covering his face against the unseasonably warm morning sun.

'Uncle John, you awake?'

'Jane, of course I'm awake,' lied John Jones as he removed the newspaper. 'I was merely resting my eyes.'

'I was just passing and I thought I'd drop in and have a word about something Don heard at the office.'

It was lovely to see Jane, but passing Glanddu? One did not pass through Glanddu, not if one was on the way to anywhere.

The mention of Don's office made him uneasy. He went into the kitchen and made them both a cup of tea.

'Don got a call from the Swansea Office, who got an anonymous call accusing the Glanddu club of making under-the-counter payments,' Jane said, leaning against the kitchen door frame.

'Someone did what?' Jones slammed his cup down with such force that it spilled. 'Why would anyone do such a nasty thing? I'd like to get my hands on the bastard, who called - I'd give him what for. Who was it? Did they say? No,' he said answering his own question, 'they wouldn't have the guts.'

'It was a woman.'

Jones' jaw dropped open in surprise. Jane nodded her head.

'Yes, Uncle John. Though the caller's voice was disguised and barely audible, the Swansea officer was adamant that he recognised a Bryntowy accent.'

'Good God,' John gabbled, 'they recognised the caller's accent? Do they now have special training to recognize regional accents? I've seen those American cop programmes where a machine analyzes the smallest components of person's voice. Do you have those machines now? And is it evidence in court? Talk about Big Brother. Remind me never to make an anonymous call. Still, you could identify the woman, right?'

Jane laughed. 'No, there's no specialist accent training and no ultra-expensive speech machine; just old fashioned human skill.'

'I promise you that it's not the club but individual supporters who, out of the goodness of their hearts, pay the players a winning bonus. Everyone does it. In case your husband is thinking of making a wider investigation, all the local clubs are in the same precarious financial situation as we are.'

'I know.'

John frowned. 'I'd like to know why the call was made? Surely not just sour grapes because we are above Bryntowy in the League? And it seems far-fetched for a woman to make the telephone call.'

'That is a sexist remark, Uncle John. Remember, you have a woman chair and women are even playing the game, though why a woman would want a cauliflower ear, I have no idea.'

'Obviously, to go with their tattoos and their body piercings. Any idea of her age?'

'Possibly late forties but fifties, more likely.'

Jane's face lit up in a grin. 'Perhaps this woman is a jilted lover of one of the Glanddu players. She reported the club to cover for what she really wants, which is for Revenue to investigate every player and their tax returns, including her Don Juan.'

'Clever, except for one thing: you said she was in her fifties. How could she be involved with one of our players?'

'Ever heard of toy-boys?'

'In Glanddu? Have you seen our players?'

'Uncle John, could it be something else entirely? I assume there are some Glanddu players who are "hobbling" or, "working on the dark?" Jane said, using the local expressions for people who claimed unemployment benefit whilst working.

'I doubt it,' John joked, 'we're all on the straight and narrow in this village.'

Jane mused, 'But why report the club to the Inland Revenue rather than the individuals receiving the dole? I guess that if she reported specific players they could figure out who shopped them. Another reason might be that someone in the club did a real cowboy job on a piece of building work for this woman. Am I right in thinking that most of the hobbling is building work?'

'Yes, Colin Mabbutt is a bit of a cowboy and he does use our out of work players to help him, but you'd have to have a mind like Machiavelli to come up with that as an excuse for dropping the club in the mire.'

A thought struck John. 'Isn't true that the people who report tax dodgers can get a reward for a successful prosecution?'

Jane shook her head, 'Yes, but no name was given.'

'So all she gains is revenge. What will happen now, Jane?'

'I'm not sure, Uncle John. I'll tell Don what you've said. Probably, he'll write a report saying the complaint has been investigated and the allegation is unfounded. He'll pass the case back to the Swansea offices and the tape will be conveniently mislaid.'

Jane stood and buttoned her coat. 'Uncle John, if you can find out anything about the woman let me know.' She turned at the door, 'Will you tell Auntie Gwladys I was here?'

'As it was about club business of a particular type, I think not.'

Less than five minutes after his niece left Jones slammed his front door and set off briskly down the road. In the distance he saw the milk van disappear over the brow of the hill. He cursed and, to make matters worse, it started to rain.

'Bloody hell, Dai,' gasped Jones a couple of minutes later when he arrived puffing beside the van where Williams was updating his order book. Dai motioned Jones to join him in the cab and he drove into the next road.

Dai loaded his milk tray from the side of the van. 'I could do with some help when you get your breath back, John.'

Dai reached in through the driver's door and retrieved a spare raincoat for Jones. For the next twenty minutes the two men delivered milk in tandem and concentrated on how many bottles of skim, semi-skim or full fat milk went to each house. Dai made sure that John walked downhill with the full bottles because he still hadn't quite recovered from running down the road. Eventually Dai parked the van and took out his thermos flask.

'Thanks for the help, but what triggered it?'

'It must be nearly fifty years since I helped your father with his deliveries. Happy days.'

Jones eyes grew misty before his look changed as he recounted his morning's conversation with Jane. Dai sat in silence before he emptied the tea dregs out of the window.

'I don't understand why the call was made because the Bryntowy team are also getting a win bonus paid for by this English chap, Tommy Joy. If anyone from the Bryntowy club dropped us in the mire with the Inland Revenue, they would end up in it, as well. The whole thing is a can of worms.'

'I was wondering if your wife, Marilyn, coming from Bryntowy, could ask her family about it?'

'We'll see.'

Jones normally telephoned Gloria before visiting her so when she opened her front door, she was surprised to see him. Gloria ushered him into her sitting-room where he perched on a leather chair and rejected her offer of tea.

'I've had contact with someone from the Inland Revenue about our bonus payments.'

'Swansea Inland Revenue has contacted you. Why?'

When Gloria saw Jones' face she realised that something was wrong. She felt her heart sink and knew she had just made the mistake that would expose her.

'Have Swansea Inland Revenue been in touch with you about this?' Jones said, panic in his voice. Perhaps his niece had been wrong and the Swansea office was doing an investigation after all.

'Oh no, John, I just assumed the Revenue Office was in Swansea.'

'No, ours is in Llanelli – I thought you knew.' Jones relaxed back into the chair. 'Funny that you should mention Swansea, because that was the Revenue Office the informer telephoned. From the accent the Swansea office identified the informant as from Bryntowy, but handed the complaint over to Llanelli for investigation.'

'It is utterly despicable that someone should betray us to the tax people. Can I assume that the call was made because, against all the odds, we are top of the League and we have just beaten them?'

'Possibly, but the investigator thought it might be a jilted lover of one of the players trying to get back at him in a clever way. The problem with that theory is that the woman sounded in her fifties, much too old for one of our players.'

'Absolutely.' Gloria faked a shudder. 'Could it be someone on our committee she was after?'

Jones laughed, 'Of course - you're thinking of Arthur! He's had quite a few dalliances over the years and the law of averages says he must have had paramour in Bryntowy, but damned if I know who it might be.'

For a few moments they sat in silence. Then the striking of the grandfather clock galvanised Gloria. 'If the club was investigated, then you and I, as officers of the club, would be in trouble.'

John started to calm down. 'If the Revenue investigates us we can stir up the local papers. The Revenue would then need to examine every sports club, not just in West Wales but throughout the UK; every club pulls the same financial stunts.' Again he laughed, 'They have bigger fish to catch.'

'May I remind you that in this part of Wales the biggest businesses are the rugby clubs. So don't be so sure that this investigation won't proceed,' Gloria said, wondering what she could do now.

'True,' replied Jones. 'Oh God, I must go,' he said. Without another word he leapt from his chair and rushed out of the house.

'I'm home,' shouted Gwladys, slamming the front door. She sniffed then marched into the kitchen. 'What time did you put the oven on? Three o'clock, like I said?'

'Well, no, I was out till four.'

Gwladys went to look at the kitchen window and then disappeared to look at the sitting room window. She returned, exasperated.

'The windows are still dirty. You said you were going to clean them. What happened? You forgot?' She went over to the sink. 'As always you haven't washed up your things. Wait a minute, what is this cup with lipstick on it? You had a woman round?'

'Jane Devereux.' He took a very long breath. 'She came on official business.'

'And that stopped you cleaning the windows that you have been promising for ages.' She paused, 'Don't tell me it was something to do with the club?'

When her husband rolled his eyes she shrugged, 'I told you that one day they would catch on. I'll come and visit you in Swansea Gaol, but my visits will be very infrequent if you end up in Maidstone or Parkhurst.'

'I think those are both prisons for violent offenders. Anyway, Parkhurst is on the Isle of Wight and you like it there.'

Against her better judgement, Gwladys laughed and after Jones told her the full story, she immediately surmised that the caller was one of Arthur Davies' many floozies. John said whilst that was logical, no sightings of the man in that village had been made.

'I rest my case; he has abandoned whomever he was chasing,' replied his wife. 'Now, lay the table. Remember knives go on the right.'

Jones gave his wife gentle smack on the bottom before laying the knives on the left and the forks on the right. He glanced at his wife and promptly rearranged them.

CHAPTER 25

As usual Dai went to bed at the end of his milk round for an hour's sleep, despite John Jones' revelations. He awoke to the smell of roasting beef and the sound of the TV in the lounge broadcasting the latest string of calamities collectively known as the news. He quietly he opened the bedroom door and crept down stairs into the kitchen. Marilyn was peeling Brussels sprouts.

'You are moving very quietly, David Williams. Were you expecting me to be watching TV so that you could steal a piece of the meat without my noticing?' She turned and saw Dai's look of guilt. 'Do I or don't I know you, and the answer is no, David. The food will be ready in twenty minutes and not before.'

'Good day?' Dai said, as he took a can of beer from the fridge. He was just about to sip his drink when Marilyn glared at him. He retrieved a glass from a kitchen cabinet, poured in the can's contents and dutifully placed the can into the plastic re-cycling bin.

'Good. You?' Marilyn went back to the sprouts.

'I lost another two customers today. Both are going to work part-time at Sainsco. They said they would pick up their milk at the shop, and who can blame them? Since July I've acquired the Wilsons but lost,' he looked at the ceiling as he calculated, 'eight of my faithful.'

Marilyn thought out loud. 'Long ago the only the reason we lost customers was because they were leaving the village in a pine box.' She sighed and put the sprouts in a saucepan. Then she sat down opposite Dai.

Dai held his glass up to the light and studied its amber colour for a moment. 'I was out on my round when who should appear but Le chef de books, who proceeded to help me deliver for a while.

He said it took him back to when he helped my father. It's sad that kids can't help milkmen anymore.'

Helping the milkman used to be a countrywide tradition that introduced children to work, responsibility, and meeting people. It was fun and after a day's work the milkman paid them sixpence or a shilling. Nearly all the children who had worked with Dai had fond memories of those times, and many old enough now to have youngsters of their own wished the latter had the chance of doing a milk round.

Now milkmen must be vetted by the government to ensure they are not paedophiles. And, in the unlikely event that today's milkman allowed a child to accompany him on his rounds, if a child splashed milk and ruined his shoes or caught pneumonia because it rained, an ambulance-chaser would contact the parents and say, "Let's take him to court."

'Health and bloody safety,' muttered Marilyn. 'So what did Mr Jones want? To get back into trim? Re-live his childhood?'

'No. He told me that a woman with a Bryntowy accent had reported player bonus payments to the Swansea Inland Revenue, and Swansea sent it over to Llanelli to investigate.'

'And? He thought it was me or one of my brothers' wives?'

'No.' Dai thumped the table hard enough to make his beer spill. Marilyn tossed him a dishcloth. 'John wondered whether you could make some discreet inquiries.'

'Anyone in particular or is the whole village under suspicion?' Marilyn plonked down in a chair opposite Dai and folded her arms.

'Could it be Miriam White getting back at Will?'

'Miriam and Will were divorced twelve years ago and Will has been on the Glanddu committee for at least thirty years, so why would she say anything now? I know her well. She's not vindictive.'

'Not vindictive!' Dai exploded. 'We're talking about the woman who threw her husband's clothes out into the street, scratched his car and moved his father's piano out into the garden to rot in the rain. We are talking about that Miriam.'

'He *did* run off with that woman.'

That woman was Betty Rees, but Dai knew better than to mention the name of Marilyn's mortal enemy. Dai went out with

Betty a few times before he started dating Marilyn, and that still rankled his wife.

'Anyway, John thought we ought to hear about this call because it might lead to an investigation of our business.'

'How so?'

'Like where our sponsorship money comes from. But John did say that he was sure that there was absolutely nothing to worry about.'

'Dai, that's a complete contradiction. As if we haven't got enough worries with the business.' Marilyn shut her eyes then, after a moment, snatched a look at the kitchen clock said, 'Now pour me a sherry, please and whilst you are up, Dai, light the gas under the sprouts. Don't look at me like that. I'll telephone my brother after dinner to see if he knows anything.'

'Would he tell you if he did?'

'If he's heard anything, he'll tell me. Have you put salt in the sprouts? Do it now, better late than never. I suppose in about thirty years you'll be able to cook.'

Marsha Bolotnikov waited until after they had eaten a good dinner and her husband had had several glasses of wine before she broached the subject.

'Boris, I had a telephone call from my mother this afternoon. She wants me to go back to Russia. Her back is so bad that she doesn't want to continue living.'

Marsha wanted to bring her to London, but Boris couldn't stand her mother and Marsha knew it.

'How long will you be gone?'

'A couple of months. I could take Mother to Cyprus where it is warm and where lots of Russians are living. Also, I could look for a holiday home for us out there.'

'We have just moved into this nice house in St John's Wood and you want another property? I don't want a house in Cyprus. I need to keep a low profile until we are well settled here.'

'Well, if not Cyprus could we buy somewhere in the West Country, perhaps the Cotswolds? Nothing big, five bedrooms or maybe six, at the most. Just somewhere we could go at weekends.

You could sell our little house in Bloomsbury to pay for it. Give you somewhere to stay when you go and watch Sergei play rugby.'

'The Cotswolds are about eighty or ninety miles from where our son goes to school.'

Boris studied his wine for a long time after he had spoken. Then he looked at Marsha across the glass.

'The Bloomsbury house is not for sale yet. We may need it for any associates who come over to work in London. However, property is always a good investment; I'll start the ball rolling. The Cotswolds, I hear, are overpriced.'

He held his hand up to stifle her protest. 'I'll have a look at what's on the market.'

The investigation of who in Bryntowy might have grassed on Glanddu was undertaken with as much discretion as possible. Len Penry bearded Arthur Davies in his car showroom to find out if he ever had a girlfriend in Bryntowy. Arthur said he didn't think so, but he would check. He led Len into his office and retrieved from the safe, not one but two black address books. He found Bryntowy's area code in the telephone book. Then he scoured every entry in both address books, but he drew a blank.

Euros Thomas, the playing sub-committee chairman, undertook the investigation as to whether the players had any love interest in Bryntowy, but he also found that Bryntowy was a love desert.

John Jones met his niece Jane Devereux for a lunchtime sandwich at a pub in Llanelli a few days after her visit to his home. He told her that no one could identify the squealer. To John's relief, Jane told him that no investigation by the Revenue was currently planned. John celebrated with a gin and tonic. His niece had the same, except her tonic was slimline.

CHAPTER 26

The storm that had started on Sunday evening got stronger throughout Monday until, by that evening, the wind was rattling the Glanddu clubhouse windows almost out of their frames. The rain left mini-lakes and ponds where there was level ground and elsewhere water gushed in torrents to find lower land. It was seven thirty pm and four men with grim faces occupied the committee room of Glanddu's otherwise empty clubhouse. There was a pungent smell as all four silently dried the bottom of their trousers in front of the room's single electric fire. Jones shivered, blew on his hands, took off his raincoat and nearly put it back on immediately except he imagined Gwladys saying, "You'll not get the benefit of the coat when you go back outside if you keep it on inside." He pulled a small table close to the fire and a chair even closer, looked at his watch and, with a snap of his fingers, brought the others to join him.

On Saturday the club had recorded its eleventh consecutive win, resulting in a twenty-two pound bonus for each player and the coach. Before that Saturday Granville was instructed not to use the substitutes (to avoid paying them) unless someone was injured. During this game Granville cocked a snook at his paymasters and used both substitutes, not to replace injured players, but as part of his game plan. When Len and Dai challenged Granville's use of substitutes Granville, using basic Anglo-Saxon, told them exactly what they could do with their complaint. The coach's view was that he was in charge of the team and its tactics, and he would do whatever was necessary to go on winning. The coach's action added forty-four pounds to the bonus bill, bringing it up to a total payment for the week of three hundred and ninety-six pounds. Tommy Harries' bequest and the money the club had set aside for the bonus had evaporated sooner than expected. For the last three weeks Dai, Arthur, Len and Colin had provided the money, amounting to ninety-nine pounds each - virtually the limit the sponsors had agreed at the start of the season.

'You all know why the meeting has been called,' Jones said, rubbing his hands to get the circulation going.

Everyone knew.

'Meeting our financial commitment to the team,' said Mabbutt. 'I must tell you, John, I cannot afford to pay any more money. If the team wins again this week it will be the last time I can pay out.'

'Ninety-nine pounds means that I lose the profit from delivering scores of pints,' exclaimed Dai, his voice rising to deliver the next sentence. 'My wife and I will be working for nothing soon. I'm with Colin. This coming week will see my last contribution.'

'Me, too,' added Len. 'I know that I promised I would go on paying, come what may. But we are not being helped by Granville's seemingly wanton use of substitutes, costing us so much more money than is necessary.'

Len shrugged, looked at the table with an air of resignation and slowly sank back into his seat.

'The proper term is replacement, not substitute,' said Jones.

'Don't be so pedantic, John, we've always called them substitutes or subs,' Dai grunted.

'Thank you, Dai. Now, can I get back to Granville?'

Len answered his own question. 'Granville seems to think that money grows on trees. He is coaching Glanddu, not Llanelli or Manchester United. We've told him what the money situation is and he deliberately ignores our instructions.'

'He is doing a fantastic job,' muttered Mabbutt. 'The players love him, so what do you suggest? That we sack him and the team reverts to their normal playing standards?'

As with any group of men sitting in a rugby club with something serious to discuss, it was inevitable that they turn their backs on the important subject and get on with what they like to deliberate: the team's current performance.

'If only we had made the team accept a joint league and cup bonus system,' Len mused, referring back to the cup game Glanddu had lost five weeks previously. 'The boys would be on a bonus now of,' he paused whilst he made the calculation, 'eight pounds.'

'Ifs and buts,' said Jones and then, just as he was refocusing on the reason for everyone's presence in the room, the sound of heavy footsteps reverberated and a moment later Arthur Davies appeared through the door wearing a camel-haired coat with a velvet collar. Dai and Len together made a great production of looking at their watches, which Arthur cheerfully ignored. Arthur took his coat off, shivered and then put it back on; his current wife was no Gwladys.

'Selling cars is an evening business which requires a little finessing, unlike dealing with the great unwashed public like you two,' Arthur said. He turned to the others, 'Good evening, John and Colin.'

Len erupted, 'Arthur, you are full of shit. I saw your car parked outside a certain woman's house on my way here. You have kept us all waiting three-quarters of an hour. You're involved in this issue and you would complain loud enough if we had decided something you didn't like.'

'Actually, Arthur, all we've been discussing is the team's performance,' explained Mabbutt apologetically, but when he saw Dai eyeing him he thought he had better add, 'whilst waiting for you to arrive.'

Arthur took out a cigar but after glancing round the room he put it back in the packet; those in the room were not worthy to inhale the aroma of fine tobacco.

Dai waited for Arthur's theatrical performance to end before he spoke.

'Arthur, whilst you were satisfying your lady friend the lads here said that if we win, they cannot afford to go on paying. Are you prepared to go on supplying money?'

'Not if you lot drop out. However, I am prepared to go on for another,' he hesitated whilst he thought, 'three games. I don't like (please excuse the phrase in consideration of our nationality) welching on a commitment. Am I the only one prepared to make the sacrifice for a team that we all played in? Have you no honour?' Arthur sat back in his chair and smirked at Dai, who visibly bristled.

Jones interrupted quickly. 'Come on now, Arthur. None of us here has the level of business success that you have achieved.' He looked round to see if any of the others had taken offence at his remark.

'What about the club? Can it find some extra money?' asked Mabbutt, trying to diffuse the tension in the room. 'I mean, thanks to Wilson, our takings across the bar must be up.'

'They are up and the takings from the slot machines are up, too. However, I must keep money back to repay the bank loan due at the end of the season; I can't rob Peter to pay Paul.'

Jones looked at the faces round the table and felt he had to add, 'A chef de books I may be; a conjuror, unfortunately, I am not.'

Dai said, 'I say, despite Arthur's comments, that we bite the bullet and agree this is the last week we pay the bonus, even if we lose this game and win in the following week. No matter what, I will not pay a penny more; we simply cannot afford it.'

'Nor me,' said, Len looking as though he was about to burst into tears.

Mabbutt hesitated, and then said, 'Absolutely no more money after this weekend, win or lose.'

Arthur made a great show of looking disgusted at his colleagues' remarks. Inside, though, he was relieved. His earlier remarks criticising the others were just contrariness. He enjoyed keeping the pot boiling.

'I agree under protest.'

'So then, boys,' said Mabbutt looking straight at Dai, 'who is going to tell the players?'

'Why me?'

'Because you are so wonderfully good-looking,' Arthur cracked.

'That's as good a reason as any,' Len said, thanking the Almighty he had not been selected for the task.

'Before we tell them, can we just see if there are any alternatives?' Jones asked. 'You experienced businessmen might have some ideas on how the club could raise money for the bonuses. Because I think we all know what will happen if we just stop paying it.'

'Plant money trees,' replied Len to laughter tinged with despair.

Out of the ether, a thought hit Mabbutt. He wondered if the others would think his idea was a masterpiece.

'Graffiti,' he blurted out. 'We could say graffiti artists are targeting the rugby stand every week.'

'Why would they do that?' asked Dai.

'You think people who produce graffiti need a bloody reason for doing so?' spluttered Arthur, his face red as he recalled the graffiti sprayed on his garage walls. 'All these bastards do is to enjoy filth and chaos. They force us, the general public, to share it, whether or not we want to. Who is left with the bill to clean it off? Us!' Arthur hammered his chest several times and glared round the room in case there was any misinterpretation of how he felt on the matter.

Len remembered that the closest graffiti had got to Glanddu was in Rhyd-Ddu. The graffiti on that town's walls was always the same: "Free Nelson Mandela." After he was freed, to everyone's delight, no new graffiti appeared to replace it.

Len knew that in big cities like London graffiti appeared on walls, trains, buses and, no doubt, on people if they stood still long enough. The thing about London, though, was that the graffiti was varied; it wasn't only phrases like "Free Mandela" but decorations requiring artistic creativity. Len doubted there were local people with that sort of talent.

'Tell us more, Colin,' Dai said, glaring at Arthur.

Colin pointed at Arthur. 'You said that it costs money to remove graffiti. If graffiti appeared on the stand, then we would have to remove it. I suggest that we paint over the graffiti to clean it up with either whitewash or paint. Who, though, would know whether the graffiti ever existed?'

Arthur's eyes narrowed as he thought for a moment before he spoke. 'Wait a minute. So we are not talking about actually painting graffiti on the stand but merely imagining it, so that we can order large amounts of whitewash from Len that he does not deliver.'

'Yes,' said Mabbutt, pleased that Arthur grasped his idea, 'and I'll do the imaginary painting.' He looked at the others, all of whom were sitting staring at him in a mixture of wonder and concern for his mental well-being.

'There is no point looking at me like that, lads. John, you have fictitious accounts. In fact, we all do, right?'

'True,' his fellow sponsors replied raggedly.

Jones, however, shook his head. 'Colin, the club accounts aren't fictitious; they do have some foundation in truth.'

Arthur had no problem with the money the fiction would generate. The problem, as Arthur saw it, was that the fiction had to have some basis in reality.

'I think,' Arthur said, 'we have to paint graffiti at least once in the stand. Think about it. If we paint the graffiti and if the tax man comes to examine the club books, we can honestly say that we've had such a problem.'

'It's called covering your arse, Arthur,' muttered Mabbutt knowingly, to which Len and Dai murmured agreement as they began to warm to the idea.

'True, but I haven't finished, Colin,' said Arthur, clearing his throat. 'I think it's a good idea but having suffered from graffiti at work, we have to be very careful about going ahead.'

'One of us would put up the graffiti and that sounds fine. How long is it going to be before Colin, here, does more than fictitiously remove it?'

He held up his hand to stop Mabbutt replying.

'He's got to get rid of it. You know why? Because if we leave the graffiti on the wall for any length of time, the village youngsters will see it and, a pound to a penny: graffiti everywhere. We'll have started something we can't control. If we can't control it, then we will actually have to employ Colin to regularly paint the stand.'

'Oh, God, no,' groaned Len and got a playful punch from Mabbutt.

'Crucially,' interjected Jones, 'we will actually have to pay real, not fictitious, money for the paint and we won't generate any more bonus money.'

'We could use volunteers to do the painting, not Colin,' said Dai deep in thought. 'That would save us money and,' he looked at Colin, 'get a better job done.' Mabbutt threw a beer mat which Dai caught and tossed it back.

'So we save the money. But you are missing the point, Dai.' Arthur said. 'Who will get the blame for starting all this? The children? No, us for starting the graffiti problem. How will people know the original idea for graffiti began with us? Someone here will tell somebody that it was our bright idea.'

Mabbutt could see that if people in the village took up graffiti it might generate a good bit of business for him. He decided not to mention that now.

Sounding miffed, he said 'So now you think it's a good idea, Arthur?'

Arthur shrugged.

'I was wondering what the graffiti would actually say. Would it be something like, "Down with Glanddu" or "Arthur Davies loves Joy Lewis?"'

'She was a lovely girl,' said Arthur.

'Not you, you great oaf, Arthur. Young Arthur Davies, Ken Davies' twelve-year-old son, who has the hots for John and Linda Lewis' daughter, Joy; not one of your old bints.'

'I did know a Joy Lewis,' shouted a red-faced Arthur amidst the laughter of the others.

'We are always amazed how you remember their names,' Dai said laughing.

'She had breasts the size of the Severn Bridge, the newer one. She married an undertaker from Manchester.'

'Thank you, but we haven't got time for all your past conquests,' said Len as he stood to remove his coat.

It was obviously an inspirational night for Mabbutt because again suddenly a thought appeared: 'Got it,' he said.

The other three began to listen and they began to smile.

Colin proposed that he paint the graffiti on Monday morning. It had to be a Monday because that was the day when nobody went to the rugby ground; the Ground Committee started work on the rugby pitch on Tuesdays. Colin explained that he would paint the graffiti after the children went to school in the morning and whitewash over it before they came home in the afternoon.

Jones had been listening with increasing disbelief. At one stage he felt like suggesting that the club put up a sign outside the ground: "Come and have tea with the inmates — listen to sponsors at work." Entrance fee £2, car park £5.

'How much money could this generate? Not enough, I reckon, to pay for even one week of bonuses. Do you agree?'

John looked round the room.

'I think the idea of actually painting graffiti is dangerous, like we said. However, it is a bloody good idea for earning a small amount money for the club. Who's going to check? No one from the Inland Revenue, I'm sure. Colin, can you estimate how much paint we would need and how often we would need to paint over the graffiti? And I'll need invoices for my books.'

'Don't forget, it's got to be white paint and it's got to be exterior, not interior paint,' said Len.

Mabbutt spoke slowly. 'Good point. I have a couple of big painting jobs I'm currently working on. I could give you a duplicate of the invoices for the paint I bought for them. They should raise a hundred pounds over the rest of the season.'

'Can we get back to what we should be talking about - not bloody graffiti! Despite my commitment at the start of the season to pay the players their damn bonuses, business has been so bad at the shop that I will barely be able to pay my contribution this week. We can't pussyfoot round this matter any longer. Please let us decide how to tell the players.'

Dai snapped, 'Finally some sense from Len. Forget all this hypothetical graffiti. We bite the bullet now and tell the players that the bonus ends after this week.'

The rain gurgling down the clubhouse's drainpipes and the wind smashing raindrops against the window panes emphasized the silence in the room.

'Just before we vote on that, any other thoughts or bright ideas?'

Arthur Davies cleared his throat 'Yes. I have this mate whom I've known for a number of years. He's opening a new branch of one of his businesses in Llanelli and he shows a bit of interest in sponsoring Glanddu Rugby Club. We could use his money to pay the bonuses for a couple of weeks.'

'Why? Is he from round here?' Dai asked.

'No, he's not from Glanddu. He's from Brynhyfryd in Swansea, which has no local rugby club. He's a good friend who likes rugby.' Arthur could feel himself start to sweat as he saw the faces stare at him in expectation. 'One or two of you may have met Eurof Prosser at my Christmas parties.'

'If he was out of jail at the time,' said Len, whose look of incredulity was matched by the others.

'What sort of business is he in this time?' Dai asked after a moment's silence.

With his eyes firmly fixed on the table and after clearing his throat Arthur uttered, 'A massage parlour called Pampering Hands.'

Colin burst out laughing. The others looked disgusted.

Colin wanted to know if Eurof would give free introductory offers for the sponsors, but he decided to control himself.

Arthur expected this reaction. He pointed out that an open and above board sex industry was an accepted part of the twenty-first century. The massage parlour was just a business like all of theirs. After all, Eurof had to pay tax, council tax, cleaning bills — the last of which brought hysterical laughter. As Arthur pointed out, the club needed money. Could they be choosey about where it came from?

When Dai asked Arthur how he could contemplate accepting money from a man who had been in gaol for burglary, robbery with violence, and handling stolen goods Arthur answered, 'Eurof told me he's not going back to prison and is turning legitimate.' After looking round he said, 'Seriously, why are you discriminating against Eurof? Because, boys, may I remind you that everyone round this table keeps two sets of accounts. So what's legitimate?'

'None of us here exploit women,' remarked Len.

A gust of wind moaned round the building.

Arthur replied, 'Business is business.'

♣ 143 ♣

Again, there was silence. Dai eventually said, 'There are still chapel-going people on the committee. Will they accept money from Eurof Prosser?'

'Let them have the opportunity to reject him, not you, Mr High and Mighty.'

Jones drummed his fingers on the table, 'Come on boys, save the insults for another time.'

'What sort of logo does he want, Arthur?' Mabbutt interrupted. 'A bed with a half naked woman astride a bloke?'

'It's too late in the season to put his name on the players' shirts. How about a sponsor's billboard at the ground's entrance?'

'Don't be daft, Arthur,' everyone said in unison.

'What about sponsoring the match rugby ball and the players' meals?'

'I know what we'd announce over the tannoy system,' Mabbutt interjected: "Today's ball is sponsored by Pampering Hands, who also provide a variety of other ball services at their establishment in Llanelli."'

'Thank you, Colin, for stating the obvious,' Arthur said before adding warily, 'maybe we'll attract a new type of man to the game.'

'You mean the plastic Mac type of bloke?' quizzed Mabbutt. 'Perhaps we could get Eurof's girls to come on at half time and do a lap dance using the goal posts.'

'Lap dancing in our weather, Colin?' Arthur liked Colin but sometimes wondered how he had got a university degree.

'Well, if possible.'

Quiet descended.

'Despite my initial reaction, Arthur has a point. Unlike in our youth, today everything is sex. Everywhere you go sex is more blatant and brazen than before. Are we being too hasty in saying "no" to Eurof?'

'The thing is,' interjected Arthur, 'this is money for the club. If we don't take him up then another club will. I propose we leave the full committee to decide whether they want Eurof Prosser as a sponsor. I recommend that John talk to Mrs BT first and persuade her to put it on the agenda for the next committee meeting.'

'Thank you, Arthur. May I ask, why don't you speak to her? It is, after all, your idea.'

'Well. . .' Arthur paused, searching for reasons.

'I cannot wait to see Mrs Bowen Thomas' face when you, Arthur Davies, make this proposal,' Dai said grinning.

'I'd like to be a fly on the wall when Arthur tells her exactly what occurs in the Pampering Hands business,' added Len.

Arthur stuttered, 'You know how well I get on with that dragon. Wouldn't it be better for John or even Len to tell her? She would probably be more receptive to them.'

'Coward. I'll hold your hand when you see her,' said Len with a smirk.

'I'll come with you, Arthur, without holding your hand,' said Jones.

'Right. The meeting has generated a bit of new money through the graffiti and whitewash. Let's get back to the bonus payments, please.'

'Hold your horses and just wait a moment, John,' Dai looked directly at Arthur. 'If Eurof Prosser becomes a sponsor how soon would he put some money in?'

'Well,' Arthur responded, 'Pampering Hands is opening in March or April.'

Groans went up round the table. 'That's too late to help us now. Look, enough now. None of us can afford to pay any more. I'll tell Declan and Granville before they've had too much to drink on Saturday night: no more bonuses. I hope that all of you will be in attendance when I break the bad news.' Dai looked intently at his companions.

'I think we can close the meeting, John?'

'All agreed?'

'Yes,' came the reply in unison.

Dai stood and put on his coat whilst announcing, 'I saw June Griffiths this morning and she told me the bad news about Edgar. It seems we are looking at three months tops.'

'Christ, that is quick,' said Arthur. 'Bloody coal dust again.'

'I saw his niece's latest film the other week; she was good in it. Do you think she'll come down and see him?' Mabbutt asked, licking his lips.

'If she does, I doubt whether any of us will see her,' replied Dai.

'No,' said Arthur, 'she's bound to appear in a stretch limousine with dark windows.'

'Can we put things back into place before we go?' Jones said, as he bent to switch off the fire.

'Now,' said Dai to Arthur as he was leaving the room, 'how exactly are you going to present a massage parlour as a potential club sponsor to Mrs Bowen Thomas?'

'Good question.'

Gloria did not know quite how to react to what the two men sitting opposite her had just said. For herself she was thrilled that the bonus payments would end after this weekend, but how would the players react? Would the players strike? A strike would mean the club would fail to fulfil its fixtures. Then the club would lose league points and the club would surely collapse.

'Let's wait and see the players' reaction. I'll come down to the ground on Tuesday evening before training to hear what they say.'

'Arthur may have found a new sponsor though he might not come aboard for a few weeks yet,' said Jones, trying to keep a straight face.

Gloria's stomach sank but she managed a smile. 'Who is it and how much will they give us?'

'Well,' responded Arthur who could feel his face redden as he struggled for words, 'it is one of Eurof Prosser's businesses.'

'Our local pornographic king?' Gloria responded, her stomach rising back to its normal position.

'Well, yes. He suggested that his Llanelli establishment, Pampering Hands, might sponsor us as a personal favour to me.'

'How much is he offering?'

'Not sure,' stammered Arthur, surprised at her seeming phlegmatic reaction.

'When can he start contributing?'

'Not sure.'

'How can I go to the committee unless we know what he is proposing? Arthur, I suggest you find out.' She looked at the men with a genuine smile. 'All the old industries have gone from round here, obviously bar one. We'll put it on next week's agenda; should be interesting.'

'Item four on the agenda. Arthur Davies has a proposal for a new club sponsor, seconded by Colin Mabbutt,' announced the club secretary at the following Wednesday's full committee meeting.

There were too many men present whose wives who would brain them if they accepted anything of Eurof Prosser's into Glanddu Rugby Football Club. The proposal was defeated on a show of hands.

Chapter 27

The Glanddu players and the coach were euphoric with their twelfth straight League win. It was the first win for Glanddu at Llangoch's ground for ten years. The Llangoch bar was full of Glanddu players and supporters talking excitedly about the match — who played well, who played better the previous week, whom they were playing next week. Beer gurgled down throats. The only people in the bar who looked glum were the Llangoch supporters plus Dai Williams and Len Penry who were ensconced in the corner of the bar furthest away from their co-villagers. Neither Len nor Dai were happy because Colin, Arthur and John had sneaked out of Llangoch's ground at the end of the match without a word.

The club coach and captain analysed each game on the Saturday evening whilst events were still fresh in their minds and before the evening's alcohol took too great an effect. If Glanddu played at home, the two would sneak off to an empty dressing room for the review. When the club played away from home, the pair would drop into "The Ship Inn" on their way back to Glanddu. Len and Dai watched the pair leave Llangoch's clubhouse and five minutes later followed them to the pub.

The coach and the club captain were sitting at a table talking when Dai and Len appeared. Granville waved away the two sponsors when they approached the table but the sponsors ignored him.

'So what's so important to you miserable-looking buggers that you have interrupted our match review,' snarled Granville. 'Declan and I deliberately set aside this time for a private discussion.

Before you start, I used both substitutes today so I hope you're not going to whinge and whine about a few measly quid.'

'No, we are not going to whine.' replied Dai testily. 'We are here to tell you the bonus scheme ends this week. We are out of money.'

Len wondered whether Dai's abruptness was the right approach so he added quickly, 'We love it that the team has been so successful but things are really bad for our small businesses now. We need to pull in our horns.'

Dai and Len became aware of the laughter and conversations that were going on at adjoining tables. Crimson complexions and narrowed eyes now accompanied the Granville and Declan scowls that greeted Dai and Len earlier.

Granville saw Glanddu's success as proof of his ability as a coach. He also saw Glanddu's success as his stepping-stone to his destiny: the highest level of coaching. At the highest levels coaches were full-time, not part-time like he was now. Full-time coaches received more than the pittance Glanddu paid him and more than he earned as a panel beater at his local garage. Resigning in protest was a possibility, but until the players made a decision as to what they would do he thought he had better not act in haste. Granville also suspected that Wilson would be the key to the players' decision.

Keeping his anger under control, he spoke deliberately. 'I find this lack of commitment to the players reprehensible. However, in this instance I will be guided by the players' reaction when they are told the news.' He sat back upright in his chair, took a big swig from his beer glass and looked to Declan.

Declan had played for the club for twenty-six years as both a junior and senior player. For fifteen of those years he had played for the first team and in most of those years Glanddu had been in the lowest Division of the League. His dream to play in a league other than the bottom one – for the first time in ten years and before he retired – would not become a reality if the players' reaction was hostile to the loss of the bonus. Declan, as captain, knew he had a duty to argue against the loss of the bonus, but when Len and Dai explained that the sponsors had run out of money, he could find no counter. Declan feared that some of the players would threaten to go to other clubs when they heard the news.

'You think Wilson would leave us?' Dai said. 'He told us that he would play for the season. He gets exactly the same payment that you get - no more, despite what some people think. If he tells the team how much he loves playing down here in West Wales, do you two think he could stop any potential exodus?'

Declan and Granville exchanged glances and then nods of agreement. 'Yes, though there is one hothead who is bound to cause trouble.'

'Can you both promise not to say anything till Tuesday night training? Perhaps you can have a meeting beforehand. Dai and I will be there. We think that if everyone's present, we can iron out any issues there and then.'

CHAPTER 28

Sunday was the only day that Marilyn prepared Dai's breakfast because on every other day of the week, he left the house at 4 a.m. to collect the milk for delivery and wolfed down a piece of toast. As she lay sleepless in bed the previous evening, she tried to work out exactly what had been gnawing at her for the past few weeks. It finally came to her when Dai reported that the captain and coach heard that the bonuses were ending. Her conclusion, she realised, would have a major impact on their lives. Unsure how to broach the subject with Dai, she thrashed about the kitchen laying plates, scrambling eggs and extracting the cutlery with a crash, bang, and wallop before slamming the cabinet door. Dai, engrossed in the Sunday paper's account of all the previous day's rugby matches, eventually realised she was trying to get his attention.

'Something the matter?' Dai asked irritably, because he was halfway through a Scarlets v Ospreys rugby match report. He lowered the paper enough to peek over the top.

'Isn't it time to give up the milk rounds and sell the business?'

Dai folded the newspaper and placed it deliberately on the table. For several seconds he stared at the table then looked at his wife.

'You want me to sell out to Orion Dairies?'

'Yes,' replied Marilyn sitting down and grasping her husband's hand.

Dai and Marilyn knew three dairy businesses operating near Glanddu who had sold out to Orion in the past five years. Orion Dairies was part of a food conglomerate who was buying all individually owned dairy businesses in the region. The Orion area manager had visited Dai and Marilyn regularly, offering to buy their business. Dai had rejected all his offers. The Orion chap said that Dai would crack eventually because there was no one in his family who wanted to take over the business.

'What is the point in killing ourselves, Dai, for an ever diminishing return?'

'Could we afford to do it now?' Even rugby had now disappeared from Dai's mind this Sunday morning.

'I think, Dai, the question is, Can we afford not to? You're still losing customers and the fewer customers we have when we sell, the less Orion is going to pay us for the delivery business.'

'When should we sell?'

'I think that we should set things in motion now, which means completing the sale in the spring, giving us time to get used to the idea. Also, you know they want you to work for them for a while after the sale. Perhaps you could do so for a year, then become part-time, or act as a relief delivery man like Tony Adams and Josh Morris did after they sold out to Orion.'

Dai had not started breakfast thinking about selling the business, but now that Marilyn had broached the subject he felt relieved. He knew Marilyn's suggestion about selling was the right one and suddenly he felt happier than he had felt in weeks. 'I'll get in touch with the Orion chap tomorrow when I have finished the delivery. I think deep down I have been worrying about this for weeks. I suppose what stopped me was imagining what my father and grandfather would say.'

'They would say, "Sell it." You know they would sell because they were canny businessmen.'

Dai nodded slowly then stood, kissed Marilyn and gave her a big squeeze. When he released his grip she gave him a playful cuff accompanied with a beaming smile that further lit up his morning.

'I think it best not to tell anyone round here about our intentions until we have finalised everything. Also, I suspect that we'd lose customers immediately if they heard about it, which would then affect the price we'd get for the business. Hopefully, Orion won't leak the news.'

'No. It's not in Orion's interest to leak the news, and there's nothing we can do about it, anyway. I think you're right about completing the sale by the spring or early summer.'

He paused and looked at his wife. 'The rugby club would lose our sponsorship next year. It will be a blow to them.'

Marilyn blew a raspberry. 'It is time to think of ourselves rather than the blinking rugby club. I propose that we go away for a nice long holiday of at least a month as soon as the sale is completed.'

'That would be good.'

Dai's heart beat faster as he decided, possibly against his better judgement to say, 'Wales are playing rugby in New Zealand and Australia in June.'

'Why didn't I think of New Zealand in June? How marvellous, considering it is the depth of their winter.' Marilyn started to laugh at Dai's audacity.

'Well, Wales go on to play in Australia in Queensland whose winters are warmer than our summers.' Hope seared through Dai's voice.

Marilyn looked at Dai. 'Yes. This would be a holiday of a lifetime. I agree on one condition.'

'What? You want me to go shopping with you for shoes?' Dai's heart was in his mouth.

His wife's eyes narrowed. 'No. The condition is I get to choose where and when our following three holidays will be.'

'I agree. You really mean it about going to New Zealand?' Dai could not quite believe his ears.

'I do. I have always wanted to visit New Zealand and in particular,' she paused for effect, 'to see all its rugby stadiums.'

'Typical bloody woman,' replied Dai.

The old club blackboard placed at the entrance of the changing rooms informed the players of the meeting upstairs (if they had not read the text messages on their mobiles). By seven o'clock, the players sat expectantly facing the top table where Len, Dai, Gloria and John Jones sat stone-faced. Of Arthur and Mabbutt who had said they would be present at the meeting, there was no sign. The players' chat faded when Dai, elected yet again as the sponsors' spokesman and feeling distinctly queasy, stood up to speak.

'First, I would like to congratulate everyone on their efforts. The first team is unbeaten so far this season and the second have only lost one game. I will, however, come straight to the point.' He took a deep breath and cleared his throat. 'Being unbeaten does have its bad points — for us, the businessmen who pay the bonus, not all of whom could be here tonight.' The bastards, he wanted to say. 'I don't want to beat about the bush. Boys, we cannot afford to pay the bonus any longer.'

Dai wanted to add, 'Are there any questions?' but there was no need; bedlam followed, comprising bellowed questions mixed with curses at the committee. Jones, Dai and Len all trotted out their different reasons for not being able to continue, most of which were greeted with shouts of hostility. Only when Gloria stood was a semblance of silence achieved.

'Gentlemen,' she began, 'we appreciate—'

She stopped when the door to the room opened and she saw the man-mountain appear.

'Hey Clive, they have stopped paying the bonus,' a voice called out.

'Oh dear,' said Wilson pausing for a moment. 'I don't know about you lot, but I have come down to train for Saturday's match. I have never in my long and illustrious career gone through a season unbeaten in a league,' a smile spread slowly across his face, 'except, of course, with the English team.'

Catcalls and good natured abuse followed the latter statement but ceased when the big man held up his hand. 'I don't want to miss the opportunity now, do you? I don't care if we aren't paid. I want to go through a club season unbeaten once in my life. This, chaps, is my very last opportunity to do that.'

He turned towards the door when Huw Pugh shouted. 'That is all right for you, Clive, but we need the money.'

Wilson did not check his stride but said over his shoulder, 'You have already earned more this year from the club than you did last year. This is a small poor village, not a filthy rich one. Don't be greedy, Huw: think of the glory of promotion to the Fourth Division.'

As Wilson disappeared Declan, who had jumped to his feet during Wilson's last words, followed him almost at a run. Declan stopped at the door and waved at the others to follow him down to the changing room. Lemming-like in silence, the rest of the players followed, bar one. If there had been a survey amongst the Glanddu players or even amongst the whole village to identify the one person who would object to the loss of the bonus, the unanimous response would be: Huw Pugh.

CHAPTER 29

Huw's late father, Goronwy Pugh, had been a Communist official in the local branch of the National Union of Mine Workers and had spent his life battling for better working conditions. Goronwy had been naturally cantankerous and this, exacerbated by his work, made him a hero to the miners and a bête-noir to the bosses. Because of his argumentative nature he had never served on the Glanddu Rugby Committee; they were "management." He always opposed any proposal originating from a Glanddu committee member and supported anything proposed by a non-committeeman, even if he actually agreed with the committeeman's proposal or opposed the other side.

Brainwashed by his father but unable to follow him down the pit because it closed, Huw emulated Goronwy's anti-establishment activities. However, unable to find a regular job and thus deprived of an opportunity to become a shop steward, Huw had only one place - Glanddu Rugby Club – for his ardour. The last time Huw had opposed a club decision was about changing the colour of the team's playing shorts from white to black.

The bonus withdrawal gave Huw Pugh the first opportunity where the principle involved actually affected him and the other players. In vain he tried to stop his teammates streaming from the meeting room. Uncertain what to do, all he did was utter the words, 'This is a disgrace. We have been betrayed.' Huw wanted to add, "By the Fascist bourgeoisie," but he knew that nobody said that anymore. Huw was sure the term 'bourgeoisie' still applied to Gloria Bowen Thomas because, like his father, he felt double surnames were pretentious. Huw always referred to Gloria as Mrs

Thomas except, of course, when he was actually talking to the chairwoman; he knew if he did not add Bowen to her name, his life was in danger.

'I think training is just about to start,' replied Gloria. 'And remember there is a big game again on Saturday, Huw.'

Huw turned round; not one player was left in the room.

'Yes,' he stammered and picked his way through the seating, trying to think what his father might have said in these circumstances.

'That went better than I imagined,' said Len, once Huw had disappeared.

'It helped having a word with Wilson last night,' grinned Dai, 'and agreeing how and when he would enter the room.'

'Oh, did you?' said Gloria, surprised at such planning from a mere milkman. 'Do you think Huw will organise something?'

'He is not his father,' replied Dai.

'Indeed, a very poor quality carbon copy of his dad,' added Len. 'I doubt if he can organise anything.'

'Oh good,' Gloria said, unable to keep the sadness out of her voice — not that any of the men noticed.

'There's no point going on about it, Huw. They cannot afford to pay us and there is nothing we can do.'

Huw sniggered. 'Nothing? Have you not noticed anything in the few weeks since he arrived?'

He pointed at Wilson, who was talking to a group of men gazing up at him and firing questions as fast as a Maxim gun fired bullets.

'Like what?' Declan asked.

'More people come down here for a drink on training nights, hoping that they can see our Clive and then bore the pants off the poor sod. Look at the man - no doubt desperate to get home and see the wife.'

'Particularly with Arthur Davies on the prowl,' interjected his mate Barry Howell, one of the younger players in the team.

'Can we concentrate on the issue?' Huw said. 'Don't all these drinkers bring in loads of cash?' He waved his arms furiously at the room, smacking Barry in the mouth as he did so.

'What are you doing, Huw?'

'Sorry, Barry.'

He waved his arms again but less vigorously, scrupulously avoiding his mate.

'Bigger crowds have come to watch us play. There must have been four hundred people here on Saturday, more than double what we normally get. More people watching means more entrance money, but does that money come our way? It enables the club to sell more beer and make more profit but where does that money go? Does it go to us players?'

Huw looked expectantly at the group of players slumped round the table laden with their non-alcoholic drinks.

He answered his own question.

'No. I think we should strike.'

Huw's eyes swept the table as if he expected the whole group to jump to their feet shouting, "Eureka," and then follow him out of the clubhouse vowing not to play until the payment was restored. Nobody moved, except to take sips of their drinks.

Huw's father never had this problem; when he shouted, "strike," everyone obeyed.

Declan finished his drink, stood up, and buttoned his coat. Then his eyes met Huw's.

'Huw, the club didn't pay us the win bonus for the last few weeks because they ran out of money. The sponsors then kicked in the bonus money,' indicating with his right elbow Arthur Davies and Colin Mabbutt who had both arrived after Dai had made his announcement to the players. Now the pair stood drinking at the bar trying to join the group surrounding Wilson.

'Now even the sponsors have run out of money because we are doing so well.'

'You cannot get blood out of a stone,' put in Granville as he swilled the remains of his drink before swallowing the contents in a noisy gulp. He put the glass down with a plonk. Both he and Declan no longer had any misgivings over the loss of the bonus since Wilson's dramatic appearance before training.

Huw, like his father in this modern world, was yesterday's man.

'The fact that the club is making money doesn't mean that our sponsors are. Explain to me, Huw, how Arthur Davies sells more cars because we win a game or Dai Williams sells more milk or Len Penry sells more stamps because Clive Wilson is playing for Glanddu?'

Barry said, 'But if they cannot afford to pay us, Huw expects someone else to come up with the money.'

Declan looked down at Barry. 'Oh, yes, Barry, who? There is no one else with money. Did you know that in England some players actually pay for the privilege of playing rugby.'

'They've got jobs in England and so they don't need the money.'

Barry's reply was accompanied by an affirmative grunt from Huw.

Huw said, 'Look at all the people who come down to talk to Wilson.'

Declan replied, turning to look at the people surrounding the giant, 'They're all retired miners. All they buy is one half-pint of beer that they eke out the entire evening. I think bar profits have gone up by about three pounds a night. That hardly makes this place a goldmine.'

'Now the pub has closed they could open this place every night,' said Huw, thinking that the tide was turning in his favour.

Declan guffawed. 'Committee thought about it but decided not to. You know why?'

Huw actually had no idea, but suggested, 'They have no vision?'

'Just the opposite. If people didn't spend money in the village pub, why would they spend money here?'

He pointed towards the shabby surroundings and the plastic furniture. 'Would you bring your girlfriend to this palace for a night out?'

'If they redecorated, had some different furniture, started doing fish and chips - that sort of thing, I might.'

'Come on, Huw. Think how much it would cost to renovate this place to a decent standard. When I played at Pontartaff ten years ago, the season they got promoted to the second division, they spent a load of money they didn't have modernising their clubhouse and revamping their changing rooms. And what happened? The next season they were demoted back to the third division, and the season after that they were relegated to the fourth division. Now they play on the local school's pitch and their old ground and clubhouse have been converted to a supermarket.'

Declan added, 'Look. Despite the bigger gates and more drinkers on training nights, the club has huge debts which apparently it has to clear this year. People like Dai and Len and are not multi-millionaires. You also know bonus payments are illegal according to the League. I suspect,' he dropped his voice, 'people like Dai and Len, as well as the club, have had to pay the bonus out of money they have hidden from the Inland Revenue. Would you want these blokes to go to gaol? Do we really want the Inland Revenue getting involved? What if they were to come and do an inspection here? Do you think that they would stop at only the club's officials? They'll find out that we players got payments without tax. You want them coming round to your houses to see what you do, or what you claim you are doing or, to be more accurate, what you claim that you are not doing — namely, working? I doubt you would welcome them very much. Finally, imagine going through the season unbeaten, as Clive says. Although Granville and I felt aggrieved on Saturday night about all this, we're fine about it now.'

Declan stalked off and as he passed Arthur and Colin at the bar he said out of the corner of his mouth, 'Huw is trying to stir things up.'

'Par for the course,' acknowledged Arthur and then to Declan's departing back he barked, 'Is he getting anywhere?'

Declan shook his head. 'So where are our other sponsors? I thought that they would stay to see if our Huw might have any impact.'

Mabbutt laughed, 'Dai and Len were positive that Huw would have about as much success as a lead balloon would float in the sea. Dai has gone to see Edgar Griffiths. Len went home.'

In his playing days, which coincided with those of Dai Williams and Len Penry, Edgar Griffiths had been a burly fifteen stone six footer. Now the ravages of cancer had reduced him to a bag of bones and his height was little more than five feet nine inches.

Whenever one of his old playing cronies dropped round to see Edgar, his wife Sheila would leave them alone to chat in the front room where Edgar spent virtually the whole day in an armchair. Sheila knew that very shortly his bed would be moved downstairs into that room.

When Dai Williams arrived, one look at the gaunt face of the woman he had known for over thirty years told him things were grimmer than on his last visit.

Dai accepted a slice of home-baked jam tart with alacrity. As he ate the tart the two chatted about their children, the weather and even the rugby club before Sheila went to see if her increasingly lethargic husband was awake. Dai heard Sheila enter the house's front room and then speak her husband's names three times before Edgar responded. When she told him Dai Williams was here, Edgar was extremely pleased.

Edgar was fully dressed in a suit. Dai wondered why he wore a suit when all he did each day was slump in front of the TV. Perhaps Edgar was trying to get full value out of the suit before he died; Dai thought he would do exactly the same thing.

As soon as Dai entered the room and shook Edgar's limp hand, he loaded a DVD into the player. The club recorded each match it played onto DVDs and the club made sure each week that Edgar received a copy. In silence the two men watched the match re-played in front of them. From time to time Edgar purred with pleasure at Glanddu's play, interspersed with hostile comments about Glanddu's opponents or the referee. When they were about seventy minutes into the tape Dai heard his friend begin to snore so he pressed the pause button on the DVD machine and silently left the room to look for Sheila before he left.

Dai found Sheila at the kitchen table talking to a young woman with hair the colour of the setting sun. Sheila saw him and, with a smile as wide as a barn door, she beckoned him to sit beside her. Without asking she poured him a glass of champagne from the open bottle sitting between her and the visitor opposite.

CHAPTER 30

'You remember my famous niece?'
'Of course,' stammered Dai, staring spellbound at the exotic creature before him. He didn't know whether to kiss her on the cheek or shake her hand so he stood uncomfortably, shifting from foot to foot. With a giggle Rhiannon stood and gave him a peck on the cheek.

'Bet that's the first time you've been kissed by a Hollywood actress,' said Sheila.

Dai opened his mouth to say it was, but he could only emit a gurgling sound, making both women laugh.

Rhiannon's father had been killed in the pit not long after she was born, leaving his brother, Edgar, to act as her father would have done: taking her to watch Glanddu play rugby. Rhiannon was no older than three or four years when she first watched the game and had continued to do so as she grew up, probably because there was nothing else to do in Glanddu on a Saturday afternoon. Rhiannon's mother remarried and moved the family to London when the girl was about twelve. Since then, Dai had only seen Rhiannon heading out of the village at the speed of light in a variety of sporty cars.

Dai and Marilyn watched all of Rhiannon's TV programmes and films. The latter they normally saw on rented DVDs, but once or twice they actually went to a Swansea cinema.

Dai concentrated hard on remembering every bit of conversation; he knew he'd get a grilling from his missus if he left out any detail Rhiannon mentioned about this actor or that actress, her home in California and her other house in London.

Dai concentrated so hard that his brain hurt.

He almost fell of his chair when Rhiannon switched her gaze to him and said, 'I'm thinking about acquiring a property here, Mr Williams. Of course, because of my status I do need something that is very private. Any ideas?'

'Why do you want to come back here?' Sheila's voice betrayed the shock she felt.

'Well, I was born and raised here. I need somewhere quiet.' Rhiannon grinned at Dai. 'And my rugby team is here.'

'I didn't think you were that interested in rugby,' Dai exclaimed.

'She always asks her uncle how Glanddu are doing,' Sheila interjected, unable to understand how her niece could be so keen about a stupid game.

'Aunt Sheila, I watch all the games that Wales play and all the big tournaments like the Rugby World Cup. I even thought of dropping into the clubhouse this evening on my way here and see if I could recognise anyone.'

'The clubhouse will be exactly as you last saw it. As for the team,' grinned Dai, 'there are a few people you might remember from your schooldays.'

Rhiannon asked, 'Huw Pugh is playing these days?'

Dai fluttered his eyes in exasperation, to which Rhiannon gave a wry smile.

'God, he was a nuisance when we were in school. If you said black he would swear it was white.'

'No, Huw Pugh hasn't changed. He's an exact replica of his father.'

'At least Goronwy Pugh had a full-time job, unlike Huw,' Sheila exclaimed.

'I can't blame him for that, Sheila, with the lack of jobs down here.'

Dai switched his attention back to Rhiannon. He realised that he might get Rhiannon to put her hand in her pocket.

'Though we're unbeaten, we're still having major financial problems. These days money seems to be the be-all and end-all of everything. Anyway, we told the players tonight that after this week we can no longer pay them a winning bonus.'

'Huw Pugh, no doubt, immediately jumped to his feet. . .'

'Shouting strike,' Rhiannon finished her aunt's sentence. 'I remember his father coming to the house when daddy was killed. I think every third word was strike. He was nice, though.'

Sheila had no interest in discussing rugby or money tonight and changed the subject back to a local property. After two seconds she and Dai came to the conclusion: the only large property was Gloria Bowen Thomas's house, but it wasn't currently for sale.

Dai finished his champagne but when Rhiannon offered him more, he covered his glass with his hand. He sensed that Sheila wanted her niece to herself.

Dai took his jacket off the back of the chair and stood.

'I must go because I promised the boys down at the club that I'd give them the latest news on Edgar.'

Just as Dai awkwardly started to broach the subject of money, Rhiannon said, 'Auntie Sheila, would you mind if I went down with Mr Williams to the club? I promise I'll return shortly, so keep the champoo cold.'

Rhiannon smiled when she saw her aunt looking perplexed. 'It's a slang expression for champagne. I've just had an idea that I'd like to discuss with Mr Williams.'

Without waiting for an answer, Rhiannon drained her glass and headed out of the kitchen. Like a lapdog Dai followed, leaving Sheila still sitting at the table, nonplussed.

Rhiannon put on a long, dark green suede coat whose value was probably quadruple what Dai collected on a Friday afternoon when his clients paid their bills. Rhiannon then covered her glorious hair with a scarf that matched her coat. She looked in the hall mirror and tucked a wisp of hair under the scarf. Then she took a pair of dark glasses out of her pocket and opening the front door, she peered suspiciously at the street. Dai moved behind and began to sweep the street with his gaze.

They saw only the lights shining from the houses on their street. There was no movement at all.

Parked in front of the Griffiths' house and the house next door was the first real-life stretch limousine that Dai had ever seen in the village. Leaning with his back to the car was a man in a peaked cap who was chatting to a gentleman with an obviously bored dog slumped at his feet.

'That's Nigel Newlove,' whispered Dai as he led the way forward. 'I bet he hasn't got his teeth in; beware of spit.'

'Evening Nigel, evening Jack,' he said to the dog as he patted its head.

'This yours?' asked Nigel, who somehow managed not to notice the chauffer ushering Rhiannon into the back seat.

'Only for the evening, Nigel. Just a little treat for the girlfriend.' He bent down to whisper in Newlove's ear, 'Don't tell Marilyn.'

'Mum's the word,' replied Newlove. 'I never liked this one or her films.'

He inclined his head towards the limousine and then began to shuffle up the street at a pace normally associated with snails.

Chapter 31

The entrance of Dai and Rhiannon into the clubhouse was electrifying, even outdoing Wilson's arrival. When Dai initially entered the bar the noise decibels were deafening, but when Rhiannon glided through the door the room went silent. As Dai looked round the room he could scarcely stop smiling at so many gaping mouths. Even the old men clustered round Wilson had switched their attention to Rhiannon as quickly as rats desert a sinking ship.

Rhiannon smiled as she looked round the room that was every bit as unprepossessing and ugly as she remembered. Faces from the past loomed up before her gaze. The last time she had seen many of the men they had hair, or had hair of a different colour, but their clothes hadn't changed at all.

She gave everyone a gracious smile which faded as Huw Pugh rushed to her side and looked as if he was about to try and force his tongue down her throat. What stopped Huw was the sight of the chauffeur who had followed Dai and Rhiannon into the room. By his size, hairstyle and shape Huw deduced that the man was ex-special forces.

'Just popped in to see if the photographs of my father are still hanging on the wall,' she quipped. Then she said to the room, 'Hello, darlings.'

Rhiannon accepted an offer of a drink before going over to the wall covered in photographs of the first teams dating from the late nineteenth century to the present day. Huw watched her study the photographs hung in horizontal and vertical lines from the ceiling to the strip of wood four feet from the floor.

A scrum of men followed her saying, 'How's your uncle? I played with your father. How's your mam? Lovely lady, I haven't seen you for years. You haven't altered. Does it rain much in Hollywood? I see all your films. You'll win an Oscar. Any marriage plans? Wait till I tell my wife. My daughters – Bethan – Victoria – Susan - Bronwen. . .you remember them? They were in your school class. They'll never believe that you were down the rugby club.'

Some of the names hurled at Rhiannon she did remember. She had nothing in common with them now, only memories of skipping, playing hide and seek, or blackberrying. She stood staring at the ten photographs containing her father. He was always standing in the back row except in his last three years when he progressed to a seat, perhaps to compensate for his clearly diminishing thatch and increasing girth.

She went over to the most recent photographs, scanning to see how many faces she recognised, and was surprised at how many she did remember. Then she returned to look again at her father. There were copies of some of these photographs somewhere at her mother's house but not with all the players' names nor with the number of matches won, lost and drawn in that season.

'Can I get copies of the ones with my father?' Rhiannon asked, turning round and seeing a face she remembered as a member of the club committee.

'Mr Probert?'

It was a toss-up as to who was more surprised, Mr Probert or Rhiannon.

Brian Probert, an ex-miner in his middle seventies, had retired at the end of the previous season from thirty-five years of continuous service on the Glanddu Rugby Club committee. Because of this year's winning streak he regretted not going on for one more year. Without fail every Saturday he told his wife, 'Rome wasn't built in a day you know, Mabel. The club is having success now, thanks to the efforts of blokes like me laying the groundwork over many years.'

'Yes, dear,' Mabel would reply and raise her eyebrows in supplication. Brian's broken gramophone comments sometimes made Mabel envy her sister, Jean, whose husband had died ten years before.

'It will have to be a committee decision, won't it boys,' announced Probert to the surrounding mob who murmured their agreement, eyes glued to various parts of Rhiannon's body.

'Of course, you'll bring it before the committee won't you, Mr Probert?'

'As the village's most famous person. . .'

Probert then nearly added "after Tommy Harries" but thought better of it.

'I am sure the committee will approve.'

Probert knew that there would be a problem at meeting Rhiannon's request. Lewis, the photographer who had taken the photographs in question, had been dead ten years, his business sold and his old premises were now a charity shop. Since Lewis' death the club had used three or four photographers, and Probert doubted that any of them would have the old negatives.

Removing the ten photographs from the wall in order to copy them would cause ructions at the club. First, the wall would show the marks where they had been hanging and everyone would see that the whole wall needed cleaning. He could hear Mabel's voice saying, 'Clean the wall? Oh, yes, who at the club wants to do that? None of the youngsters will volunteer, not like in your day.' As for painting, that was last done only six years ago so it was not due to be repainted for another four years at least.

Then Probert wondered if removing the ten photographs destroyed the symmetry of the wall. Would the remaining hundred photographs be temporarily re-hung? This was turning into a tricky problem. Probert would recommend that the committee *not* approve of the photographs' removal until the rugby season finished.

'You'll leave a telephone number?' Probert requested, but it was hardly surprising when she didn't answer, deep in conversation with the five men jostling round her.

Probert wandered over to a quiet corner and began to mutter to himself while sipping the remains of his half-pint ration of beer. Just as he was ready to move back to join the scrum round the girl, she burst through them with a laugh and with a wave headed for the door. As she passed Probert, he said, 'I'll get in touch about the photos.'

Rhiannon didn't stop. As she hastened through the door held open by the chauffeur, she called over her shoulder, 'Just leave them with my aunt, Mr Probert.'

'Might not be able to do anything immediately,' said Probert to the swinging door as it closed behind her.

Huw, who had had to answer the call of nature, came out of the gentleman's toilet and was genuinely disappointed to find that his favourite film star had not said goodbye to him.

'Did she say anything about me, Lloyd? She hasn't seen me since school when she had a bit of a crush on me because I was in the school cricket and rugby teams'

Lloyd Price looked at his friend's serious face and burst out laughing.

'I was in her class and she never fancied you! And with the passing of the years she hasn't appeared to change her mind. Anyway, you were in those teams about six years after she left, remember?'

His tone softened as his friend's face fell.

'If it's any consolation, though, she didn't remember me, either, and I sat only seven desks away from her. What she did say was that she might come down to see us play this Saturday. So, even if any of the players agree with you, we can't go on strike this week in case she turns up.'

Huw pondered how his father might react. He murmured, 'No. We'll play, not because her majesty might come down to see us, but because I need time to win the players round.'

'That's about thirty or forty players. I wish you luck but I'm not interested in any strike. I'll see you Saturday?'

'Definitely,' Huw replied to his teammate's departing back. 'I'll have a speech prepared.'

Over at the bar Dai Williams and his cronies had been amusedly observing the antics surrounding Rhiannon's flying visit. As they watched, Dai told them about Edgar Griffith's condition and how he had come down to the club with the Hollywood star in a stretch limo that was as big as his parents' old house. Dai didn't mention what he and Rhiannon had discussed in the car because he wanted to talk to John Jones about it first.

When Dai got home, he saw the light in the kitchen where he expected to find Marilyn. The room was empty but their laptop's screen saver with the current Welsh Rugby Captain's photograph flickered. The laptop sat in front of an empty chair and beside a pile of papers. Dai drank a glass of water and turned off the laptop and the kitchen light before he went upstairs.

As soon as he entered the bedroom, he knew something was wrong. Marilyn's bedside light was off. His light was on, but she lay with her back to him.

As he got into bed she said, 'Where have you been? After you visited Edgar Griffiths we were going to do the VAT return together. You told me you were coming straight home. I can smell the drink on you.' She half turned in the bed and said over her shoulder. 'I'm waiting, David Williams.'

Marilyn moved round in the bed so that she could glare at him so he went on quickly. 'Rhiannon, their niece, was there to see Edgar. Come all the way from London specially. Anyway, she brought some champagne. Did you know that champagne is the only thing she drinks? Anyway, I had to stay for a chat with her, ask how her mam was, that sort of thing. Then she wanted to go down to the club.'

'Oh, and she didn't know where it was. What did she think? That it had moved?'

'No, but she had a stretch limousine with her and as I had never been in one. . .'

'And?'

'OK, she had a proposal about how she could help the club get some money.'

Marilyn exhaled air in a near scream. 'That bloody club. Our business can go hang as long as that club keeps bloody going.'

'The VAT return does not have to be submitted to Customs till next week – we'll do it tomorrow.'

'I am going to my sister's tomorrow night. Don't you men ever listen? I have entered all the data so all you have to do tomorrow is check it, print out, sign it, write a cheque, put it all in an envelope and post it. That is, if you are not doing something for the club like riding in a stretch limo. Good night.'

After a pause, she said, 'Did she say anything about Hollywood?'

Dai smiled into the darkness. 'That's the real reason I missed doing the VAT return. She talked to Sheila and me for ages.'

Suddenly the room was bathed in light. Marilyn plumped up her pillows and sat upright against them. She poked her husband in the back. Marilyn looked down at him and raised her eyebrows. Dai cleared his throat, sighed, then slid up beside his wife and put his memory into gear.

Chapter 32

Rhiannon thought about her future on the drive back to London. Her time with her uncle had been all too brief and his appearance and her aunt's haggard look had shocked her. But the thing that surprised Rhiannon the most was her own upbeat reaction at being back in the village after five years.

Rhiannon was a Hollywood star at the moment, but she was shrewd enough to know that she needed another two or three film hits to cement herself permanently into the big time. There was always the chance of one of her films failing, though the three films she had lined up all looked like winners. In the meantime she wanted to cash in on her current fame. That was why she had accepted the chance to be the face, body and voice in a series of TV commercials for a new fragrance called, "Ohdour."

Rhiannon thought Ohdour was revolting, but the exorbitant fees she received made dousing herself in it an unalloyed pleasure.

Rhiannon had already made three Ohdour commercials in the States. The first commercial, which launched the product in the USA, filmed her at a racetrack approaching the horse viewing area right before the race. Just as the jockeys walked their mounts past the crowd, Rhiannon strolled by. The next scene showed the finish line as the horses thundered past, riderless; Rhiannon was sitting in the driving seat of a bus jammed full of jockeys, grooms and trainers. At the commercial's end a huge crowd of men surged after the bus as it drove away.

The second advertisement showed her at a rodeo and the third, at an American football game. In both commercials Rhiannon enticed men to follow her even more gormlessly than the children followed the Pied Piper of Hamlin - and she did it with the fabulous Ohdour perfume, rather than a flute.

The award-winning series of commercials generated huge product sales and attention.

Ohdour was going to be launched in Europe this coming summer. Naturally, because the sporting theme seemed successful in the States, the manufacturers wanted to use the same theme for Europe, though with sports reflecting European interests. The horse racing scenario would be adapted for Europe and cycling and soccer were the likely choices to replace the rodeo and the American football.

Whilst she was talking to Dai Williams and her aunt, Rhiannon had a brainwave. Perhaps she was silly to mention the idea to Dai Williams when they were chatting in the car because its impact on him had been electric. She had to contain his excitement and talk to the right people to see if it could work.

Of course, the person she needed to talk to was Jackson Greenbaum, Ohdour's European head man. If Jackson did not like it, then there was always Banker Z Heinemann III who would ensure that Jackson changed his mind. Banker Z Heinemann III was the Chief Executive Officer of the Omnia Corporation of America, which manufactured and marketed Ohdour.

Banker, at a meeting of Omnia's directors, had insisted that Rhiannon was going to be the spokesperson for Ohdour, whatever the cost.

The only trouble with getting Banker involved was that there would be a price to pay. The thought of the three-hundred-pound Banker in his boxer shorts made her stomach turn and her affection for Glanddu Rugby Club pall.

About halfway back to London she switched her thoughts to why she wanted to have a house in an old mining village when she already had homes in Hollywood and London. The only option in Glanddu seemed to be the Bowen Thomas place, and she probably would have to pull it down in order to build something more befitting her station. The only time Rhiannon ever visited the Bowen Thomas house was to attend a Christmas party when she was a young child. As a child Rhiannon had thought the house enormous but after Hollywood, the place was tiny. As she stared out at the lights of a passing town she pondered what she could do to expand the house. She only needed about five bedrooms and five bathrooms, a cinema, servants' quarters - nothing too grand. All this would need planning permission, surely not too difficult for a famous film star.

Rhiannon was having difficulty reading the latest script her agent had sent her. On her arrival back from Wales last night she started to read it but quickly got bored. It was the usual fare of lots of explosions, lots of karate, no plot - written either by a computer or plagiarised from a hundred-and-one previous films. But with Rhiannon starring, it would make buckets and buckets of money. This morning, another attempt at reading the script failed as thinking about living in Glanddu occupied her mind.

Living in Glanddu had some seriously negative points. Where would she get her hair done? The nearest celebrity hairdresser was in Cardiff; she might even need to drive to Bristol, miles away. And where would one shop for food when one was accustomed to Harrods or Fortnum and Masons? But then she remembered her mother telling her that all supermarkets now delivered, so at least her fans wouldn't be gawking at what she put into her trolley. If she wanted retail therapy she would have to travel all the way to London, a royal pain in the derriere.

What were the advantages of living in Glanddu? Although Rhiannon loved the trappings of stardom, sometimes she needed a break from it. Having a house in Glanddu would give her that relief; her home village would never attract hordes of the nouveau riche and turn the place into the new Cannes.

Then there was the weather in Wales. Why did everyone go on and on about the wonders of the Californian climate? Sure, Rhiannon enjoyed the blue skies for a while but even blue skies become boring. She yearned not just for clouds but also for rain. She also loved walking in the hills and she didn't get a thrill from cactus and bare soil. She dreamed of sheep and green, green grass — well, at least, some of the time.

CHAPTER 33

In the two weeks following Rhiannon's visit the team continued its winning streak. It was only now that the loss of their bonus was beginning to rankle some of the players. Part of the reason was that Huw Pugh had been busy in his shop steward role, trying to ferment trouble with the rallying cry, 'Boys, this will be a demonstration of player power against committee oppression.'

Despite the growing unease in the team about the loss of their bonus, only six players sympathized with Huw's proposal, sympathy that seemed unlikely to lead to action.

The only person that Huw knew who had been in a similar situation was Wilson. Wilson had been in the England team that, in the week before they were due to play an international match, threatened to strike over pay. A strike would have had cataclysmic results for the game; no doubt the TV Company due to broadcast the game would issue a breach of contract lawsuit against the Rugby Football Union. It would have cost the Rugby Football Union a fortune to fight the lawsuit, and if they lost they would have to pay compensation to the TV Company and lose the lucrative sponsorship deals that were now part of the modern game. To cap it all, the team would lose the goodwill from the thousands of paying supporters travelling from all over England to attend the match in London. Days before the match, concessions to the England players were made and the threat of a strike disappeared.

The Thursday evening after training Huw asked Wilson how the England team organized their strike and what advice would he give Huw to arrange a strike by the Glanddu players.

Wilson replied, 'Don't do it. Frankly, the England situation was in a different time, place, and scale to what you have here. Our threatened strike occurred just as the game of rugby union was about to move out of the old amateur days. Players felt they were treated badly because the committee men, who ran the game, were still rooted to the ideals of the old amateur era.'

Wilson paused whilst he remembered.

'In the old days, the average committee man had a high and mighty attitude: "I wear a blazer and tie so I am important. Ask the committee; only the committee can make a decision. Free drinks for the committee; make mine a gin and tonic. We administrators travel first class; players go second class because youngsters put up with the discomfort better than we can. Who the hell do the players think they are to complain about anything? Hells teeth, players are merely players and if they don't like it we'll drop them from the England team."'

Wilson's tone softened, 'TV companies were fighting with money to put International rugby matches on their prime TV channel. Twickenham, our home ground, was full to capacity every time we played, the tickets and corporate boxes cost God knows what, and international sponsors were falling over themselves to pay enormous sums of money to put their logo on our England shirts.'

Wilson inhaled noisily.

'All we wanted was a fair share of the cake. Compare that with what you have here, Huw. Nobody round here has any money whatsoever.'

He paused and looked down at Huw.

'I won't support a strike in this economic climate.'

Huw thanked Wilson and said he understood Wilson's stand on a possible strike but he still wanted the players to take some action.

Wilson said, 'You're living in cloud cuckoo land if you think a strike would do anything other than wreck the team's spirit and end their hopes of promotion and playing a better standard of rugby. Is that what you want?'

'Not really,' replied Huw, 'but there's one thing I forgot to mention.'

When he saw Wilson look quizzically at him, he said with a smile, 'You. Since you started playing here, crowds for home games have increased and people come here to drink on a training evening, not because of the beer but to see you and to speak to you. The club is making more money.'

'Ah,' said Wilson, 'how much more are they making?'

'Enough money to put tarmac on Grindley's old garage site, a site not owned by the club, but by Mrs BT.'

'The club probably had to repair the tarmac for insurance purposes before they could use it. I heard she's just leasing it for the club. Look, Huw, there is no more money, just like there are no more mines. Forget it and concentrate on winning next Saturday's game. If you can't do that then I, as an assistant coach, suggest you leave the club and go and play elsewhere. And by the way, it is the club captain's job to discuss payments, not a self-appointed shop steward.'

Huw rankled at Wilson's last remark. He had talked to Declan O'Grady earlier about the situation. O'Grady's attitude had been blunt: there was no way he would ask for more money from the club. And by complaining and whining to the other players, Huw was undermining the team's morale.

When Huw pointed out that the younger members of the team were hardest hit because several of them had no regular jobs, O'Grady replied that there was plenty of work out there if the players would just get off their backsides and make an effort.

The day after his discussions with Wilson and O'Grady, Huw went to see his father. Huw could not get to talk to his father until the afternoon because he had a morning's work at Arthur Davies' garage, cash in hand.

Huw arrived at his father's place during a spell of weather that seemed incapable of making up its mind. One minute the sun was out, the next it was behind a cloud, interspersed with showers varying from drizzle to downpour, and all the while a chill wind blew off the hills.

Huw came to see his father to talk things through or to get advice. He had two methods of communication with his father: speech and telepathy. He cleared some weeds from the grave and then, after looking round the graveyard and seeing no-one, he summarised his conversations with Wilson and O'Grady in a low voice. Then he asked his father what to do about the money. Huw stood in silence and studied his father's headstone waiting for a revelation.

Suddenly, there was a kerfuffle and Huw whirled round to see an old lady trying to pick up her walking stick that had fallen from her grasp. He watched the woman put some flowers in a jar underneath a headstone five or six graves away. Her hands were claw-like as she struggled to pick up her stick, so he walked over and picked it up, and then gently offered his hand to help the woman straighten as best she could.

The woman smiled and looking up at Huw said, 'People say graveyards are places of peace. Not for my David. Thirty years I have been coming here every week to tell him what is happening. He never said much when he was alive and he hasn't altered. You get anything from your —?'

'Father,' Huw interjected.

'I know who you are,' she snapped back. 'I'm not senile. I just have a touch of arthritis. My youngest daughter was in school with your dad.'

She pointed at Goronwy Pugh's grave and barked, 'Well?'

'Nothing yet. I'll go back and see if he's got anything to say.'

'Don't be soft,' said the woman. 'You have to listen to yourself. This place gives you silence in order to let you think and hear your own thoughts.'

The woman turned back to her husband's grave, 'David, I nearly forgot. Our Audrey's son Trefor is getting married to a girl with a double-barrelled name. I'm sure she's nice, despite her posh name.'

She looked up at Huw and waved her stick at Goronwy's grave.

'Give my regards to your father. He was a good man. Last time I saw him was in the miners' strike. You were this high.' She held her arm out level with her shoulder. 'Ah, well, my lift is waiting to take me to the home. Oh God,' she sniffed, 'I smell of shit, excuse my French, but what can you do when your children can't be bothered to look after you? Money isn't everything, you know.

Even when your Dad was leading strikes they were never only about the money.'

Then as she hobbled away, she said over her shoulder, 'Be nice to see the club up in a higher division. I've waited a long time for that and David will be thrilled.'

Huw stood and watched the woman's slow progress through the graveyard and waved to her when she got to the gate and looked at him. He turned and, looking at her husband's headstone, saw that the man died when he was only fifty years old. Huw presumed the dust had killed him as it had his father, to whose grave he slowly returned.

'I have just been chatting to David Emyr's missus and she sends her regards. I know a players strike is not just about the money. It's more about the club respecting the players. Perhaps that's the tack I should take.'

The wind gusted through his too thin coat and he shivered. Eventually he grunted, 'If you think so. Ah, we are playing Cwmtawe tomorrow down there on that hillside that they call a pitch. They are unbeaten at home this year so we'll have our work cut out to win, particularly if the weather stays like this. You're probably better off down there out of the wind and rain. Still time to go and thanks for listening.'

'Oh,' he stopped, 'bit of gossip. David Emyr's wife has just told me her grandson is getting married to a girl with a double-barrelled name. Now don't fret about that, apparently she's a nice girl. I'll be up again soon. '

Huw pulled his hood over his head as the latest shower swept in hard, then jogged back to the cemetery entrance where he stood sheltering until the rain abated. As he waited for the next break he used his mobile to tell Granville and Declan that he was looking forward to the game and that he was abandoning his strike talk. He did not mention on whose advice; they never would have believed him.

Chapter 34

Unable to think of anything in reply, Gloria nearly dropped the hall telephone at the shock of hearing who was speaking. Steadying herself, she asked the caller to wait. Gloria put the phone down on her hall table, went into the kitchen and picked up the cordless instrument. In her excitement she knew she would have to march up and down, and the hall telephone's cord would prevent her pacing around the room.

The caller suggested that she come to the game televised in two weeks time on Friday evening. Transmission, as always, began half an hour before the game kicked off at 8 p.m.

Gloria knew the programme, Rygbi Nos (Rugby Evening), having sat through it with Duncan often enough. She knew the programme's strict formula. Half an hour before kick-off was spent in such fascinating chat as who was going to win, what the results between the two teams had been since about 1898, and what the result would mean to the two teams: crisis or elation.

The studio guest was usually an ex-player from one of the combatant teams who had put on a lot of weight. The guest inevitably wore a matching shirt, jacket and tie that his wife made him purchase specially for the programme. The programme's researcher told Gloria that she was the first female rugby guru to appear on the show. Gloria agreed to discuss her successful role at Glanddu and the future of female executives in Welsh club rugby.

'Of course, Mrs Bowen Thomas,' the researcher went on, 'you stay in the studio to view the game. There is absolutely no need to go out and sit in the cold stand to watch it. The producer asked if you would be happy to comment on the game at the half-time break. If you are not happy to do so then —'

'Happy?' Gloria interrupted, and smiled to herself as she envisaged what she would love to say at half time — that Dewi Jones needs a new barber and Geoff Lewis' shorts are far too tight. 'I would be absolutely delighted. I know enough about the game to make some pungent comments.'

Gloria was not sure about her last statement but she was not going to admit that to a mere researcher. She knew how she could avoid making glaring errors: listen to the match commentators and their critical comments during the game and re-gurgitate their utterances in her own words.

'I don't suppose you speak Welsh, by any chance, because we're the Welsh-speaking channel. If you don't, then don't worry. We do have the odd guest on the programme who can't speak Welsh.'

Gloria had to think about her reply. Gloria wasn't born in Wales. Her parents were English. They moved to Wales when she was nine to run a post office.

Gloria learned Welsh in school and spoke it with her brother, particularly if her parents were in earshot. Duncan was a Welsh speaker from birth. Gloria and Duncan, after their children were born, used Welsh only when they didn't want the children to understand what they were saying. During Duncan's terminal illness, the pair switched back again to Welsh.

'Yes, I've got enough Welsh to get by, I think.'

'I'll send you a letter, Mrs Bowen Thomas, giving you all the details of the match and I'll enclose tickets for the car park and the ground. We look forward to meeting you on Friday week. If you arrive no later than half past six that gives us an hour before the broadcast begins.'

What on earth would she wear?

Once her caller rang off Gloria realised she'd have to comment on the game's technicalities. She telephoned Toby who suggested the obvious: watch all the games on TV, regardless of the language of the commentary; borrow DVD copies of rugby games from all and sundry; listen to what the pundits say at half time and during the post-match review.

Gloria had just put the telephone down after her conversation with Toby when the mail arrived. In the mail was a letter from a Mr Lord, and when she saw what his company did a shiver went down her spine. She immediately telephoned Mr Lord to agree to his proposal.

CHAPTER 35

Mr Lord arrived exactly on time. He told Gloria that he was looking on behalf of a client but he could not reveal the identity of the buyer, not even the gender.

Lord's visit struck her as odd when she sat down later to think about it. The man spent little time inside the house but once he went into the garden, he was thorough.

Lord asked if he might be alone whilst in the garden and Gloria agreed, though she watched him avidly. The man stalked round the garden looking at the house from every conceivable angle. He took photographs, not only of the house but the layout of the garden.

The first thing Lord asked on his return to the house was, 'Who owns the field behind the house and have you ever tried to buy it?'

Gloria replied that she had never tried to buy the field known as "Caefach" (little field) from its owner, Mr Rhys, the sheep farmer. Gloria expected Lord to ask where Rhys lived, but the only question he asked was, 'What amount do you want for your house?

Gloria dodged the question. She told Lord first, that she expected him to make the valuation and second, that she had not devoted any time to researching the market. Lord had accepted her reply with a grunt and when pressed to give a valuation, he pleaded that he needed time to think.

As soon as Gloria saw Lord's Mercedes disappear out of sight, she picked up the telephone.

'Good afternoon, Betty. Is Bob there by any chance? No. No sheep loose in the garden today. The last fence repair Bob did is fine. Has a Mr Lord been in touch with you? Well, keep this under your hat but he was looking at my house and he asked after Caefach. No, I am not thinking of selling just yet. This chap told me he was down here on a whim for someone. He categorically would not say. Let me know what you and Bob think when he contacts you. That's right a Mercedes . . . really. . . Would you mind letting me know what he says? Thank you.'

Gloria returned to Lord's website and studied it more thoroughly than she had done before. Most odd that he should be looking at her house.

Then she sent emails to the three estate agents used for the Grindley site evaluation before trawling through a list of houses in her price range in Swansea and Cardiff.

Afterwards, she felt horribly depressed.

When Evelyn telephoned her mother that evening, Gloria told her of Lord's visit.

'And?' said Evelyn, excitedly.

'The way he looked at the house made me think he either wants to completely overhaul it or pull it down. Who would want to do that in Glanddu?'

'Could it be our friend, Mr Ball?'

Gloria had not thought of Mr Ball because she assumed that Rhiannon Griffiths was the likeliest buyer.

'Ball did not seem enamoured with the place, so I doubt it. His reaction could have been a blind, but I think not.'

She hesitated.

'I had a look at Lord's company's website and, of course, they give no details of any of their exceedingly wealthy customers.'

'Sounds like Toby should still probe his friend, Mr Ball. Shall I ask him?'

'It can't do any harm. Please. When Toby speaks to Ball, tell him not to volunteer too much.'

'I will. I read in a newspaper recently that the second home market has crossed the border into Wales because the West of England is all snapped up.'

'Maybe I could get a good price?'

'Sadly, Mother, there are good prices for England and good prices for Wales. There is no correlation between them.'

'That is no comfort,' replied her mother.

Toby met Ball to play squash and when they were changing before the game, Toby asked Ball if he knew Lord. Ball said that he knew him only by his reputation of dealing exclusively in property for millionaires and above. Lord's clients used to be Arabs, ex-patriot American businessmen and people in show business. Recently, his clients were Eastern Europeans whose chief priority was security.

When Ball asked why Toby was asking about Lord, Toby said that he would tell him after their game, giving himself time to concoct a story. Toby won the match so easily that Ball stomped off the court, collected his clothes from his locker and then, without showering, disappeared with not a word to Toby.

CHAPTER 36

A knock on the door interrupted Rhiannon's thoughts. Steve Sly, her manager, came in and scuttled over to the chair opposite her. Sly put his calfskin briefcase on his knee, clicked it open, removed a paper document in an expensive looking cover, and retrieved his laptop.

Sly opened the document and flicked through a couple of pages. It all looked promising. He placed the document on the coffee table in front of him and said, 'Looking at this report by the estate agent, the one thing that strikes me is that you need be in no rush to act.'

Sly thought Rhiannon barmy to be thinking about buying anywhere in Wales. He had spent several holidays as a child in Wales and had a low opinion of the country and an even lower opinion of its weather. Still, if the woman wanted to waste money on a house in an old mining village, that was her problem.

'Rhiannon, if you do decide that having a house in your home village is what you really want, then I think we can trust Lord to handle it discreetly. The last thing we need is for this Thomas woman to hear that you're the one interested in buying her place, because then the price will just go —'. He raised his forefinger to the ceiling.

Rhiannon nodded and said, 'True. Is this estate agent coming today? Always assuming I have some spare time.'

Sly keyed into the laptop. 'I will just check your schedule. Yes, you have a couple of hours this afternoon before your personal trainer arrives. I'll email Lord now.'

'You spoke to Jackson?'

Sly stopped keying and smiled at his employer. 'He absolutely loves it. So does Banker. Both of them are very impressed that you could dream it up.'

What had given her the idea for the advertisement was her own experience as a girl in Glanddu. When she first went down to the ground to meet her friends and compare the physical attributes of the players, Rhiannon always got to the ground early and stood outside the changing room window. If the window was open she would shut her eyes and breathe in the air as it wafted out of the room, filling the immediate area with the pungent smell of the liniment. Rhiannon still thought the liniment smell was rather more attractive than Ohdour.

'And?'

'They both thought that this would be an ideal advertisement given your personal interest in rugby. Looking at your schedule, you have time in April and early May,' Sly replied.

'We should be able to shoot it in a day,' Rhiannon mused, 'though being Wales, there is always the issue of weather.'

'Perhaps allow two days and make it the first week in May?' Sly interpreted a small shrug as "yes" and keyed into the laptop. 'Whom do you think the ad agency should contact at the rugby club? David Williams?'

'No, he's just a milkman. I don't know this Bowen Thomas woman but since she is the chair, a businesswoman and the brains of the club, she is definitely the person to contact. Also, tell the Agency to make it clear to Mrs Bowen Thomas that using the club's ground for the advertisement was my idea. That will get me into her good books.'

Rhiannon paused for a moment.

'My acquiring her house will bring loads of visitors to the village just to see where I live. My fans are bound to spend money in Len Penry's shop when they come; perhaps we should think about what souvenirs he could stock. I see myself as a one person economic boom which will surely encourage the local council to get on my side.'

'Like if you wanted planning permission to alter the house?'

'Of course,' snapped Rhiannon. 'Leave the folder. I'll have a look at it now. Lord is definitely coming this afternoon?'

Sly looked at Rhiannon and stammered. 'I'm positive he will cancel any other appointment he might have to see such an important client. Shall I sit in at the meeting with him?'

Rhiannon raised her eyebrows at Sly before she picked up Lord's report and began to read. Lord's findings were in a file bound in a gold cover with black calligraphic script; the report look like a work of art.

Rhiannon was pleased that everything Sly got for her was of the very best quality — or at least looked like it.

Lord arrived and took the seat opposite Sly whilst Rhiannon sat in a chair set at a forty-five degree angle from the estate agent. Sly had instructed Lord never to make eye contact with her unless she spoke directly to him; she did not like strangers gawking at her.

Rhiannon jabbed a finger at the report lying on the coffee table and signalled Sly to begin the conversation whilst she listened.

Sly waved an arm at the report. 'You must appreciate, Mr Lord, Ms Griffiths is a very busy person. Will you summarise your findings?'

Lord's raison d'être was to please his clients and ensure they call on his services again and again. And perhaps, equally important, he wanted them to refer their rich friends to his company.

With his longevity in the property market, Lord was rarely surprised at what rich people expected. Lord's visit to Glanddu, however, was more than a surprise; it was an abomination.

'The best and most obvious place to suit your requirements is the Glanddu Rugby Ground. It would give Ms Griffiths a huge garden but unfortunately it is surrounded by houses, so privacy might be an issue.'

'That could be solved by building a wall with barbed wire to stop Ms Griffiths' fans from disturbing her,' Sly stated firmly.

'No, it's now illegal to have a high fence or wall with barbed wire or broken glass cemented into the top. You would need a top class security system for the grounds.'

'Nobody told me that the rugby ground was for sale when I was there,' snapped Rhiannon at the estate agent.

'Well, it isn't yet. If the rugby club goes bankrupt, a real possibility since it can't meet its outstanding bank loans, then its one asset, the ground, will have to be sold.'

'I'm not going to wait years for a possibility which, as the club is riding high at the moment, seems unlikely. And as I hope to raise funds for the rugby club to ensure its survival, don't waste my time with talk of buying the ground.'

'I just thought that the rugby ground would be the most appropriate place to build a decent sized mansion for someone of your status.'

'I've said, "No chance." I hope he's found something else,' Rhiannon said, looking at Sly.

Lord was used to rich clients speaking to him as though he was not in the room. Not in the least fazed he went on.

'Yes. Another possibility is a three-acre field owned by Mr Bob Rhys called, "Caefach". It is, however, beyond the edge of the village boundary so I doubt that even someone as famous as you would get planning permission to build a house on it.'

Sly could see Rhiannon beginning to anger so he snarled, 'Why mention it then, Mr Lord? Ms Griffiths does not like negativity. You're wasting time.'

'I apologize. It was just background information.'

'I am sure you have been thorough,' Rhiannon snapped. 'Just tell me something positive. My time is precious.'

'Yes, of course it is, Ms Griffiths. I don't intend to waste it. I visited Mrs Bowen Thomas and asked whether she might be selling her house. At first she said she wasn't interested. But then Mrs Bowen Thomas admitted that she wants to move to London to be with her children, not that she would be able to get anything much in a decent area for what she would get from her Welsh property.'

'You found nothing else?' Sly asked, seeing the disappointment on Rhiannon's face.

'The interesting thing is the three-acre field that sits behind Mrs Bowen Thomas' house. Mr Rhys said he might sell the field when I spoke to him. If he sells the field and you buy the house, you would get a very big garden and the level of privacy that you require.'

Sly looked at Rhiannon and saw her look interested for the first time. Rhiannon looked directly at Lord. 'The house has just five bedrooms, if I recall.'

'So it is a bit small for Ms Griffiths,' anticipated Sly.

'If you knock the current house down you are allowed to build a new house ten percent larger. The current house is several feet higher than its road entrance, so if the new house could be built at road level you could get a three-story house instead of the current two.'

Rhiannon grunted, 'Did you discuss a price?'

'No, but I got some estimates from a local contact. They're in the report. The good thing is that because the house is not on the market, you have no competition. I think Mrs Bowen Thomas badly wants to sell and you, if I may be so bold, are a Godsend.'

'Undoubtedly, as I am commonly referred to as a goddess,' Rhiannon said, laughing at her own joke.

Sly sensed that Rhiannon was becoming bored. He was just about to open his mouth to ask if she had any more questions when Rhiannon said, 'Mr Sly will see you out.'

Rhiannon dismissed the estate agent with a movement of the head and then picked up Lord's report and began to flick through its pages.

'What do you think?' said Sly when he returned a few minutes later.

'No doubt this report will cost me a fortune to tell me what I already know. She threw the report on to the table from whence it bounced onto the floor.

Sly tried to think of a response as he bent down to retrieve the report.

'Well, we had to be sure of the facts. But Lord is a shrewd operator and he does think she will sell it to you,' he stammered.

'She had better.'

CHAPTER 37

It was ten minutes before the match kicked-off and people were making their way from the Glanddu clubhouse to where they were going to watch the game. Colin Mabbutt and Arthur Davies were deep in conversation when Colin looked over to the car park. What he saw caused him to jab Arthur on the arm. Arthur stopped and turned to see a huge Mercedes edging into a parking space.

'Must be Rhiannon Griffiths showing off that she's got a second stretch limousine. Obviously, she wouldn't park at Grindley's old place because she couldn't show off that car and make a grand entrance. Christ, look at the size of her bodyguard, and he's a different one from last time.'

'And how would you know it's her, Colin?' Arthur's grin faded. 'And now I can see that she's changed gender since her last visit as well as put on a few years,' he said, indicating the man getting out of the car. 'I've never seen him before. Presumably he supports the opposition?'

'Indubitably, with that car. Doubtless he's another Englishman with pots of money ready to pump into the local club. How come we don't get immigrants to Glanddu like him, Arthur?'

Arthur pointed disparagingly at the village.

'Because of this less than exotic place.'

Arthur's words got a resigned shrug of agreement from Mabbutt before the two men continued on their way, greeting friends from Glanddu and acquaintances from their opponents of the day, Llanlas. The pair sat in their usual spot in the third row of the stand and all they could hear were spectators commenting on the Mercedes' occupants and wondering out loud who they were.

There was also laughter as they watched the strangers, two men and a boy, desperately try to get to the stand without getting their shoes muddy. Of the stand's occupants, ninety per cent were wearing some sort of boot; the others, waterproof trainers. As the interlopers got close to the stand, the laughter died as the size of one of the men became apparent. Whilst the man was tall it was his shoulders, roughly the size of the Severn Bridge, that made people stare.

The strangers stopped in front of the advertisement for Arthur Davies' garage and studied it. The man wearing the fur coat and clearly the boss said something to the goliath who took out a notebook and, glancing several times at the hoarding, wrote something down.

'Hey, Arthur,' said Dai Williams, leaning back from his seat in front of the garage owner. 'Perhaps he wants to buy a little runaround from you. Know him?'

'If I did, he wouldn't be writing down what I suspect is my telephone number,' Arthur replied as he began to explore his pockets for a business card.

As the three unknowns climbed the steps into the stand, the seated spectators fell silent.

'Do you think the fur coat that bloke is wearing is mink?' Mabbutt whispered in awe.

'I think so. God, the others are wearing cashmere coats! I should guess that what they're wearing would pay for our team for a year,' speculated Arthur.

Brian Probert had sat in the front row in the same seat for forty years but when he caught the look of the giant as he stood at the top of the stairs, the old man slid along the bench to make room for the newcomers. Yuri nodded at him before scanning the stand as the other two slipped past him and sat in the area vacated by Probert.

Before sitting down Yuri said something to his boss who turned and waved at someone sitting further up the stand. Everyone turned to see to whom he was waving, but no-one could work out who it was.

Clarification followed within a minute as Yuri climbed to where Bob Rhys was sitting and then bent and whispered in Bob's ear. Bob got up and followed Yuri down to the boss man who shook his hand and, after a brief conversation, the former sat down.

Such had been the fascination of the stand with the three strangers that they had not noticed that the two teams had run onto the field in virtual silence.

During the game Bob Rhys was heard explaining the finer points of the play to the two men. The boy who sat on the far side of the men also explained what was happening in a tongue that nobody in the stand had ever heard before. The debate between Glanddu and Llanlas supporters as to who the three newcomers were was carried out in Welsh to avoid upsetting the fierce-looking Yuri, but no one knew who they were or why they were watching the game.

At the end of the game the foreigners left the stand first, partly because they had been sitting close to its entrance, and partly because Yuri stood and looked at anyone who threatened to get in front of his charges.

The three again picked their way slowly through the mud back to their car with Bob Rhys in attendance. When they reached the rutted cinder and shale car park, mink-man and the boy shook Bob's' hand.

A few moments later, the cavernous car carefully extricated itself from the jam-packed, badly parked mass of vehicles and drove off down the club drive and out into the road. Bob stood and watched the car until it disappeared and then headed into the clubhouse for what he expected would be a grilling.

Bob had not intended to go to the clubhouse after the game as he and the wife were going out to dinner with the local sheep farmers association. However, he knew if he did not tell everyone who the foreigners were immediately, he would be answering phone calls from the nosy and the curious from that evening to the unforeseeable future. Bob had the longest discussion in the bar with Gloria Bowen Thomas because she had seen the Russians talking to Bob in Caefach earlier in the day.

Lord had just started eating his Lobster Thermidor when his mobile phone rang. He smiled weakly at Eric Rudd, his long-suffering partner, as he answered it.

Eric's glare of annoyance at Lord faded as the latter's face changed from happiness to concern. Lord snapped the telephone shut and stood up gasping.

'I don't understand people. I sent the man to view four properties. All are mansions with acres of land in beautiful Gloucestershire, Somerset and Wiltshire. I mean, the smallest has twelve bedrooms; the youngest is late eighteenth century. What happens? The man likes an ugly Victorian house, in barely three-quarters of an acre in some shit hole up a lane in Carmarthenshire. I had never even inspected a property in Carmarthenshire before I saw this house, let alone sell anything as tiny as a five-bedroom dwelling. This house is not even for sale, yet it has the interest of two of my clients. If this happens and word gets out, I'll end up getting all sorts of people asking me to look at terraced houses in,' he searched for an unlikely town, 'Wigan. It will ruin me.'

'I promised your mother to look after you, Larry. So eat your lobster then we'll watch a nice DVD, go to sleep and, as always, when we wake up bright-eyed and bushy-tailed and in the morning things will look completely different.'

Chapter 38

Leon Zisserson waddled over to the chair opposite Bolotnikov, but before he sat down he stretched over the desk and shook Bolotnikov's hand. Leon was a middle-aged man whose handmade suits did a magnificent job of disguising the mounds of fat encasing his body.

Once Zisserson sat down Bolotnikov leaned forward, put his elbows on the desk and then his chin on his hands.

'Leon, I want the name of a sports agent.'

Leon did not bat an eyelid as he wrote himself a note.

'A greedy one, of course,' he suggested.

Bolotnikov merely smiled and did not bother to answer the obvious.

'I assume you are thinking of taking over a soccer team? May I ask which one?' Leon said, raising his eyebrows in anticipation of an affirmative response.

'I am not an oil man or a banker so no, not a soccer team,' Bolotnikov grinned, 'yet. The village of Glanddu, where I intend to have a small country home, has a rugby team.'

'Rugby?' Leon looked shocked. 'Wales? Why would you want to go there, Mr Bolotnikov? It is always raining and it is full of sheep shaggers.'

When the Russian raised an eyebrow, he added, 'It's a term for people who have sex with sheep. Wales is alleged to be full of them because there is nothing else to do there. And to get involved with rugby and not soccer where we know there is big money...'

The lawyer shook his head.

'From the business point of view, just forget Wales completely. If you want to get into the sporting world, stay in England, forget rugby and go for a soccer team. I can start right away to acquire one.'

'Mr Zisserson, one of the reasons why you are sitting on the employee side of the desk is that your vision is only about money. If I try to buy a soccer team in England, it will be in all the newspapers. That would be fine if I wanted publicity, but I do not.'

'Now,' Bolotnikov opened his diary, 'I am having lunch at The Quail Egg the day after tomorrow at one o'clock. Let me have at least three names of businesses, say within a twenty-mile radius of Glanddu, which you think might be available to buy. You know what I prefer.'

'Car dealers, scrap metal dealers, filling stations and any other cash-oriented businesses?'

'You already know that, so why bother to enunciate it,' replied the Russian.

Then he thought for a moment.

'To start you off, here is the name and telephone number of a car dealer in Swansea. Find out all about him and the price for his business. Find out all you can about a Mrs Bowen Thomas who lives in the village of Glanddu and is the chairwoman of the local rugby club. I also want you to investigate the rugby club's finances and find out who owns the ground.'

He snapped the diary shut and leaned back in his chair.

Leon, furious at the tone of the Russian's voice, hid his face whilst jotting down his instructions.

He stammered, 'There's not much time to do all this.'

Zisserson looked up at Bolotnikov's face and knew exactly what it meant. Zisserson sighed, nodded, snapped his notebook shut and shot out of the room.

Bolotnikov waited till the lawyer had closed the door then made two telephone calls.

John Smith arrived at Bolotnikov's house, as forewarned by Zisserson, dead on time. Yuri opened the front door and ushered Smith into the house where he stood and stared.

Smith had often ogled the grand houses in the road that, as a young boy, he walked past on his way to Lord's cricket ground. In those days he could only guess at what their opulence was like but now he could see for himself. He sniffed the air and smelt something he liked: money.

Smith rubbed his hands together in anticipation, though when he saw Yuri frowning at him he blew on them as if they were cold. Then surprisingly, Smith had to raise his arms while Yuri frisked him. Yuri did a far more thorough job than Smith had experienced at any airport security check-in. With nervous anticipation he followed Yuri into one of the rooms.

Smith would like a library like the one he entered. There was a log fire burning with real logs whilst the walls were hidden behind bookcases filled to the brim with books - or at least they looked like books. The antique desk at which Bolotnikov sat was vast. Smith thought the desk would look nice in the Georgian house he was going to buy someday. To buy that Georgian house, he needed clients like Bolotnikov who would use him to make surreptitious transactions of which the taxman would be blissfully unaware.

Bolotnikov was busy on his laptop and shook Smith's hand peremptorily before continuing what he was doing.

'I gather you have handled the transfers of soccer players from abroad to English teams. I gather that when many of these players arrive, their ability does not match the sums of money paid for them,' Bolotnikov said as he switched off his laptop.

'Not all of them, Mr Bolotnikov. How these players perform on the pitch is not my responsibility. My job is to bring the club and the player together to talk about wages and conditions. How they perform on the playing field is not my responsibility.'

'Overvaluing players is not necessarily bad,' said Bolotnikov.

Smith could see his dream Georgian House becoming a reality. The Russian was clearly his sort of client.

'With which football team are you involved, sir?' Smith said, emphasising the last word.

'I am expecting to be involved shortly, not with a soccer club but with a rugby club.' Bolotnikov mused for a moment. 'Football may well come later. I actually prefer soccer but my son plays rugby at his school in Wales. Have you handled rugby players?'

'Yes.' Smith decided not to admit that he had not done so for several years because this opportunity was too good to miss.

'Which club are you interested in?'

'Glanddu.'

Smith saw his Georgian House rapidly fade from view.

'Oh, that Welsh club where Wilson is now playing.'

When Zisserson told Smith before the meeting that the Glanddu rugby club was what held Bolotnikov's interest, Smith just had not believed him. And he still could not comprehend that Bolotnikov wanted a rugby team - who would? Something underhand was happening and he wanted in. Just play along, he told himself.

'Glanddu is a firm favourite to win its league this season and to stay in the higher division next year. It will need new players. Those players will come from France.'

Smith thought to himself, what about players from New Zealand, South Africa and Australia? What about an all-expenses paid trip to some of those places and perhaps Fiji and Samoa, as well?

The Russian, though, was too imperious to be open to suggestion. It meant he must have some sort of scam going on in France.

Smith disliked negotiating with the French because none of them seemed able to speak passable English. But the good thing about French rugby is that it is mainly played in the southwest where the wine and weather is infinitely better than in England. He would definitely need all-expenses paid trips to France to meet and discuss terms with prospective players. This project was sounding very, very good.

'The players I see coming over would be good players, but close to retirement and looking to earn some easy money. You have connections in France?'

Smith nodded, but as all his recent connections were related to the soccer world he needed to telephone Pierre Domenech as soon as he got home. Pierre was his best contact in France, and he would know local agents who specialised in rugby players.

'If Glanddu doesn't win promotion, Mr Bolotnikov?'

Bolotnikov thought for a moment. 'Glanddu are unbeaten and they are several points clear of their nearest rivals. In the unlikely event that Glanddu does not win promotion, the club will definitely need three or four players to ensure they win next year. Whichever it is, you need to start to find potential candidates now.'

'Any particular positions you are thinking about?'

Bolotnikov shook his head. He did not have a clue about what the team required.

'It is too early to say. I just know that if I get control of the club I will be bringing players in.'

He cleared his throat and stared hard at Smith.

'At this moment, my involvement with the club is "hush, hush." If I hear any mention of my involvement then there will be serious consequences for you. Thank you for coming to see me.'

Bolotnikov did not bother to get up but merely waved a hand at Smith and picked up some papers from his desk and began to read. Smith stood uncertainly for a moment, his hand offered as if to shake the Russian's. After a moment, he returned his unshaken hand to his trouser pocket and quietly slipped out of the room without a backward glance.

As Yuri opened the front door he whispered to Smith, 'Remember what Mr Bolotnikov said about mentioning this meeting to nobody.'

'I understand fully.'

After seeing Smith leave the house, Yuri returned to Bolotnikov's study, accompanied by Ivan Bolotnikov and Zisserson.

Ivan sat whilst his brother explained what he had been discussing with Smith.

Ivan asked puzzled, 'Boris, why move to Glanddu and get involved in a rugby team?'

'Buying this woman's house would give me a useful hideaway from London. It would provide a good base to expand my activities in an area where I would have little competition. It is an area where my activities would stir less interest than in London. And supporting the local team would be good public relations.'

Boris went onto explain his latest thinking. If he brought players in from overseas, he would pay their wages and buy houses for them in the local area using off-shore money from one of his holding companies. When a player leaves he would sell that house and remit the proceeds to his English company. A turnover of just a couple of players per season would provide a small but useful way of laundering money.

He then reminded Ivan of what their father had said: 'One should never be too greedy because greed so often leads to a downfall.'

Ivan conceded that Boris' idea was sound. They turned to Zisserson who was champing at the bit to tell Boris what he had found out.

'I'm sorry that I couldn't make the restaurant the day before yesterday but I actually went down to Wales to do some of the investigation. The car dealer,' he looked at his notes, 'Mr Arthur Davies, trades in a full range of second hand cars, making him an attractive proposition for you, particularly as his showroom is on a good site on a main road into Swansea. He owns houses which he rents to students and he has a small scrap metal business which is struggling. Davies is friendly with Eurof Prosser, a man well-known to our associates. I met Eurof Prosser who told me Davies intends to sell up and retire to Spain. Prosser thinks Davies wants to do this sooner rather than later. Davies has had several wives and is always keen to keep his money hidden.'

'Sounds good for us.'

'Yes. The one legitimate business I thought might interest you is an estate agency. It is one of the few independent agencies left in the area and is owned by William Isaacs, who spends more time in amateur theatricals than in buying and selling houses. You've told us about your plans to bring French rugby players into Glanddu. They will need housing.'

'An estate agency would be ideal, not just for buying and selling houses to our own players, but also to channel legitimate sponsorship money to the club,' Ivan said, looking approvingly at the lawyer.

'No,' said Boris shaking his head,' you miss the main point. If the club goes under, as we hope, and the ground is sold for housing, then who better to help with the sale of the houses built on the land?'

'Brilliant. The club will have to sell you the ground because you will make sure it owes you lots of money.' Zisserson's statement got a nod from Boris and a grin from Ivan.

Boris stood and walked round to where Zisserson was seated. Boris leaned down and stroked the shoulders of the man's jacket. Thrusting his face close to the seated lawyer, who dared not turn away from the Russian's garlic-smelling breath, Boris said, 'Leon, luckily for you I am feeling generous because you have done well. Next time when I say I want the information on a certain day, that is when I want it. Clear?'

'Absolutely.'

'Anything else?'

'Yes,' interjected Ivan, 'Zisserson and I have been discussing Mrs Bowen Thomas.'

Chapter 39

The Friday that Gloria was to commentate on the televised match was a red-letter day in every respect. On the previous Tuesday she had shown Bolotnikov the house, and was puzzled by his enthusiasm for it and flabbergasted by his zeal over the Glanddu Rugby Club.

Afterwards she boldly asked him if his business had any openings for senior IT staff. He shook his head, but asked for a copy of her CV to take away with him.

On Friday, Gloria was surprised to have a telephone interview for an IT job with an agency. Gloria felt she had interviewed well but she had no expectations. Surprisingly, the agency's client, a bank in London, wanted a formal interview on Monday. She had little time to reflect on how the interview had come about or why the agent was so positive – she had been down that road too often.

As soon as she put the telephone down, she began to worry about the evening and how she would look and sound.

'So, Mrs Bowen Thomas, can I assume you think that behind every successful rugby team there should be a strong woman? And do you see a trend towards female chairwomen at rugby clubs?' Maldwyn James said earnestly.

Gloria's smiled under the bright studio lights and tried not to blink.

'Well, Maldwyn, all I know is that we at Glanddu remain unbeaten this season whilst our closest rivals have lost one or two games – obviously, against us. And we currently have a sound financial system.'

Gloria had debated with John Jones on the words she should use when referring to the club's financial status and they decided she should not lie outright.

'With my business background and in conjunction with my late husband, we designed a modern, well-organised club administration. This increased efficiency and the well-established club management structure resulted in the club being able to concentrate on what it does best: playing rugby.'

Gloria ensured that she gave herself a plug; there was always the hope that a Welsh businessman or woman would be watching. And she emphasized that Glanddu were unbeaten, so nobody on the committee could complain.

She couldn't fathom if Maldwyn James was interested in her comments because he nodded his head with his eyes fixed on the floor. No doubt he was being told, via the tiny receiver lodged in his ear, what his next question was to be. The question was one she had anticipated.

'How has Clive Wilson fitted into Glanddu and what impact has he made to the club?'

'He has fitted in well and obviously his vast experience has been of great use to us. We will be sorry to lose him at the end of the season because unfortunately for us, his University course ends.'

'If Glanddu wins promotion, you won't be offering him a contract to keep him in Wales?' Maldwyn laughed at his own joke.

Then before Gloria had a chance to reply, he said, 'Who do you think is going to win tonight?'

Gloria looked serious. She and Dai Williams had discussed this very issue earlier in the afternoon when he came to collect the milk money.

'They are two evenly matched teams. I think whichever side stamps its authority on the game early on and maintains its concentration will win. Of course, whichever team has the greater determination has a greater chance of winning. The avoidance of mistakes is crucial in the modern game particularly, like tonight, when the weather will have a major impact.'

Gloria turned to look out at the floodlit ground. 'If the wind increases, the match could well be a game of two halves.'

She turned back to the camera. 'Finally, I think the ability to accept any scoring opportunity when it arises may be crucial in deciding the outcome because in the modern game, such opportunities seem seldom to happen.'

'Thank you, Mrs Gloria Bowen Thomas, Chairwoman of the Glanddu Rugby Club currently at the top of their League here in—' he turned to look at the glass windows of the studio that were being splattered by rain, 'typical wet West Wales weather. We will be getting Mrs Bowen Thomas' comments on the game at half time.'

'Well, Mrs Bowen Thomas what are your thoughts so far?' Maldwyn asked when half time arrived.

'I doubt that either coach will be happy. It is a game where there have been too many dropped passes by both teams. The kicking by both teams has generally been so poor that the coaches will be disappointed. None of the key players has stamped their authority on the game. It is a game of missed scoring opportunities, which will disappoint both players and coaches. I know the wind and the rain are making playing good rugby difficult, but the players are professionals, and at this level their skills should be higher. All in all, this is a game littered with the mistakes that the coaches won't be pleased with.'

'What do you think the coaches will be telling the players in the dressing room, Mrs Bowen Thomas?'

'Cut out the mistakes, improve your kicking, catch the ball and take all scoring opportunities.'

Maldwyn pursed his lips nodded and replied, 'Thank you for those deft comments, Mrs Bowen Thomas.'

When the dismal match thankfully ended, one of the match commentators had the task of announcing "the man of the match award." The commentator picked the referee for the award since both teams had played so appallingly.

In the studio, the commentator's strange choice of man of the match produced such a mixture of consternation and amusement that the discussion about the match was forgotten, much to Gloria's and everyone else's relief. Gloria had practiced her post-match remarks in front of the mirror but she didn't have to use them.

Gloria was wending her way through the parking lot to her car when a voice called out, 'Mrs Bowen Thomas, is that you?'

'Yes, Watcyn, it is,' Gloria said, and turned round with a smile.

'Dreadful game. To think I paid to watch it. I would have been better off going with my wife to her sister's house and watching it on TV. Not only was it a lot of money down the drain but I have got a soaking into the bargain,' said Watcyn, holding his trouser legs as he splashed through the puddles towards her.

Watcyn came and leaned against her car. 'Someone told me you were doing an interview on TV so I've taped the game to see how you did.' Watcyn smiled and the smell of drink wafted out through his open mouth towards Gloria.

'You must be a glutton for punishment to sit and watch that rubbish again, Watcyn.'

'I'll probably fast forward through most of it and just pause when you are on camera.'

'Good,' replied Gloria, retrieving the car keys from her handbag and then opening the car door. 'It is always a pleasure chatting to you, Watcyn, except on a night like this,' she said, thinking just the opposite. 'I'm getting wet, so please excuse me; I must get home.'

Before she could shut the car door, Watcyn leaned in.

'I understand that you're using Grindley's old place for extra parking for your club. Do you and your family now own the site?'

Gloria put the keys into the ignition then looked up at Watcyn.

'Yes, we are using it for parking but no, my family do not own the property. We leased Grindley's for the club and the club then paid for the tarmac.'

'Oh.' Watcyn then pushed his head into the vehicle. 'You know we talked about amalgamating our respective clubs all those months ago?'

'We are getting promoted at the end of the season so we won't need Brynddu,' Gloria said, as the alcoholic fumes nearly suffocated her.

'Maybe. That doesn't mean that we at Brynddu won't need you as the senior, not junior, partner. If we play at the Brynddu ground you won't need to pay to use the Grindley plot as a car park.'

'Hadn't thought about that,' Gloria muttered as she switched on the ignition. 'Perhaps you have some ideas about what we could do with it. Houses, you think?'

'I wouldn't want new houses. I would prefer a little garden or a children's playground.'

'Well, it won't happen because we'll be parking in Grindley's for years to come. I must be off, Watcyn. Good night.'

'Good night, Mrs Bowen Thomas.' Watcyn slammed the car door.

Gloria started the motor and turned to wave goodbye to Brynddu's chairman, but he was already picking his way through the puddles in the car park, holding his trouser legs at half-mast.

When Gloria got home her answering machine had over twenty messages. All but two congratulated her on her appearance before the cameras; some expressed surprise at her Welsh-speaking capability. There was a sole, unpleasant message from a caller who expressed an interest in sharing a sexual experience she had only ever read about. The last message on her machine was to confirm Gloria's formal IT job interview on Monday afternoon in London. The message advised her that a second interview might be required the following day.

As she lay in bed listening to the wind and the rain, Gloria reflected on what the TV programme's producer had said to her. First, he told her how good she had been. That was what she had expected, but when he pointed out that there might be the possibility of developing a media role for herself, she began to get excited. Second, he suggested that they might get Gloria back on TV towards the end of the season if Glanddu won promotion.

As for the Monday interview she tried, valiantly, not to let her nerves get the better of her.

Gloria believed that any chance of a career in television depended on Glanddu's gaining promotion. During Saturday's match Glanddu won, but its talisman did something stupid.

CHAPTER 40

Boris and Ivan Bolotnikov sat at their regular table in their favourite Italian restaurant in Covent Garden, surrounded by people who were dining prior to attending the Royal Opera House round the corner.

'I see your team won again on Saturday. You must be pleased.'

Then, after his brother merely smiled a reply, Ivan added, 'I must thank you for your recommendation.'

'So you think Mrs Bowen Thomas will be the answer to your problems?' Boris said, sipping a glass of fine Barolo wine on the table between them.

'I think so,' replied Ivan. 'I telephoned several companies and talked to senior managers who remembered her and all were positive. One chap said she was the best manager he had ever worked with. When I dropped her name at a management meeting at our office last Friday, three managers knew her and two were exceptionally positive.'

'The other?'

'A man called Dave Prentice said he was dreading working with "the dragon" again. I suspect he knew that if she arrived, he would be going.' Ivan laughed. 'His suspicion was right. I fired him this morning. We had complaints about his work from everyone.'

Ivan shook his head.

'Sometimes, I wonder if managers don't check applicants' CVs or telephone previous employers like I did with Gloria. I expect Gloria will bring some gravitas to the place and, more importantly, years of relevant experience. It will also be nice to see an older person round the place, a sort of mother figure.'

'I don't quite see her like that,' laughed Boris.

'What happened when she saw the house today?'

Boris' answer was forestalled by the arrival of the waiter.

Gloria was already in Evelyn's flat with a goblet full of gin and tonic when her daughter and son-in-law, Ron, walked in.

'Mother,' Evelyn said, raising her eyebrow at the size of her mother's glass.

'Evelyn, if your mother has left any gin in the bottle would you like one?' grinned Jon.

'Yes, but in an ordinary sized glass,' Evelyn replied to Ron's departing back. She then turned to her mother.

'Don't say anything until Ron comes back, Mother; otherwise, you'll only have to repeat it.'

Evelyn removed her shoes and plonked her feet on the table before wiggling her toes.

'It was like Christmas in Oxford Street. All the shops were jam-packed.' She turned and hollered over her shoulder. 'Hurry up, Ron. I'm dying of thirst in here, and I'm desperate to hear Mother's news.'

Ron's reply was unrepeatable, but he made sure that he rattled and clinked everything he touched in the kitchen to indicate progress. He reappeared carrying a tray with the drinks, nuts and crisps. Immediately everyone dived into the nibbles without saying a word. Gloria drained her goblet and waved it at Ron.

'Same again and don't look at me like that, Ron. It was virtually all tonic, honestly.'

When Ron returned and gave her the goblet, Gloria took a sip and pulled a face. 'Any gin in here, Ron? Just kidding. This will be fine. I'm not sure why they bothered with a second interview. It was a complete waste of time and effort.'

Gloria stopped as her daughter and son-in-law clucked their tongues in sympathy. Gloria remained poker-faced as she went on.

'My interviewer was Ivan Bolotnikov, who is in charge of the bank's London operations.' Gloria could feel the excitement flushing her face. 'He is Boris' brother. I have a contract job beginning next Monday!'

Ron and Evelyn jumped up and kissed her in delight.

As she hugged her mother Evelyn told her that she was welcome to stay in their London flat for as long as she liked. To obtain her husband's agreement, Evelyn merely smiled and raised her eyebrows at him.

Even though no son-in-law wants his mother-in-law to stay indefinitely, Ron didn't say a word; he nodded his head whilst his heart disappeared into his slippers.

Once Gloria disentangled herself from her hugs she said, 'Ivan was efficient enough to have telephoned several of my previous work places and they gave me glowing reports – of course.'

'Hard to believe,' interrupted Ron, causing Evelyn to give him a playful slap. Then to his surprise, Gloria threw a nut that hit him bang on the nose and bounced back onto the table. Ron made everyone laugh as he scooped down with his mouth and made a great play of sucking up the nut while leering at his mother-in-law.

Ron remarked. 'The interview was just window dressing?'

Gloria beamed, 'Yes. As always, this proves it is about whom you know, not what you know. Actually, I knew the chap I am replacing and he was always useless.'

Suddenly Gloria changed her tone.

'The agency the bank uses to handle all their contract workers telephoned me within half an hour after the interview. The agent wanted all sorts of information like my VAT number, bank branch sort code, the bank account number, etcetera and etcetera. I told the agent that I would send them when I got home. Then he started shouting at me that if I did not get the details to him immediately we might lose the contract. I said to him, "Your agency is going to get a nice percentage of my earnings merely because you're the bank's preferred supplier of contract computer staff. Don't have the cheek to tell me you might lose this contract when the Bank found me directly and brought me to you. Your agency has done nothing to get me this job yet it will earn you a fat fee. Now unless there is anything else, I have to go." Of course he could say nothing,' she laughed. 'The snotty-nose brat started off calling me Gloria as if he had known me the whole of his life, but ended up calling me Mrs Bowen Thomas. I would love to get my hands on him.'

'Mother, he was just a typical agent: grasping, greedy and selfish, and never learning that one should use surnames when talking to people of a different generation.'

The group then sat in silence with their drinks and nibbles. Evelyn took her feet off the table and announced that tonight she was not going to cook but instead would be microwaving several rice and curry dishes from Waitrose, drawing a cheer from Ron. Just as Evelyn began to clear the table, Gloria announced that she had something even more important to tell them — something else that concerned Boris Bolotnikov.

Ron burst out, 'He proposed marriage.'

'No, he is already married as you well know, so do not be stupid, Ron,' Gloria replied.

'This afternoon he showed me a property near Tottenham Court Road. He said that he would swap it for the house in Glanddu.'

This announcement was met with deafening silence and looks of amazement and even Ron's hunger pangs took a temporary leave of absence.

Before they could say anything Gloria told the whole story. The property was in a wonderful location but she couldn't afford it. Boris had replied, "Not so." He was sure a deal could be arranged. One of Boris' offshore holding companies actually owned the house. The property was a company house that was surplus to requirements. It was useful sometimes, from a tax perspective, to show a loss to his company.

Evelyn looked worried. 'Is he laundering money, Ron?'

Ron shrugged. 'I wouldn't know. I suspect that launderers often buy a property like this house with Swiss francs and then sell it for English pounds and then, hey presto, everything's legitimate. But this is only a guess.'

It was Evelyn's turn to frown as she spoke. 'Could it be simpler than that? No doubt, the house's value has risen and since it is company owned, they'd have to pay capital gains on any profit. Perhaps what Boris is proposing gets round that.'

Ron mused, 'Tax avoidance - yes that is a possibility. The truth is that we just don't know.'

Ron thought for a moment and then fixed Gloria with a stare.

'Is there something else that your mother has not told us, Evelyn?'

When Gloria replied that Boris wanted her to propose him as chairman of Glanddu, Ron and Evelyn were stunned again. When conversation resumed, husband and wife agreed that the Russian must be after the same thing they wanted: the rugby ground.

Gloria said that Boris also offered to take over the family's future rental payments for the Grindley site, although nothing was said about the housing development on Grindley's.

'I know the Russian's intentions aren't benign, but this is too good an opportunity for me to miss.'

'The problem, Mother, is that if something is too good to be true, then it *is* too good and something, somewhere, is wrong.'

Gloria knew what her daughter said was right.

'Evelyn, if I swap the Glanddu house for the one here, I am not the one in the wrong if Boris uses it for a tax write-off or money laundering.'

'You could say it was all because he fancied you.'

'Unlikely,' Ron shouted before bursting into laughter.

'Thank you, Ron. Come what may I intend to take the job and swap the house.'

Evelyn's and her husband's eyebrows virtually met on the ceiling.

After an exchange of glances between them, Evelyn asked, 'Tell us about the job, Mother.'

'I can do it standing on my head. The contract is initially for six months but the whole project is going to take at least another year after that. Eighteen months work; can you believe it?'

'What rate are they paying you?'

Gloria shifted uncomfortably in her seat because she believed that what one was paid was private. However, this was family and she wanted them to realise her true worth in the world of work.

'Seven hundred pounds per day which, Evelyn, is not bad for an old woman like me. I would love to see the faces of all the people who have interviewed me in the last few years and who didn't offer me a job because of my "advanced" age. Woe betide any of them if they turn up at my office looking for work.'

Her face contorted with a snarl as she said, 'I will remember each and every one of them.'

'Are we eating this evening?' asked Ron.

Evelyn slapped her hand on her knee, leapt out of her chair and disappeared into the kitchen, reappearing a moment later holding a carton of curry.

Leaning against the doorjamb she asked, 'What about the moral and ethical issue?'

'What, my earning so much?' replied her mother.

'Selling out the rugby club to the Russians,' Ron interjected.

'I don't know what you mean,' replied Gloria.

'Mother, you are conniving to get a suspicious character into the chairmanship of the club.'

'Evelyn, think of all the men who buy directorships or controlling interests in Association Football Clubs. Some of those men are not exactly straight, but they love their clubs and try to do their best for them. Morals and ethics are for people who sit in ivory towers - something I have never done. I am practical.'

Gloria looked to Ron, wondering, 'The odd thing is why would Boris want to get involved with Glanddu, which can never expect to get higher than the second division? The only logical reason is money laundering.'

'I guess he will put money into the club to buy players from overseas – probably France. Then the club could survive for however long he continues to invest in it.'

Evelyn grimaced at her mother, 'Sounds very dubious to me.'

'Well, dubious or not,' Gloria said, pointing at the curry in Evelyn's hand, 'if you are going to heat that by holding it your hand we will not eat for at least a fortnight.'

'Exciting times,' said Ron.

'What, Mother's news or the fact we're going to eat?' Evelyn said as she vanished towards the kitchen.

Rhiannon was away filming when she heard that she lost the battle for Gloria's house. This tantrum was surpassed only by the outburst she had when she summoned Larry Lord to visit her on return to her London base.

"Drama Queen" was how he described Rhiannon that night to his partner, Eric, as they were getting ready for bed.

'She threatened that she would tell all her Hollywood friends that I betrayed her trust. I can't afford bad publicity in my business, Eric. I gave the details of the house to Boris by accident. I mean, who would have thought he would go for a place in Wales? You haven't met Bolotnikov and he is even scarier than Rhiannon Griffiths.'

'Hard to believe that,' replied his partner. 'I find her bloodcurdling. Now forget it, it is done. Would you like me to scratch your back?'

Lord rolled over, lifted his pyjama jacket and began to purr as his partner scratched him with long, deft strokes.

CHAPTER 41

Gloria accompanied every Glanddu player who had to appear before the Rugby Disciplinary Committee, particularly those sent off a game for foul play.

Fond of her comforts, Gloria always insisted that they use her car to drive the miscreant player to the meeting. That way Gloria wouldn't be petrified at the speeds the players usually drove, and she wouldn't be deafened by their sound systems.

On the drive from Glanddu, Gloria would discuss —lecture was more like it — what the reprobate should say and do in front of the Disciplinary Committee. In Wilson's case Gloria made an exception, not only by allowing him to drive her, but also by skipping the lecture.

For the first few minutes the pair drove in silence before Gloria asked Wilson about his university business management course. Gloria allowed Wilson a few sentences about the subjects he was studying before she waded in to bestow upon him a full lecture on all her practical experiences. Wilson good-naturedly responded with a series of grunts and murmurs. By the time Wilson parked the car, Gloria was convinced they had developed an intellectual relationship far beyond the one she had with the other players.

Danny Gronow, the other party in Saturday's sendings off, was sitting with his club's chairman, Eric Gwynn, outside the room where the Disciplinary Committee was holding court.

On their way to the meeting Eric and Danny had discussed if Danny's eye was sufficiently damaged for him to have been off work on the Monday following the game; however, since Danny was claiming unemployment benefit, he decided against that strategy.

The four greeted one another in peremptory fashion; then Wilson and Gloria sat in silence opposite their fellow accused. On the dot of 7.30 p.m. a man leaned out of the door, glanced round the room, and focused on Danny. Then, without a word, he nodded his head before disappearing from whence he came. Gwynn and Gronow exchanged glances. With deep breaths they walked to the door. Gwynn gripped Gronow's shoulder before they disappeared.

The three-man Disciplinary Committee sat solemnly behind a trestle table on which piles of paper were stacked. Before each man was a jug of water and a glass. Looking as contrite as he could manage, Gronow sat directly opposite Tim Rogers, the committee's chair. Elis Evans sat to his right. Albert Finch, the summoner, sat to his left and both stared sternly at Gronow.

Tim Rogers glanced at each of his colleagues before beginning addressing Gronow.

'Danny, the last time you were before us I said it would be nice never to see you here again. That was only last season.' He paused and glared like a headmaster at Gronow, who shifted uncomfortably in his seat and tried to look even more abject than he had done earlier.

'Danny Gronow, this is the fourth time in six years that you have been sent from the field. We cannot keep having you appear before us.'

'Mr Chairman,' Eric Gwynn began, 'Danny has a perfectly logical explanation for what happened and it was not his fault. Why would Danny, who is ten inches shorter than Wilson, start a fight with him?'

Rogers wanted to laugh at that statement, knowing that all Danny's previous appearances had started with exactly the same remark (the only difference being the number of inches shorter Danny was than the other player).

'Thank you, Eric, but I think we would prefer that Danny tell us his story.'

'Well, both sides were scrapping for the ball on the ground when I was pushed, and to stop myself falling I grabbed onto someone's appendage. I then used the appendage to pull myself upright and suddenly I got a left hook smack in my eye, here.' Danny showed them the bruise round his right eye.

'The referee says in his report you grabbed Wilson by the balls, not his elbow.'

'I thought the appendage was his arm,' stuttered Danny.

Of all the implausible stories about why players behaved so inanely, Danny's claim was the most bizarre the Disciplinary Committee had heard.

'You thought his private parts were his arm?' Rogers sounded incredulous. He tried not to smile as he continued, 'I suggest, Danny, that the shirt material that encases an arm is very different from the feel of a pair of shorts and its contents.' He paused and said innocently, 'He was wearing a jockstrap?'

'Oh, yes.'

Danny's reply was accompanied by an audible exhaling of breath from his chairman.

Quickly, Danny added, 'Once I realised what I was gripping I let it — them — go immediately. It was a genuine mistake and no reason for Wilson to hit me, the big bully.'

'Danny and Eric, you've already seen the referee's report. His view was that your hand appeared from behind Wilson and grabbed him between the legs in a manner that does not support your claim to stop yourself from falling over.'

'Well, I suffered a blackout after the punch and I was told by teammates what had happened. I believed them.'

'Eric, did you see the incident?'

'No. I was having a wee behind the stand. Nobody I have spoken to saw the incident clearly. I know Danny to be "beyond reproach," Eric said (although he would have rather said, "a pain in the ass").

Rogers looked left and right to his colleagues on the disciplinary committee. Then he switched his attention back across the table.

'Anything else either of you wish to say?'

'Not to say, no, but something to show you.'

Eric turned to his companion. 'Show the committee the photographs.'

QUEEN OF CLUBS

Danny picked up a folder he had put by his chair and took out a photograph.

'You can see the condition of my eye there lads. . . er, gentlemen.'

Albert Finch, silent during the hearing, now whistled through his teeth.

'The quality of the photograph is incredible. What make is the camera?'

Danny shrugged. 'Don't know. One of the lads took it.'

'It has caught the blue, black and purple of the bruise really well,' Evans said, taking the photograph out of Finch's hand and looking at it with interest. 'Got any more?'

Danny passed another photograph, which had been taken from the side and showed how swollen the eye had been.

All three committeemen studied the second image in silence before handing both photographs back to Danny.

'Fair old shiner you got there, Danny,' mused Finch. 'Teach you not to play with someone's . . .'

His voice faded as Rogers glared at him.

'So there's our proof, gentlemen, that Danny was more sinned against than sinner,' announced Gwynn boldly.

'Well, we will see, Eric. You know the form, so wait outside for your verdict. But in the meantime we'll hear the other side, so please send in Wilson.'

'You have never been sent off before, Mr Wilson,' said Rogers, once the Englishman and his club chairwoman were sitting.

'No, sir.' Wilson's voice was humble without being obsequious.

'You know that you cannot go round hitting people even if they are holding onto your —'

Rogers' voice faltered as he looked at Gloria, 'Private parts.'

'I had to get him to release my — bits. Danny had been baiting me in Welsh during the entire game. I have learnt enough Welsh to know it was all derogatory. When he grabbed me I did politely ask him, in English, to very kindly release his grip on my bollocks. Clearly, he ignored my gentle request. I, therefore, thought that a light tap somewhere would be a more suitable way of communicating that what Danny was gripping was making me a trifle discomforted.'

This chap is so articulate, thought Rogers, that I can't hold it against him that he's English.

'Mr Wilson, it is the referee's job to order a player to let go of,' he looked at Gloria, 'your balls. Referees make decisions regarding such matters. You know well enough that players must not take the law into their own hands.'

'Mr Chairman, my eyes were watering and the pain I was suffering in my nether regions demanded that I take matters into my own hand. My wife's marital bliss might have been blighted forever. I was only thinking of her when I hit Danny a very light blow.'

'Thank God for that,' said Finch. 'If his eye was the result of a slight tap I would hate to see the result of a hard knock.'

'Let's not go there,' Rogers said quickly. 'Anything else you would like to add?'

'No, sir,' Wilson snapped.

'I would like to point out that Mr Wilson's record of never having been sent off should be taken into consideration. Also, I'd like to mention what a fine ambassador he is to the lower leagues of Welsh rugby,' Gloria said, looking sternly in turn at the three men opposite her.

'Thank you for your comments, Mrs Bowen Thomas. If you both wait outside we'll call you back to announce our verdict.'

Gloria was just leaving when she turned back and, in her firmest tone said, 'I would like to remind the committee that Danny Gronow has a history of on the field violence. Please take that fact into consideration before announcing your decision.'

'We are well aware of Danny Gronow's history. Thank you Madam Chairwoman,' Rogers said irritably.

The committee decided to deal with Wilson's fate first. Albert Finch, a severe disciplinarian, normally proposed a three-match ban for punching an opponent, whatever the provocation. But the night before the meeting Mike Morris, the mechanic who serviced Finch's car, telephoned him. Morris told Finch that if Wilson was not suspended from playing, he would only charge Albert for parts at his next car service - nothing for labour. Morris reminded Finch that the next car service due was a big and expensive one.

Finch was perplexed. 'Why this generosity, Mike?'

'Obvious. The Glanddu team are playing my village, Caer-y-Bont, this coming Saturday. However, it's more than that. We are holding a reunion of former Caer-y-Bont players on Saturday. Our people are coming from all over the United Kingdom. What has attracted many of them is Wilson's presence on the Glanddu team. That presence will put extra bums on seats. Caer needs the money from the extra beer sales a big crowd will generate.'

'There are three of us. I have only one vote. What happens if I lose the vote, two to one?'

'Then you pay labour costs in excess of hundred pounds. Do your best. That is all I can ask.'

Elis was more lenient over foul play than Albert Finch. On Saturday when he heard what had happened to Wilson, he thought that a two-week ban would be sufficient. That was before the Emyr family intervened.

The Emyr family of three brothers and a sister, all serving police officers, lived in Caer-y-Bont. All four were on the committee of Caer-y-Bont rugby club. They all had stopped Elis for speeding offences over the last fifteen years, though he was never booked for any of them. Why not? Elis had played in the same Llanelli team as their late father.

That Sunday evening Alun Emyr called at the Evans household in his inspector's uniform to remind Elis why he had no police record despite his numerous misdeeds on the Queen's highway. Now was the time for Elis to show his gratitude.

Rogers, in cases of foul play, always let the others have their say. Then when they disagreed about the length of sentence he would use his casting vote. Tonight he felt a two-week ban was probably adequate. Rogers looked to Finch.

'Albert, your thoughts.'

'Sending off of both players sufficient, no ban.'

'Seconded,' said Evans immediately.

Then, before Rogers could get over the shock of the abruptness of the decision, Albert said, 'That is either two to one or three nil. Whichever it is, let's wheel them both in here and tell them what we have decided. Then we can get on with the other cases we have tonight.'

He looked at his watch and lied, 'I have domestic problems and need to get home as soon as possible.

'Right,' Rogers said, 'Get them in.'

Elis moved towards the door but as he was halfway across the room Rogers called him back.

'We can't be too quick; it'll seem like we haven't discussed it.'

'Well, we haven't,' said Finch, 'and in my opinion, we don't need to.'

'I agree,' said Elis. 'His father was exactly the same when he played. It's in Danny's genes.'

'And they were more tolerant when Danny's dad played. I think he holds the record at seven sendings off. So that's enough talking, surely, Tim.'

Rogers motioned with his head towards the door, 'Elis, would you, please?'

A moment later, both offenders and their chairmen followed Elis into the room.

'Mr Wilson, we will deal with you first.' Rogers realised he had no clue what to say as the three of them had not discussed the issue. He started to scrabble on the table as if he had written down the committee's findings.

'God knows what I did with my notes.' Looking severe, 'We've had a very difficult decision to make. We took into account that you have never been sent off in a game before. On the other hand, we have to show the world that even famous ex-England players need to be punished for foul play. That said, I have to say that both Mr Finch and Mr Evans argued most strongly that being sent off was sufficient punishment. I reluctantly agreed. Please keep your hands in your pockets in future.'

'Of course, thank you, gentlemen.' Wilson said, surprised, a reaction echoed by the three people beside him.

Rogers switched his attention to Danny Gronow.

'We think you've had a major case of mistaken identity of body parts. You will elicit no ban, either. However, we warn you about your future conduct in particular. Do not swear at Englishmen; it is racist.'

'Any questions from either of you?'

Both Gronow and Wilson were intrigued about the reference to mistaken identity but according to the old adage, "Always quit whilst you are ahead," they exchanged glances and shook hands before saying in unison: 'No!'

'Because you have appeared before us there may be press outside. Perhaps it would be best if you leave the matter of your sentence for me to deal with. Our next case should be waiting outside. Would you ask David Owen to come in, please?'

'Bit difficult to play rugby with your hands in your pocket,' said Gloria as she drove out of the car park.

'Yes, but your private parts don't half welcome their protection. What did he mean by that mistaken identity remark?'

'It is a mystery.'

'Still, touch wood,' he said as he patted his head, 'I'll finish the season. Now, I hear that like me, you may be leaving at the end of the season and that the Russians are coming. True?'

Gloria laughed and put her fingers to her lips.

The following Saturday turned out to be one of Caer-y-Bont's best days for years. They had their biggest crowd for a game since 1972. The turnout of ex-players for a club reunion was the largest ever. The raffle held in the clubhouse after the match was their most successful. The only minor hiccup in the day was that Glanddu won the match by 69 points to 3.

Not present at the match was David Williams who, with Marilyn, was sorting out the paperwork their purchaser needed for completion of the sale in March. The other notable Glanddu supporter absentee from the game was Arthur Davies. Since the sponsors had stopped paying the winning bonus, Arthur had not once been to see an away game. Mabbutt said this was because his latest girlfriend had a voracious appetite. Len Penry told Dai that he believed Colin because he had seen Arthur walking down Swansea High Street, very bow-legged.

CHAPTER 42

She arrived an hour late for her lunch meeting. Rhiannon had intended to make a late entrance, but the traffic in the City of London was appalling.

The restaurant's food smelt good as she sashayed through the room. Equally pleasing was the sight of people gawping, nudging their fellow diners and uttering, "Isn't that Rhiannon Griffiths?" or, "Blimey, I could give her one."

Her dining companion she had never met, but as she moved towards the discreet tables tucked along the sidewall, a man stood, smoothed his jacket and with his hand outstretched, smiled at her.

'Ms Griffiths, so nice of you to join me. I'm sorry that I keep missing you.'

His English was without a trace of the Russian accents her fellow thespians used in the countless dramas about the Cold War or the more recent Russian Mafia films, all the rage today.

As she sat, she frowned and said, 'Missing me?'

'Every time I go to your home village I find that I have missed you, much to my disappointment.'

Rhiannon waited for the line, "I am a great fan of yours," but the usual platitudes were not forthcoming.

She said, 'You forestalled me from having a permanent residence in Glanddu by buying the Bowen Thomas house. I am so angry at you.'

Then Rhiannon looked round the room. 'Is your wife not joining us?'

'We are separated,' he said, a big lie since he was still married to Marsha, who just happened to be in Russia or Cyprus or somewhere with her mother.

Boris, at this moment, was exceedingly happy. The Bolotnikov marriage was clearly drifting apart and as Boris gazed at Rhiannon he hoped that his domestic problems were about to increase dramatically.

'Are you moving to Glanddu because the weather is much better than it is in Moscow?'

Rhiannon's sarcasm then morphed into a real question. 'Why move from sunny London? Unlike me, you have no connection there.'

'Like you, Rhiannon, I want a country cottage. I want it in a remote location. I fell in love with Glanddu when I saw it, particularly the rugby clubhouse. The clubhouse reminds me so much of the immediate post-war Russian architecture of my childhood. Also, my son is in school in Wales.'

He saw her eyes widen.

'It was his decision. Sergei never liked soccer and wanted to go to a country where rugby is king.'

'That leaves just Wales and New Zealand.'

'Yes.' Boris leaned forward and clasped his hands before resting them on the table. 'I am also developing business interests in Wales — a neglected part of the United Kingdom. I am gambling that Wales might one day attract the attention of big hedge funds and turn into another Celtic Tiger.'

'They are very parochial in West Wales. They don't take too kindly to strangers.'

'Unless one develops an unhealthy interest in rugby,' Boris continued. He sat back in his chair. 'Even before Gloria has moved out of her house she has co-opted me onto the rugby club's finance committee.'

He leaned forward and whispered, 'Don't tell anyone but I might possibly become chairman of the club if I take over the club's bank loan.'

'My lips are sealed,' Rhiannon replied.

In reality, they were sealed until later tonight when she telephoned her aunt.

During the rest of her lunch Rhiannon talked about Glanddu and her memories of growing up there.

Rhiannon found it pleasant, as always, to talk about herself but she did remember from time to time to ask Bolotnikov a few questions. The answers she got about his business interests seemed vague and ambiguous, and she began to wonder if he was the Mafioso her Aunt June thought he was. There was one way to find out.

'I already told Larry Lord that I won't recommend him to any of my Hollywood friends. No offence, Boris; I badly wanted that house,' she said as she reached over and squeezed his hand.

'No offence taken. I think you are being harsh on our dear Mr Lord. It was not his fault. When I first went to him and asked that he find me something big, he showed me large estates in the Thames Valley and the Cotswolds. Then I told him about my son boarding at school in Wales and he said that for the first time in his career, he was handling a house sale in that country. I pressed him as to where it was but he refused to answer, saying that he was dealing exclusively with an anonymous client. When Yuri —' Bolotnikov turned and looked over his shoulder at his bodyguard sitting at an adjoining table. 'That is Yuri Kaminov, my bodyguard. Do you know what they call him down in Wales?'

'"Shoulders," and I can see why,' Rhiannon replied.

Bolotnikov giggled. 'When Mr Lord handed me the details of a house in the Cotswolds, the Bowen Thomas house details were attached by accident. Larry was shocked when we showed interest in the place, but what could he do?'

'Nothing, but he compounded his error by giving you my telephone number. I don't allow that.'

Bolotnikov opened his hands in supplication. 'Yuri was there to intimidate Larry when I asked for your number.'

'I find Yuri very frightening, too,' said Rhiannon, honestly. 'As to my bodyguard, I left him outside the restaurant. I thought the food might be a bit rich for a mere bodyguard.'

'A Russian businessman always needs his bodyguard close at hand.'

Rhiannon seized her moment. 'Why, have you made lots of enemies? Are the Russian Mafia after you? Is the Russian Government looking to extradite you?'

Boris stroked his chin and looked pained. 'My dear Miss Griffiths, you must not believe everything you read in the papers about Russian businessmen relocating to the West. London is one of the major financial capitals of the world. Where else would someone like me go?'

'America?'

When Bolotnikov responded with a grimace, she said, 'So exactly what businesses are you in here?'

'I am a multi-faceted businessman. My interests are motor vehicles, property, entertainment and clothing.'

'What sort of entertainment? Films? Theatre?'

'Perhaps I'll expand in those directions. At the moment I do some specialist retailing of DVDs and CDs. Right now I am thinking, not about specific businesses, but areas like Wales that are ripe for investment by an entrepreneur like myself.'

'Going back to your interests in —'

Before Rhiannon could say "film," Bolotnikov interrupted.

'There were three reasons for my asking you to lunch. The most important was just to meet you, a delightful experience and perhaps something we can do again. The second reason was that Lord is most upset with me for pinching the house from under your beautiful nose. I have asked him to look again for you and said I would pay his expenses.'

'If he finds something suitable, then he did not do a good enough job in the first place.'

When she saw the Russian raise a questioning eyebrow she went on, 'He only found the Bowen Thomas house.'

Bolotnikov nodded his agreement. 'Yes, this is why I have asked him to look at the surrounding villages for you.'

'I'm from Glanddu. My fans want to see where I was born and raised. They won't care about the other villages.'

Bolotnikov waved a hand in supplication. 'I said to Lord that I would ask you to forgive him. Will you do that as a favour to me?'

As if having teeth pulled Rhiannon replied, 'I suppose so, since you've asked me nicely.'

'Thank you. The third reason for lunch was to ask about the advertisement you are shooting on the rugby ground.'

'Well, the head man, Banker Z Heinemann III, is coming over from the States next week. Can you believe that name? Banker insists on going to see the ground even though Jackson Greenbaum, their top man here, said he trusted my choice implicitly.'

'Naturally, he would.' The Russian leaned forward. 'Would you consider shooting it on another club's ground if Banker does not like Glanddu?'

Rhiannon looked startled. 'No. He wouldn't dare disagree with what I have chosen. He's only a jumped-up salesman.'

Boris explained that if the Ohdour management did not like the Glanddu ground, then she should have an alternative. Flexibility in such a situation, Boris said, showed Rhiannon in a good light. Rhiannon grudgingly admitted that what he said made sense and that another ground might have a more beautiful setting.

Bolotnikov asked Rhiannon, 'When do you plan to take the Americans down to Wales?'

After she gave him the date Bolotnikov said, 'That is fortunate because I will be down there at the same time on business. Can I take you all down to Wales in my Rolls Royce?'

'No. The Ohdour management and I will use the journey to discuss the advertisement. But a return journey to London in your Rolls might be acceptable.'

'Would you like to accompany me to see Turandot at the Royal Opera House this evening?'

Rhiannon knew that Bolotnikov was contriving to see her again. Opera was not one of her favourite pastimes but she knew the press was always present at the Opera House; it was a good chance to get her name in the papers accompanied by Bolotnikov. According to the newspapers, Russian executives now in the West were actually Mafioso but even if Boris was the Godfather, there is no such thing as bad publicity.

'I would love to go with you, but I had better check with my secretary to make sure I am free.' Rhiannon smiled graciously. 'He knows more about my movements than I do. Now I must get back home as I have several scripts to study.'

Ever since Rhiannon received her invitation to lunch with Boris, Steve Sly had been researching the Russian's background.

'Well, I've not found out much about your Mr Bolotnikov. He is married and his wife has been out of England for several weeks; I found no talk of divorce. His father was a bigwig in the Moscow Communist Party who was surreptitiously involved in the unofficial market for houses, cars and knock-offs, like CDs and DVDs. This was before the collapse of Communism. His father almost certainly had a Swiss bank account before 1989.'

'Boris followed his father into local government and was involved in planning and building houses. When capitalism became legal, Boris was in pole position to start up his own legitimate housing development company and car import company. Boris' brother Ivan worked in banking and presumably, thanks to the Communist Party's nepotism, reached high rank very quickly. Ivan came over here as director of the rapidly expanding London branch of the Moscow and St. Petersburg International Bank. Finance has never been a problem for the family.'

'So much for Boris's history. But what does he do here, Sly?'

'He has taken over car dealerships here and in France and Spain. He has a consulting company that advises Russian companies about doing business with the West. He almost certainly retains the knock-off business through an import-export company. Guess which bank provides his finance?'

'His brother's?'

A grunt confirmed that Rhiannon's answer was correct.

'But is he Mafia?'

'Not directly. The feeling, though, is that if the Russian Mafia want people like Boris to jump, Boris will reply, "How high?"'

'So what should I do about his invitation to the opera?'

CHAPTER 43

House sales in the United Kingdom usually take an eternity, with three months to complete considered lightening fast. It is also claimed that a house sale can be finalized in just one day, though most people think that a myth dreamed up by lawyers and estate agents.

Gloria's house sale was going to be completed in three weeks, thanks to Boris. Her commissioned survey of the London house showed it structurally sound. However, one night when she went out to dinner with Boris to talk about proposing him as club chairman, he showed her another surveyor's report on the house. This survey showed the London house to be damp, riddled with woodworm and suffering from subsidence. The look of horror on her face as she read the report caused hysterical laughter by the Russian. Boris explained that the real values of the Glanddu house and the London house were wildly different and that this survey gave him a way to take a tax loss.

Gloria's desire for a job and a life in London depended on this house swap; her conscience ought to have held her back but she ignored ethics and shredded her original house survey.

Gloria found that moving from her five-bed Glanddu house to the small London three-bed house consumed her weekends. She was so busy packing her worldly goods that when Glanddu played away from home, she didn't have time to travel to the games. Today they were playing in Glanddu, but she was determined to go straight home after the game without even a quick drink afterwards in the clubhouse. To facilitate an early exit from the rugby ground she watched the game from the stand, but ten minutes before the end she went to the touchline to watch the last few minutes. At game's end she strode purposefully towards her car.

Just as she stooped to open her car door Bolotnikov's voice sounded in her ear. 'You have received something from my lawyers?'

Gloria looked around, shivered in the blast of wind that tore through her sheepskin overcoat, and replied equally quietly, 'I have indeed, Mr Bolotnikov.' She hesitated and found herself blushing, 'And Mr Grindley's reaction to your offer?'

The Russian grinned and very gently removed her car keys from her hand and locked her car door. Then lightly but firmly he guided her towards the clubhouse.

'Let us just say a celebratory drink is in order.'

'Surely we should wait until next week, Mr Bolotnikov. If we win then we next week will be the league champions. I really must get home. I have so much to do there.'

'That will be a different celebration, Mrs Bowen Thomas.'

A roar from the clubhouse drowned Bolotnikov's words. 'What is that?'

'God, I bet I know what has happened - we've won the League earlier than expected,' Gloria gasped.

Gloria was right. That evening was not about packing but enduring kisses from various committee members. (The kiss from Arthur Davies was less slobbery than the rest and demonstrated why he was so successful with women.)

The general euphoria in the clubhouse, enhanced by gallons of champagne, put her in a great mood.

The only person that evening who was less happy than he ought to be was the Glanddu coach. Beck had expected Glanddu's nearest rivals, Ystrad Coch, to win their match today. Ystrad Coch were playing Llangoed, the bottom club of the League, who had not won a match all season. Before today Ystrad Coch had an outside chance of beating Glanddu to the title if the latter lost their remaining matches and the former won all theirs. But Ystrad Coch had lost - a staggering result that left Glanddu as champions.

Beck's disappointment was not that Glanddu had won the title a week earlier than anyone had expected, but that it interfered with what he hoped would be his finest oratorical moment.

In anticipation that the earliest Glanddu could win the league was next week, Beck had been researching the Winston Churchill speeches broadcast in the darkest days of the Second World War. Beck had a rough draft of an impassioned speech that he planned to give to the Glanddu team before next week's match. The speech contained references to great-grandfathers, mothers, ex-players killed in both World Wars — indeed, all sorts of people alive or dead who would be waiting on tenterhooks for Glanddu's result.

Now, no speech was necessary. Beck left the club early, a nice surprise for his wife that soon turned sour because she couldn't fathom why he was in such a foul mood. He spent most of the night drunk on the sofa in the front room and was permitted entry to the marital bed only after the third vomiting visit to the toilet had cleared out his system.

About the time Beck arrived home, only Bolotnikov remained by Gloria's side. When Bolotnikov saw Jones and Herbie chatting together he took Gloria by the elbow and thrust her firmly towards the bar manager and the club treasurer. Boris did not accompany her. She knew exactly what Bolotnikov expected her to say.

As Gloria approached the pair, Herbie pointed to Bolotnikov as he exited the clubhouse. 'He had the champagne delivered this morning, though how he knew today would be the day we won promotion, I do not know.'

'I am overwhelmed by the man's prescience,' Gloria said, holding onto the bar for support.

'Experienced businessman, that's how,' speculated Jones as he grabbed Gloria's forearm. Giving it an affectionate squeeze he spluttered, 'Just like you, Mrs Bowen Thomas. You and our Russian have foresight. I wish I had it,' he said, looking blearily at the floor. 'So does the wife.'

'I have none, either,' agreed Herbie. 'Otherwise, I wouldn't have become a schoolteacher and certainly wouldn't have remained one for thirty-odd years.'

Gloria clucked in sympathy at the two men and then blurted out as the room swayed, 'I would like Mr Bolotnikov to replace me as the chairman next year. He is prepared to invest money into all this.' Gloria waved her arms at the clubhouse then cursed when champagne flew out of her glass over Jones' head. 'Shit, I've wasted the last of my champagne.' Gloria then noticed that the room was revolving.

Ignoring the champagne trickling down his face, Jones took Gloria's glass and poured some of his champagne into it.

'I can't see you without a drink, Gloria, tonight of all nights.'

Suddenly, Gloria's statement about changing the chair of the club hit him.

'Boris, replace you as the chairperson? Wow. Why not? Absolutely brilliant idea and for us to have someone involved here with real money. He does have money? It's not just a mirage?'

'I have not actually seen his bank account but I am certain he has,' Gloria slurred authoritatively.

'I trust you, implicitly, Gloria. What do you think Herbie?'

'Sounds a wonderful choice to me, just like Mrs Bowen Thomas was.'

Herbie's smile suddenly disappeared as he clapped his hand to his mouth and raced to the toilet, arriving just in time to disgorge the champagne that he had so recently imbibed.

Jones' laughter at Herbie's hurried departure through the toilet door turned to fear when he saw who had just come into the bar: Gwladys Jones. Her gimlet eye fixed on her husband, she strode across the room, seized her husband's glass and slammed it on the bar.

'John Jones, we're late.'

Gwladys looked at Gloria. 'Good evening, Mrs Bowen Thomas. Come along you,' she said as she seized her husband's arm and dragged rather than steered him out of the bar.

Just after the Joneses disappeared, Gloria saw an ashen Herbie reappear, and using the wall of the room as a support he reeled slowly towards the exit. People in his path only needed to look at him to clear his way. Gloria's subsequent exit was rather more dignified than the others due to sheer will power. Not once crossing the room did she use a chair, a person or the wall for support. She bypassed her car in the car park and walked home, only occasionally bumping into garden walls or communing with hedges.

Gloria did wonder whether Herbie and Jones had been sober enough to remember her proposal about Bolotnikov but a telephone call to either on Sunday was probably not politic. As she sat staring at the telephone, it suddenly rang.

'Your idea about Boris becoming club chair is brilliant,' said Jones. 'I have an idea about how to smooth his path to that post.'

'Absolutely fantastic, John,' Gloria cooed after he had laid out his plan. 'I'll ask him.'

Chapter 44

On the Wednesday after Glanddu won promotion, John Jones presided over a special Finance Committee meeting. He opened the meeting by giving an overview of how promotion would affect the club's finances. Jones had contacted several clubs promoted to the fourth division in recent years and all reported little or no increase in spectators attending their matches. They received minimal extra gate money and minimal increases in spending at the bars, so crucial for their survival.

John then solemnly reminded everyone that Ffonelinc ended its sponsorship when it moved to Estonia. And now that Dai Williams had sold his business, his sponsorship was finishing. Jones, looking grave, stated the obvious: Glanddu's finances were going to be even more perilous next season.

Len then asked about the advertisement that Rhiannon Griffiths was going to make using the Glanddu ground as its backdrop. Jones replied that whilst a fee of several hundred pounds had been agreed verbally, nothing was yet settled in writing. Final approval for using the Glanddu ground rested with a man whom Rhiannon Griffiths could twist round her little finger.

The shooting scheduled for the first week in May would take only one day unless the weather was bad. If the weather was as hideous as usual and shooting went into a second day, the fee the club received would increase.

More in hope than expectation Jones asked, 'Any bright ideas about other ways of raising money?'

'Not a bright idea, no,' said Len who acted as an assistant accountant to Jones when needed. 'It may be a rumour, but I think Arthur Davies is selling up. If that's true then we'll lose his advertising revenue; I doubt that whoever is buying his business would want to sponsor a club based so far away from Swansea. Another unforeseen monetary blow.'

'At least there will be less argument,' said Dai.

'I'm sure you'll find someone else to argue with, Dai, assuming you remain on the committee now that your business is being sold.'

'If we stay in the village.'

'Where we would you go?' interrupted Jones. 'Florida, Spain, or Portugal?'

'I don't think we could afford any of those but perhaps a nice flat by Swansea's marina might be possible.'

'Too noisy,' Len asserted.

'Can I steer you back to something relevant?' Gloria looked round the table. 'Good. I have some news that may negate the loss of the various sponsorship monies. Boris is setting up businesses in Wales. He has bought my house whilst I move permanently to London at the end of this week. That means I will not be standing again for the club's chair. I will continue in the role till my replacement is selected at the annual general meeting.'

'We will miss Gloria, won't we lads,' announced Jones and received a chorus of agreement from everyone.

'I thought Rhiannon Griffiths was trying to buy your house?' Dai Williams asked.

'Boris' offer was better.'

Len interrupted the murmuring and grunts of support for Jones' words.

'The rumour is that Arthur Davies is selling out to Mr Bolotnikov.'

'I have no knowledge of Boris' business. I only talk rugby to him,' replied Gloria.

'So that is why he is so knowledgeable about the game.'

Even Gloria joined in the general laughter at Dai Williams' remark.

'Does it matter what businesses he owns?' Herbie said, still looking green from the effects of the previous Saturday.

'Herbert is right. The key point is that Boris has money. When we first discussed Boris' buying my house he said he wanted to integrate into village life.' Gloria felt herself redden as she went on with a little white lie. 'One reason I wanted him to have the house was because he was immediately willing to put money into the club to ensure our survival next season.'

She looked at Jones.

Jones continued, 'For that reason I recommend that we co-opt Boris onto this Finance Committee immediately. I have already asked Boris if he will so serve, and he has said "yes."'

'Is he a club member?' Dai Williams asked.

'He has been since January of this year,' Jones replied.

'Is it necessary that we get him on the committee now?' asked Len Penry. 'We only have one or two more meetings of this committee before the Annual General Meeting in August. Couldn't he wait till then?'

'We need him and his financial muscle immediately; we need to begin our financial planning for next season now. Having a chap with Boris' financial resources on this committee may be the difference between survival and oblivion. Leaving things until August is too late.'

'Why?' uttered Dai Williams.

'If Boris sponsors the club, we can bring in new players to ensure that we don't get demoted back down to the Fifth Division. Training starts in July so we need to have the money to pay the players from then on. If we are spending his money, then he should have a say in how we do it.'

'Fair enough,' Dai said, nodding his head.

'I propose that we co-opt Boris Bolotnikov onto this committee forthwith,' said Herbie.

'Seconded,' said Penry, catching a nod from Jones.

'Any against?' Jones looked round the table where nobody moved. 'Right. Then Boris is elected to the Finance Committee. Anything else? Dai?'

'Yes. What I really wanted to say earlier is that I won't be able to stand for the committee next season, now that we have sold Williams & Sons Dairies Ltd. to Orion Dairies. I will work for Orion fulltime for a while so I'll be otherwise engaged on Saturday afternoons. I should also like to announce,' his face suddenly burst out with a grin, 'Marilyn and I are going to see Wales play in

Australia and New Zealand in June. It was Marilyn's idea, of course.'

'Really?' Gloria said, bringing roars of laughter from the men.

'You lucky bugger.' Colin's words were his first contribution to the meeting. 'Can you take me?'

'You'll be too busy making the many alterations to Gloria's old house when Boris takes it over. I'm sure Gloria mentioned that you were our reliable and honest local builder,' Dai Williams said.

'I have told Mr Bolotnikov, myself.'

'Perhaps, Colin, you can increase your sponsorship next year,' Penry said with a grin.

'If he signs a six-figure contract with me, I will.'

'Best wait a while in case he has to get someone to undo all your efforts and sues,' sniggered Herbie.

Jones moved on to the second subject for the meeting.

'People in the village have been asking how we can reward the players for winning the league.'

'We haven't got any money to buy them anything. Winning the league should be their reward.'

'Dai, it is special what the team has done and it is a different world from when we played. Youngsters today expect a reward for whatever they do,' Penry said sadly.

'Do they? Or is it that we think they do?' Dai said, slumping back sullenly in his chair.

Jones broke the silence that followed.

'Mr Bolotnikov has suggested a commemorative pewter tankard pint,' Jones announced.

'Good idea,' everyone exclaimed except Dai.

'We've just said that the club has no money so please tell me, John, how the club can afford to buy anything?' Dai asked.

'Dai, Mr Bolotnikov said he would pay for the tankards. Every player who has played for the first team should receive one.'

'Fantastically generous,' injected Herbie.

'More money than bloody sense,' grumbled Dai.

'Still, if that is what he wants to do, David,' said Gloria, 'let us not look a gift horse in the mouth.'

Herbie then said what Jones had asked him to say.

'Do you think we should suggest to the full committee members when they are elected, that Boris replace Gloria as our chairman?'

Jones felt himself redden. 'Good idea.'

'I wish I had thought of that,' added Gloria.

CHAPTER 45

'So then, Leon, where did you take Watcyn? What did you say? And how did he reply?'

Zisserson wiped his brow because as usual, he found being in front of Boris exceedingly nerve-racking. His wife constantly suggested that the anxiety he felt was not worth the job, to which Leon always replied, "I like the money and you like the shopping."

There was no comeback from her on that remark.

'As you suggested, Boris, I took him to a nice pub, bought him a pie and just chatted about inconsequential things until I could get him on the subject of money. Moving the advertisement from Glanddu to Brynddu would generate the money they need. When he knew that I worked for you he said how lucky Glanddu were to have such a benefactor, and he was sure that Glanddu's financial difficulties would be eased by your presence there.'

'What about him?'

'He has connections to some local developers but not much has been built in the area for a long time. Watcyn hasn't been getting backhanders, unlike some of his colleagues on the planning committee who make use of the "opportunities" in their council business. Hard to believe, but he seemed straight. What he did say was that he had found a plot near his house that might be suitable for a certain young woman. He has invited her aunt to discuss his suggestion.'

Zisserson saw his boss frown and his gaze shift from the lawyer up into space.

'Good. That suits us.'

'How?'

Bolotnikov stood up and walked round his desk until he was perched on his desktop looking down at Leon. He folded his arms and said, 'You know I want to develop houses on the Glanddu Ground. The best way for me to do that is to take over the club's debts from the bank and increase their liabilities, for example, by buying players and improving the clubhouse. They will be heavily in debt. When the time is right I will demand my money. When they don't cough up, I get the ground instead.'

Boris pursed his lips. 'I am not really a bad person. I've heard that informal talks about amalgamating the Glanddu and the Brynddu Rugby Clubs have already occurred. The Brynddu ground, anyway, is more attractive than Glanddu's and I am sure everyone will thank me for pulling down the eyesore commonly known as the Glanddu clubhouse (which reminds me of some of the ugliest places back in Moscow). So, my good man,' he reached forward and squeezed Leon's shoulder, 'I do not want any money accruing to Glanddu from this advertisement. I want you to telephone Watcyn once I know Miss Glamour Puss has fallen in with my plans. I will want you to ask him to go to the Brynddu ground to show these Ohdour people all its facilities.'

Boris began to laugh at his little plan.

Leon joined in the laughter when Boris looked at him but said anxiously, 'But what about the film star? I understand she is totally one-eyed about a Glanddu house.'

He shook his head in bewilderment. 'Those Welsh are so parochial; she thinks that buying a home as far away as the next village is as remote as another planet.'

'That can be to our advantage. Divide and conquer, my dear Leon.'

'She is so used to demanding her own way. How can you get her to go up the road?'

Boris grinned, stood up and walked back round his desk and plopped himself into his chair. 'I'll deal with her.'

'It looks promising,' said Watcyn Watkins to Ray Bevan, the local farmer, as they walked with June Griffiths round the site.

'It's not overlooked. I'm sure the planners would welcome both barns being converted into living quarters for your niece, Rhiannon.'

'They do a lot of barn conversions in England,' said Bevan, whose sheep farm barely earned him enough to live on.

June Griffiths looked at the churned up mess surrounding the two stone barns. She tried to imagine her niece living up here. The site was set back from the road with an impressive view across the hills. Also positive was that the nearest Brynddu houses were at least eighty yards away.

However, a big negative factor was the perennial Brynddu wind which reminded her that it was always colder here than down in the Glanddu valley. Rhiannon was not a woman who liked the cold.

As she stared at the view, June could not help smiling at how people down in Glanddu would react if Rhiannon were to come and live here.

'You know how narrow-minded we Welsh are. Despite her moving away to London when her mother remarried, and despite her Hollywood film star status, she is still a Glanddu girl.'

Poor Bevan looked crestfallen at her words. June knew hill farmers were suffering dreadfully in the current economic climate. She turned and looked at the barns again. One would make a big but not a huge house, whilst the smaller could be transformed into a garage with servant quarters above. She squinted and imagined how they might look once converted. She nodded her head vigorously.

'It does have possibilities. Mr Bevan, I will suggest that Rhiannon have a look at this plot when she comes down next week. She is bringing some Americans with her to look at the Glanddu ground prior to shooting her advertisement.' She laughed. 'It will be interesting to see their reaction when they arrive, knowing that Rhiannon might live up here in these barns.'

Watcyn motioned with his head that they return to the car. He and June thanked Bevan for showing them the barns, and then they stood and watched the farmer trudge through a field towards his farmhouse.

As soon as Watcyn reckoned the farmer was out of earshot he said, 'Be nice to get Rhiannon up here to live. Perhaps she would switch her rugby allegiance to us. She would certainly put bums on seats if people thought they might see her at a Brynddu match. It would make us a lot of money.'

'Is money all you rugby committee men think about, Watcyn?'

'Yes.'

'I can't believe it, Rhiannon. Ray Bevan came to my door, the first time since your father's funeral. Bevan wants to sell a piece of ground up on the edge of Brynddu with two barns. He has applied for permission to convert both into dwellings. He heard that you wanted to have a place down here and he wondered if you would be interested in buying them both.'

'Brynddu? Christ, Auntie June, it's always bloody freezing up there. They think it's boiling hot if the temperature up there is sixty degrees Fahrenheit.'

Her aunt chortled down the telephone. 'Anyway, I went and had a look for you just in case. The barns are at the end of the track that runs alongside the Brynddu Methodist Chapel cemetery. Your only neighbours will be sheep. The plot is about two acres with good mountain views. It would cost a lot of money to carry out the conversion but you could get what you want, within reason.'

'I do like barn conversions. You know I want a big house, so what size house could I get?'

'I think you could get four bedrooms, three bathrooms and a large lounge and kitchen in the larger barn. The small one would make a nice guest flat over a garage. Councillor Watkins was present when I visited the plot and he thought that planning permission for the conversion is likely to be granted.'

'That sounds a bit small, but I'll have a look at the barns when I show Glanddu to the perfume company people next week. So how is my uncle?'

'A couple of months ago the doctor said your Uncle Edgar would be dead by now. Shows how much that doctor knows. Uncle Edgar actually went and watched Glanddu's last two home matches. He walked from the car to the stand. People were amazed, particularly Len Penry and Dai Williams who saw him at his worst.'

'Did he manage to have a drink afterwards in the clubhouse?'

'Rhiannon, we're talking about your uncle.'

Boris thought that Rhiannon had enjoyed his company when they went to the opera, but she had turned down all his subsequent invitations. Still, he thought, as he sat in the car at the Glanddu ground waiting to meet her and the Ohdour executives, today gave him another chance to impress her. Half an hour later than expected a stretch limousine appeared in the clubhouse drive. As soon as the limo stopped, Boris buttoned his raincoat and got out of his car, followed by Jones.

Boris tried not to smile as the two Americans followed Rhiannon out of the stretch limousine and peered with bewilderment at the clubhouse and the rugby field with its many bare patches still awaiting rejuvenation.

'You have got to be kidding me, Rhiannon.' The larger man growled over his shoulder, 'This place?'

'I think it is a typical homely rugby ground,' Rhiannon replied, looking anguished at Boris who quickly introduced himself.

Rhiannon kept her eyes on the two Americans conversing in low tones and squelching across the pitch. Behind the men their two PAs followed, repeatedly extracting their high heels from the mud.

'They've never been to Wales?' Jones asked, indicating the two women with his thumb.

'Probably not,' said Sly, who had been the last person out of the stretch limousine. He introduced himself to Jones and Bolotnikov.

'I'd better go and sweet talk those two,' Rhiannon said, and set off after the Americans.

Rhiannon was wearing the sensible shoes that she had slipped into when her guests had set off without her.

As she trotted over the field, Sly pointed at her shoes. 'Local knowledge counts.'

Once Rhiannon was out of earshot, he whispered, 'It doesn't look too promising.'

♣ 243 ♣

'Sadly, not,' lied Boris.

After the Americans spent a few minutes looking at the ground from different angles, they climbed into the stand and sat huddled forlornly whilst Rhiannon spouted at them. All three principals in the stand then entered into a discussion at a decibel level capable of being heard ten miles away.

Sly, Jones and Boris stood by the latter's car watching events unfold. When Banker's voice boomed out across the field, it did not have a happy cadence.

Boris told Jones and Sly to get into his car out of the rain whilst he went to see how things were going. Sly wanted to accompany him but Boris said that Rhiannon probably needed help from a Glanddu Rugby Club official, i.e., himself. Jones smiled at Boris' identifying himself with the club.

Turning up his collar, Boris set off towards the stand, gingerly avoiding the larger patches of mud. As he came within earshot of the group he heard Rhiannon explaining that today had unusually bad weather and that when the sun shone (as it would since summer was due any day now), they would see how attractive the place really was.

The men's groans implied that Rhiannon was not winning her argument. Boris climbed the stand steps only for Rhiannon to angrily wave him away but Banker Heinemann called him over. Ignoring Rhiannon's glare, Boris climbed to a row above the Americans and sat down.

'You are a club official, right, Boris?'

Heinemann pointed at the ground. 'We're unimpressed with the visual aspect.' He turned back to Rhiannon. 'We do still love your idea for the advertisement. We just envisaged something more picturesque.'

Heinemann's idea of British villages was medieval thatched cottages, painted white, grouped round a village green - not slate-roofed, Edwardian houses built of drab brick.

Boris caught Rhiannon's eye and transmitted a message to keep quiet before he started speaking.

'Well, one way of looking at it is that Ms Griffiths' beauty would be enhanced by setting her against such a backdrop.'

Everyone looked at Heinemann, who nodded. 'There *is* that, I grant you.' He rubbed his chin and sat silent for a moment. 'I don't like this place. I'm sorry, Rhiannon. This just won't do for our luxury creations.'

Before Rhiannon could reply, Boris burst out, 'A key problem here is that Ms Griffiths is being completely unselfish.'

Boris smiled at Rhiannon who raised her eyebrows and looked back questioningly.

'She is a devoted fan of this club and knows that the money you're going to pay for the use of the ground will help the club enormously. Now, let me check: are you happy that the backdrop to the advertisement is rugby?'

'Yes,' said the two American men in unison.

'I suggest that we take you all directly to Glanddu's deadliest rivals, the adjoining village and rugby club, Brynddu. Brynddu does have a very pretty ground. Rhiannon might hate me for saying that, but I think she will agree with me.'

'I've never looked at it like that,' replied Rhiannon reluctantly.

Rhiannon had not thought the Americans would disagree with her choice of rugby ground, but there was too much money involved for her to have a tantrum. She wondered if the home of Welsh Rugby, the Millennium Stadium in Cardiff, was available and how much that would cost to hire. Her thoughts were interrupted as Boris went on.

'In a few moments I will be meeting the chairman of Brynddu Rugby Club about a business matter at his club's ground. Why not come with me and have a look at that ground instead? It is only two miles away. Let us all have a coffee before we drive up there.'

As the group trudged back across the field, Boris said to Rhiannon, 'I will give the Glanddu club the fee that they would have earned if the advertisement is filmed up the road at Brynddu.'

'I would want to use Glanddu players if we do switch grounds,' said Rhiannon.

'That's no problem if we like the ground,' said Jackson, with a curt nod of support from Heinemann as he lifted up his trouser legs to prevent mud splashes.

The arrival of the cars at Brynddu's ground were greeted not only by a surprised Watcyn Watkins but also, even more surprisingly, by a gleaming sun in an ever increasing blue sky. Brynddu's ground was regarded as one of the prettier rugby grounds in West Wales provided the wind was not blowing (about one day a fortnight). The ground stood at the edge of the village overlooking moors towards the distant sea whilst sheep, not houses, rubbed up against its whitewashed boundary walls.

As soon as Watcyn saw Rhiannon step out of the car, he put on a turn of speed to get to her side that he had not demonstrated since running out of a London Indian Restaurant without paying his bill thirty-five years ago. To Rhiannon's horror he kissed her on each cheek, saying how wonderful it was to see her again and how he had recently seen her Auntie June. Boris rescued her by introducing the two American businessmen.

Watcyn looked bewildered at the party. 'I didn't know you travelled with such a large entourage, Rhiannon.'

'What do you mean, "Large?"' Heinemann snapped.

Watcyn blanched and stammered, 'I meant the number of people, not anyone's girth.'

Heinemann grinned, 'Just a joke,' putting his arm round Watcyn and steering him towards the moor side of the ground.

'Wow! This, Watcyn, is what I call pretty. What do you think, Jackson?'

'Gorgeous,' Greenbaum replied, and their two PAs nodded, as well.

Rhiannon ruffled Boris' hair as she went past him. Then she indicated where cameras should be set up and what the background shots would be. After a few minutes, Watcyn detached himself from the group and returned to where Boris was standing.

'Amazing that Rhiannon thought about using our ground instead of Glanddu's.'

'My idea, actually,' Boris said as they watched Rhiannon walking backwards with her hands forming a square as if filming. 'It was my idea to come here, wasn't it, Rhiannon,' he shouted as she came within earshot.

Rhiannon, keeping her back to the pair, raised her thumb in agreement high above her head.

'This will generate some much-needed revenue for the club. Thank you for that, Mr Bolotnikov. Why did ask to meet me here?' said Watcyn.

'Boris, please call me Boris, Watcyn. I had to be at Glanddu this morning and I knew that there was a chance the Americans would not like what they saw.'

He put his hand on Watcyn's arm and steered him towards his car. 'Have a cup of coffee with me.' Boris made a drinking motion with his hand to Yuri sitting in the driver's seat.

'As you know, I was recently co-opted onto the Glanddu Finance Committee and I am in the process of moving into the old Bowen Thomas house. I fervently hope to be elected to the full Glanddu committee at their next annual general meeting. Being elected is so much better than being appointed. It makes you feel you are wanted, don't you agree?'

Before Watcyn could reply the Russian continued, 'I will naturally be putting most of my financial support into that club. However, I may be amenable to putting some cash up here in Brynddu for one of my businesses.'

'In return, you want the Local Council Planning Committee to approve alterations to your Glanddu house?' Watcyn looked quizzically at the Russian.

'I assure you that any alterations to the house that need planning permission will only be done after I gain that approval. You are right to be suspicious, but I assure you I am a man who sticks to the letter of the law,' Bolotnikov said with a saintly smile.

'Now, Watcyn, Mrs Bowen Thomas told me of your pre-season chat about amalgamating the two clubs. If amalgamation occurs in order to save the clubs, then so be it; I will support the local organizations where I live. I will stay in the area depending on how kindly you locals treat me. I am one of those people who likes to be liked. I am happy to help my local area with a little financial clout. Is that so wrong?'

'No.'

Boris patted Watcyn on the shoulder, took the coffee cup from the latter's hand and poured the slops on the ground.

'I mustn't keep you.'

Yuri opened the car door, took the coffee cups and closed the car door after his boss had slipped inside.

Boris was suddenly gone. Watcyn walked over and joined the others.

CHAPTER 46

The Brynddu Rugby Ground was packed with people acting as extras for Rhiannon's advertisement. At the director's signal from behind the camera, everyone began shouting and screaming with gusto. At another signal they stopped. Then the director shouted for someone in each row to stand and go berserk. The crowd followed orders a couple of times. Then the huge throng stood idle whilst Rhiannon talked and gestured at a screen.

'I thought Arthur would be here. I heard he suddenly went to Spain a few weeks ago, but I thought he would be back by now,' Dai Williams said, taking a packet of sweets out of his pocket and passing them round his neighbours.

'He's bought a house near Marbella and is retiring there. The business and house are being sold,' Mabbutt dejectedly responded.

'What, the Inland Revenue finally got him?'

'Nothing so bad. It seems that he got an offer for the business, saw a house in Spain he liked and has been busy flying to and fro over the last few weeks sorting everything out. I spoke to him last week and he said he would be here.'

Dai Williams sniggered, 'So he's late as usual. What about his wife?'

'That is the biggest surprise. She has gone with him,' Mabbutt replied.

'You know who bought him out, Colin?' Len asked, looking at his watch and feeling increasingly bored standing around with the other extras.

'A certain Russian has bought Arthur's business and his mate Eurof Prosser's in Llanelli,' said Police Sergeant Llewellyn, turning round from his seat in the row in front.

'Is Bolotnikov being investigated, Llew?'

The policeman shook his head. 'Not by the CID or the regional crime squad. He seems to have a clean bill of health. You did not hear that from me. Clear to you all?'

'Yes,' was the unanimous reply. Before anyone could ask any more questions, the director requested the stand's occupants to shout and scream louder and look more animated. The director didn't seem impressed by the crowd's performance; he made them rehearse it three times before they shot the scene four times. Once the scene was completed the director and some of his minions went into a huddle and stared at the takes whilst the crowd in the stand waited.

'You're renovating the late Mr Morlais Lewis' place on the main road, Colin. Who has bought that?'

'Boris.'

Dai Williams looked surprised. 'Why would Boris buy Morlais' house, Colin, when he has the Bowen Thomas place?'

'Boris hinted, and I say hinted, that if he gets elected to the committee, which I think is a foregone conclusion, that he will pay for some famous French player to come over to play for Glanddu next season. The house is for this unknown Frenchman.'

The policeman, whose uniform could just be detected under his raincoat, turned round and spoke in a conspirator's whisper. 'You've got French players coming to Glanddu, have you?'

'No,' Colin said anxiously, thinking how to change the subject. He leaned forward and grasping the policeman's raincoat pulled it open to display more of his uniform.

'You're in uniform, Llew. You haven't been demoted down from plainclothes?'

'No. I'm wearing my uniform especially for the advertisement in which I have a starring role. My role is . . .'

Llew's audience leaned forward and listened intently as he spoke.

'When the crowd rush out of the stand because they smell the scent on Rhiannon, I'll be at the foot of the stand steps trying to control them. I fail and they trample me in the dust.'

'It could lead to a Hollywood career, Llew.'

'I am coming up to retirement so it would earn me a bit of pocket money,' Llew replied, then leapt to his feet and removed his coat to reveal a uniform jacket that no longer covered his expansive backside.

'I'm on,' he added, pointing to an assistant director who was waving frantically at him from the front of the stand. Llew slowly picked his way along the narrow seating of the stand and down its steps to a cacophony of catcalls about the police from the packed crowd.

'Anybody got any other titbits about Boris, now that our nosy friend has gone and we await further instruction from our director?'

'John Jones told me that Bolotnikov may take over the club's bank loan if the bank won't extend it. I'm not sure that is a good thing,' Len said, his head swivelling to look first at Dai on his left then Colin on his right.

'Beggars can't be choosers,' said Colin profoundly. 'I may have a big job up here.'

'And?' Dai and Len spoke together.

Colin lowered his voice. 'You know that Ray Bevan put in for planning permission to convert his old barns beyond the chapel. It looks extremely likely to be granted.'

Dai interrupted, 'Since I started delivering milk for Orion, I've lost touch and missed all the excitement.'

Len spoke eagerly, 'Come on, Colin. Don't keep us waiting.'

'I heard Rhiannon has put in an offer to buy the barns. If her offer is accepted I'll get the job, according to June Griffiths.'

'Have you ever done a conversion before?'

Colin shook his head. 'No, and believe it or not, I know my limitations. I'll sub-contract the work out and act as the site manager. I'll make more money that way.'

The assistant director's voice suddenly boomed through the loud speaker, asking the crowd to come down to the pitch for their next scene where they chased Rhiannon. After the fifth take, the crowd parted to reveal the assistant director coming towards them.

'Sorry, chaps. Ms Griffiths has decided that she does not need you two anymore.' He pointed at Dai and Len.

'Len, we must be thought too old to chase after Rhiannon.'

The assistant director shook his head and replied. 'No, no. Just surplus to requirements. Ms Griffiths said nothing about your age.

Anyway, we would appreciate it if you could leave the area quickly. There is tea over in the clubhouse if you would like something to drink. It would be very helpful if you could go round behind the camera and not in front.'

As he turned to go he checked himself and whirled round.

'Ms Griffiths says thank you for coming,' he said and jogged back to Rhiannon.

'You fancy a cup of tea?' said Len, as he and Dai plodded round the field towards the refreshment van.

'Not really. I think I'll go home and pack for New Zealand.'

'Enjoy yourself. I think I'll hang around for a while and watch the filming.'

The two men shook hands. Len went towards the clubhouse and Dai strolled through the car park heading for home. As he arrived at the gate, a car pulled up beside him and honked. Dai turned, saw the driver and walked round to speak.

'Not staying for the filming?' Mrs Bowen Thomas said, leaning out of her window.

'Apparently, I am surplus to requirements.'

Gloria raised her eyebrows and nodded.

'Welcome to the club.'

Acknowledgements

To my wife, Lynn, who has spent an inordinate amount of time, patience and effort editing this novel. Lynn, when she worked in IT, had the nickname, "The Rottweiler," because of her doggedness in seeing not only a job done, but a job well done. Lynn's gifts as an artist are shown here on the cover illustration. Lynn has a website that shows the full range of her work: lynnblakejohn.com

To my sister-in-law, Andy Blake, who designed the book and my website, simongjohn.com, I give heartfelt thanks for all her creativity and ingenuity, particularly since I had to wake her up in Seattle, Washington, where there is an eight-hour time difference between us. Andy's website is tomboywebdesign.com.

To David Trace, an old school-mate, who bought the first copy of the book after seeing the cover of the proof copy.

THE COTTON SPIES
By Simon Glyndwr John

This forthcoming novel is inspired by actual events in Central Asia in 1918.

Germany and the other Central Powers impose the humiliating peace treaty of Brest-Litovsk upon Russia in March 1918, and their armies continue to invade the country looking for raw materials. In the midst of these invasions revolutionaries, counter-revolutionaries, Cossacks, bandits and subject peoples roam and plunder Russia.

A Revolutionary Soviet Government rules Tashkent in Russian Turkestan. The city houses hundreds of thousands of released Prisoners-of-War, Indian Nationalists en-route to stir up insurrection, and thousands of tons of cotton. The cotton is particularly important because it is used in munitions.

Three military officers under the command of Lt-Colonel Edrich and a British Politician, Surridge, are sent to Tashkent to discover its government's intentions. Upon arrival the British group tell the local Soviet commissars that they are on a peaceful, fact-finding mission. Edrich and Surridge are shocked when the local Chief Commissar informs them that British troops have fired on revolutionaries in Western Turkestan and Allied troops have invaded Murmansk, North Russia. He then accuses Edrich and Surridge of spying for the advance group of a British invasion force. The Chief Commissar wants to shoot them but he must wait for Moscow to confirm their execution.

Despite the danger the mission roves through the city with the Cheka Secret Police dogging their every step. Edrich and Surridge manage to hoodwink the Cheka and prevent German agents from buying the cotton, and they liaise with local counter-revolutionary groups. When the mission's position becomes untenable they are all allowed to leave except Edrich.

A coup brings more violent revolutionaries into power in the city. Edrich, now hostage, must somehow find a way to leave the city and save his life.

The Final Year Project
By Simon Glyndwr John

This forthcoming novel is set in the early 1980s. Email is the latest technological advance whilst the mobile telephone is a mere speck on the horizon.

Londoner Byron Hughes returns to his hometown to look for work. As a favour to his cousin he observes an insurance fraudster to see if he really has a bad back.

Whilst watching his old rugby team at a game, he casually mentions his "detective" work and within a few days the word has spread that Byron is Sherlock Holmes incarnate.

Byron is offered a temporary job at a college where he once lectured. He is hired to teach and to investigate email misuse – despite protests that he knows nothing about security.

As part of his teaching role Byron acts as tutor to final year degree students. One of his students, an Asian man, is killed. Other Asian students believe that the "racist" police are ignoring the case. They persuade Byron to look into the death. Byron has no idea how to investigate but fearlessly sets out to discover the killer.